Lovecraft's Pillow

WORKS BY KENNETH W. FAIG, JR.

As Author

H. P. Lovecraft: His Life, His Work (1979)
In Memoriam: Howard Phillips Lovecraft: Ethel M. Phillips Morrish (1987)
Life and Death: A Hoax and a Retraction (1989)
Tales of the Lovecraft Collectors (1989; revised edition, 1995)
The Parents of Howard Phillips Lovecraft (1990)
Edward Francis Gamwell and His Family (1991)
Some of the Descendants of Asaph Phillips and Esther Whipple of Foster, Rhode Island
    (1993; *Corrections & Additions*, 1994)
Boy in Summer (1996)
When Grandma Went A-Courting: Ancestral Romance in the Poetry of
    Jennie E. T. Dowe and Edith Miniter (1998)
Big Heart: Remembering Robert Earl Hughes (2001)
Devonshire Ancestry of Howard Phillips Lovecraft (2003) (with Chris J. Docherty
    and A. Langley Searles)
The Dating of the Rebel Press Edition of The History of the Necronomicon (2006)
The Providence Amateur Press Club: 1914–1916 (2008)
Quae Amamus Tuemur: Ancestors in Lovecraft's Life and Fiction (2008)
Leviathan: Some Notes on Martin "Blimp" Levy (2009)
The Unknown Lovecraft (2009)*
George Elliott Lovecraft: Lost Scion of the House of Lovecraft (2010)
The Site of Joseph Curwen's Home in H. P. Lovecraft's The Case of
    Charles Dexter Ward (2013) (with Jason C. Eckhardt)

As Editor

Edward W. O'Brien, Jr., *Insidious Garden: A Look at Modern Horror Fiction* (1988)
Josephine Richardson *et al.*, *Within the Circle: In Memoriam Franklin Lee Baldwin*
    (1988)
Sam Moskowitz, *Howard Phillips Lovecraft and Nils Helmer Frome* (1989)
Duane W. Rimel, *To Yith and Beyond* (1990)
Dirk W. Mosig, *The Miskatonic: Lovecraft Centenary Edition* (1991)
Charles C. Beaman and Casey B. Tyler, *Early Historical Accounts of Foster, Rhode
    Island* (1993)
Edith Miniter, *Going Home and Other Amateur Writings* (1995)
Franklin C. Clark, *Susan's Obituary* (1996)
H. P. Lovecraft, *Criticism of Amateur Verse: A Selection from the Critical Department
    of the* National Amateur (1998)
Louise Imogen Guiney, *Memories of an Old Girl* (1999)
Edith Miniter, *The Coast of Bohemia and Other Writings* (2000)
The Fossil (quarterly journal 2004–2012, text available at www.thefossils.org)
Edith Miniter, *Dead Houses and Other Works* (2008) (with Sean Donnelly)*
Edith Miniter, *The Village Green and Other Pieces* (forthcoming) (with Sean Don-
    nelly)*

* published by Hippocampus Press

Lovecraft's Pillow
and Other Strange Stories

Kenneth W. Faig, Jr.

Hippocampus Press

New York

Published by Hippocampus Press
P.O. Box 641, New York, NY 10156.
http://www.hippocampuspress.com

Cover illustration © 2013 by Daniele Serra
www.multigrade.it

Cover design by Barbara Briggs Silbert.
Hippocampus Press logo designed by Anastasia Damianakos.

First Edition
1 3 5 7 9 8 6 4 2

ISBN 978-1-61498-063-6

FOR EDIE AND WALT

"Tell me strange things."
—*From the tombstone of Rev. Montague Summers,*
Richmond Cemetery, Surrey, England

CONTENTS

PREFACE

Most of the stories in this collection were originally published in the amateur press (specifically, the Esoteric Order of Dagon (EOD) and Necronomicon amateur press associations) between 1977 and 2006. I collected the first four of the David Parkes Boynton tales under the title *Tales of the Lovecraft Collectors* in 1989 (Moshassuck Press). Marc A. Michaud published a revised edition of *Tales of the Lovecraft Collectors* from Necronomicon Press in 1995, with a striking cover illustration by Jason C. Eckhardt. (Eckhardt's cover illustration showed that he read *all* the stories carefully. He included an apt element for each story in his cover illustration.) I next ventured a collection of my fiction with *Lovecraft's Pillow and Other Strange Stories* from Moshassuck Press in 2011.

After reading my 2011 Moshassuck Press collection, Derrick Hussey of Hippocampus Press wrote to me that he wanted to publish a collection of the best of my fiction. S. T. Joshi and David E. Schultz have assisted in selecting the stories for this new edition of *Lovecraft's Pillow and Other Strange Stories,* which has different content than the earlier Moshassuck Press edition. (There are eight stories in common between the two collections.) The Moshassuck Press edition included only one fugitive David Parkes Boynton story not included in either edition of *Tales of the Lovecraft Collectors,* but the present collection gathers all five Boynton adventures together for the first time. I am grateful to Messrs. Joshi and Schultz for allowing me to include the fifth tale, which has hitherto seen publication only in the EOD amateur press association (1991) and Peter A. Worthy's electronic magazine *Black Book 3* (2003).

I'm especially grateful to David E. Schultz for recovering a copy of "Innsmouth 1984" from the March 1985 mailing of the Necronomicon amateur press association so that it could be included here. The stories "Leng" and "Gothic Studies" are exceptions to the statement that most of the stories collected here were originally published in the amateur press. These two stories were original to the Moshassuck Press collection *Lovecraft's Pillow and Other Strange Stories.* I am not sure that H. P. Lovecraft, whom R. H. Barlow described as the most asexual person he ever met in his correspondence with August Derleth, would have appreciated the erotic bent of "Innsmouth 1984," "Leng" and "Gothic Studies." I can only plead that I as author bear sole responsibility for what I have written.

The title story of this collection was my response to Stephen King's challenge, in his introduction to Michel Houellebecq's *H. P. Lovecraft: Against the World, Against Life* (2005), to take up his story idea concerning the presumed survival of the very pillow that Lovecraft slept on. The late Rick Hautala and Mark Steensland also took up the challenge and published their version of "Lovecraft's Pillow" in Danel Olson's Ash-Tree Press anthology *Exotic Gothic* (2007). Steensland also made an excellent short film of the story, which can today be viewed on the internet. I suspect that other writers have developed the story idea which King cast into the public domain. My own version is not intended as more than an entertainment for the Lovecraftian reader. I hope its version of H. P. Lovecraft toward the very end of his life will ring true with some readers and Lovecraft aficionados. My protagonists Andy Kot and Ben Silver probably both reflect aspects of my own personality.

Perhaps I would do better to let the texts speak for themselves, but I'll offer a few comments on some of the other stories, for whatever help or insights they may provide.

When "Life and Death" was originally published under H. P. Lovecraft's byline in the Necronomicon amateur press association in 1977, it was not accompanied by the acknowledgment of authorship which I had intended. Whether it is a fair imitation of Lovecraft's Dunsanian-style stories from the 1919 era, I leave for each reader to judge. By the way, I intended no disrespect to my late friend George Wetzel in writing my own version of "Life and Death." Such is the scarcity of amateur journals from the 1918–22 era that it is still very possible that Lovecraft's actual story will one day be rediscovered. I would rejoice to live to see such a discovery.

"The Squirrel Pond" was based on a visit my wife and I paid to Graceland Cemetery in Chicago. I don't care much for its inverted sentence structures and florid prose today, but I have decided to let the story stand much as it was originally written. It's probably a good example of my attempt to write a Lovecraftian story in the mid-1980s.

Frankly, I think I did a better job with "Life and Death" nearly a decade earlier.

"Boy in Summer" was written to celebrate the one hundredth anniversary of the two-week visit that Lovecraft and his mother paid to James W. Phillips (1830–1901) and his wife Jane A. (Place) Phillips (1829–1900) in Foster, Rhode Island in 1896. Everyone in the story is a real person except for hired man Paris Shippee who is my invention. (For example, James W. Phillips was the elder brother of Lovecraft's grandfather Whipple V. Phillips.) Readers interested in all these people are invited to consult my Phillips family genealogy (1993), which is available for reading on microfilm at LDS family history libraries.

After falling silent fictionally for ten years, I conceived the idea of a lady psychic detective, Wilmott Watkyns, headquartered in my own native city, Cincinnati, Ohio. I think I was inspired in part by Jonathan Valin's marvelous series of Harry Stonor detective stories, which are also set in Cincinnati. Both of my Wilmott Watkyns stories (of which one is reprinted here) draw on Cincinnati's rich background of German settlement. My great-great-grandfather John J. Faig (1843–1909), a shoemaker, emigrated to Cincinnati from Wuerttemburg, Germany in the 1860s to escape the then-raging German wars. Two generations of his descendants, including my grandfather Walter A. Faig (1894–1983), continued in the shoe and leather business. Then my father Kenneth W. Faig, Sr. (1918–2003) and his brother John L. Faig (1923–1990) decided to go into the laundry and chemical businesses, respectively. Unlike Frederick Allroth in "The Haunting of Huber's," the Faigs were not Nazi sympathizers. My father was a stateside Army laundry officer during World War II, while my uncle, a graduate of the Naval Academy, saw action in the Pacific theater. Huber's Teepee is a dim echo of the now sadly closed Schuller's Wigwam restaurant in Cincinnati's College Hill suburb where my Uncle John and Aunt Betty lived for many years.

"Leng" reflects the sense of alienation I have always felt on long-distance automobile journeys, especially at night. "Gothic Studies" tries to fit a weird story into an academic setting.

The five David Parkes Boynton adventures have always been the most popular of my stories. I've never visited Boynton's home town (Fall River, Massachusetts), but it was the setting of the notorious Borden family murders of 1892 which have always fascinated me. R. H. Barlow's career as an anthropologist in Mexico always claimed a strong hold on my imagination, so naturally I worked a Mexican setting into the first Boynton adventure. The mostly submerged Suffolk village of Dunwich, anciently a great city, also fascinated me, and formed the setting for the second Boynton adventure, which also drew upon my fascination with the Borden murder case. The third adventure set in Providence was inspired by my fascination with HPL's "Nyarlathotep" and my respect for Providence's black community. In the fourth adventure I had Lovecraft falling in love and begetting a child with a young Italian girl from Federal Hill who was his fellow evening high school student. I hope the fourth adventure reflects my respect for Providence's Italian community and shows some respect for Lovecraft and his family as well. Of course, all of Boynton's adventures are completely my invention and have no basis in fact.

The alternative version of Lovecraft's ancestry in the fifth and final Boynton adventure is also my own invention and similarly has no basis in fact. I am inclined to accept Pardon T. Howard's version of Lovecraft's direct maternal (Phillips) line: Howard P.(9) Sarah S.(8) Whipple V.(7) Jeremiah E.(6) Asaph(5) James(4) Jeremiah(3) Joseph(2) Michael(1). But the link between James(4) and Asaph(5) remains to be proved. I don't know of any family historians who accept Lovecraft's claim that Michael(1) Phillips (1668 freeman of Newport, Rhode Island) was a son of Rev. George Phillips (1593–1644) of Watertown, Massachusetts.

I hope Lovecraftian readers will find some fuel for their imaginations in the stories collected here. In a sense, all Lovecraft's readers are collectors, because they share a strong predilection to correlate the contents of the author's imaginings. I can't claim the genius of Lovecraft, but if I have provided some pleasurable reading for the Lovecraft devotee, I am amply rewarded. I thank Derrick Hussey of Hippocampus Press and his collaborators S. T. Joshi and David E. Schultz for giving my fiction the opportunity for a wider readership than it has hitherto enjoyed.

I don't know how my writing will develop in future years. There are younger, brighter, more talented researchers of Lovecraft's life and associates active today who will accomplish more than I could ever hope to achieve. However, I hope to keep adding my own small bit to the story of Lovecraft's life. At one point, I contemplated an extended account of the life of HPL's erstwhile amateur rival Frank Graeme Davis (1881–1938) and his circle, including Elsa Gidlow (1898–1986), but for now I have decided to let the subject rest with what I have already written.

Since its foundation in 1973, the EOD amateur press association has served as my eyes and ears for perceiving the Lovecraftian world, but today websites like those maintained by Donovan K. Loucks, Chris Perridas, and David Haden are expanding the information available about Lovecraft. Electronic resources for family history are expanding so quickly that I wonder whether a collection of Lovecraft family records would be outdated before it was published. It is hard to realize that I worked almost exclusively with microfilm and print resources in compiling my own Phillips family genealogy twenty years ago. Technology is changing the world so fast. What is not changing is the fascination of Lovecraft's work for an ever-expanding body of readers.

As for fiction, I doubt whether I will write any more adventures of David Parkes Boynton. For one thing, it's hard to keep dates consistent if one writes too many adventures of a single character. I had the idea that Annie Gamwell and her friend Edna Lewis decided to treat H. P. Lovecraft to a week's visit to the Chicago World's Fair of 1933 in gratitude for all the time he spent caring for his aunt after she fell and broke her ankle shortly after moving to 66 College Street. I thought I could fit such a visit into the chronology of Lovecraft's life in 1933. My father and my uncle attended the 1933 Chicago fair (which celebrated "A Century of Progress") with their parents, and of course I was going to try to work the Faig boys into an adventure with HPL on the fairgrounds. Any Chicago visit by Lovecraft would also have to have included a rendezvous with *Weird Tales* editor Farnsworth Wright. I thought that Lovecraft might also meet with his old amateur nemesis Frank Graeme Davis, who by 1933 was pastor (in fact bishop) of his own Old Catholic Church of the Mystic Way on Chicago's North Side. For now, I have put my manuscript on the shelf to season. Whether parts of it will ever see print, remains to be seen.

It will be a treat to see a generous selection of my fiction in print from Hippocampus Press to celebrate my sixty-fifth birthday in 2013. I hope the diehard Lovecraftian will find many points of fascination in these stories. For the Lovecraftian reader with time for only one story, I recommend the title story "Lovecraft's Pillow." Perhaps the Lovecraftian reader might also want to look at "Life and Death" (it is short) to see whether he or she can imagine Lovecraft's writing that story. The general ghost story aficionado might try "The Haunting of Huber's" to see whether it pleases or not. The dark fantasy/weird fiction/horror aficionado might try "Leng." I hope that my stories will find both male and female readers. Despite her silence, I intended Delbertine Loomis of "Leng" as a strong character. The same applies to Professor Ann Giunta and her subject Frances Lawton of "Gothic Studies," Marina Kot of "Lovecraft's Pillow," and Wilmott Watkyns and Christine Allroth of "The Haunting of Huber's." I see more and more female names—Caitlin Kiernan, Lois Gresh, Ann K. Schwader, Faye Ringel, Silvia Garcia-Moreno, Rachel Gray are a few examples—in the Lovecraft domain. I hope that Lovecraft's ever-expanding readership will eventually include equal numbers of males and females. Lovecraftianity and cosmicism are not for adolescent males only!

Whether they are sleeping on Lovecraft's pillow or their own, I wish for all my readers pleasant dreams.

Tales of the Lovecraft Collectors

Introduction

When David Parkes Boynton died in his grandfather's house in Fall River in the spring of 1956, aged fifty-nine, the brief obituaries that appeared in the local newspapers mentioned nothing to hint that he might ever be of interest to a science fiction fan. They recited the story of the fortune that his grandfather Ezekiel Boynton (1828–1904) had amassed in the screw manufacturing business in nineteenth-century Fall River. Left with no descendant whom he considered capable of continuing his business, Ezekiel Boynton sometime before his death in 1904 at the age of seventy-five arranged for the sale of his interests for the sum of $3,500,000, which he left in trust for his son Arthur Clough Boynton (1857–1908) and his two daughters. Born in 1897, David Parkes Boynton was the only son of Arthur Clough Boynton and the socialite Ann Cullen McClintock. Upon his father's early death in 1908, David Parkes Boynton was left the beneficiary of nearly $2,000,000 in trust, the remainder of the fortune falling to his father's sisters. Encouraged in his intellectual endeavors, David matriculated at Harvard University in 1916 but dropped out in 1917. In 1918, upon the attainment of his majority, he acceded to a regular income from his grandfather's trust, which he continued to enjoy throughout the remainder of his life. Thus, despite the economic decline that Fall River suffered in the early years of this century, Boynton and his mother (who lived until 1938) were able to maintain their gracious home and standard of living. David spent his time in travel and in the pursuit of his diverse intellectual interests. He never married, and upon his death in 1956 his share in the trust income fell to his cousins. These promptly disposed of David's effects and sold the old mansion on Cowper Street in Fall River.

This much I was able to learn about David Parkes Boynton after my friend Lou Bellows inadvertently steered me onto him at the New England Science Fiction Convention in 1971. Knowing of my interest in H. P. Lovecraft and his work, Lou cornered me briefly in the dealer's room on the first day of the convention.

"There's a dealer here you ought to meet," he said. "Has something rather obscure related to HPL which no one has really been able to place." After I readily agreed to his proposal, he introduced me to the dealer, who specialized in comic books and related material and only rarely handled a fantasy item.

"I don't have it with me," he said, "but on Lou's recommendation, I'll send it to you if you'll leave me a $25.00 deposit. I don't know quite what it is. On the face of it, it's the diary of a fellow named David Parkes Boynton for the years 1919 through 1956. A lot of it, however, is quite obviously his attempts at fiction in the Lovecraftian mode. Some of it is rather good of its kind, I'm told by a few people I have had look it over. John Vetter, Jack Chalker, and Roy Squires have all examined it and pronounced it of only associational interest. When you've had a look at it, I'll let you have it for $50.00 if you want it. I have had it since 1962, when I picked it up as part of a lot of books that I bought at auction in Boston. I don't believe David Parkes Boynton was a pseudonym either, for many of the books that I acquired had his bookplate. I may have one or two of the books around still, and if so, I'll send you a sample along with the diary. I believe the fellow was from Fall River, Massachusetts—home of Lizzie Borden, you know. The books were mostly travel and history, no fantasy or supernatural fiction. Because of the obvious Lovecraftian references in the diary, I inquired of the auction firm whether they had had consigned to them any more material from the same source; however, they had not, and in fact the present lot was part of a group of material being sold by a storage firm in Boston for storage charges. I suppose that whatever fantasy or supernatural books had been left by Mr. Boynton had long ago been sold. John Vetter did, I believe, ask August Derleth for me if he knew anything of David Parkes Boynton; and John later told me that Derleth told him that there was such a Lovecraft collector and that he had had some correspondence with him. John called the diary a fine associational piece, but it didn't fit into his pattern of collecting only original material by Lovecraft. He said that Derleth himself had evinced no interest in the diary, saying that he was swamped with fiction in the Lovecraftian mode to read. Several other Lovecraftians to whom I have shown the diary have expressed no more than mild interest. I think it's rather vivid stuff, though, and I hope you'll give it a try. I think a Lovecraftian who read it through would thoroughly enjoy it. It has a ring of authenticity to it. Of course, I realize that it's fiction, but I think this fellow David Parkes Boynton must have had a special background to write it. Several comics collectors have offered me my price, but I have been holding out to interest a Lovecraftian in it. If you'll risk $25.00 on me and the manuscript, I think you'll at least have a good read."

I think both Lou and the dealer realized that no such sales presentation had really been necessary. The transaction was soon completed, and by March the ledger-sized black leather-bound diary of David Parkes Boynton had arrived in my mail. For more than twenty years I have pored over it and pondered its authenticity. Whether fiction or nonfiction, it is surely the greatest $50.00 bargain I ever acquired in my collecting career. Inquiry has failed to turn up much more about David Parkes Boynton than I related at the beginning of my introductory essay. I did finally locate one of his nieces, who had visited her aunt Ann McClintock Boynton and her cousin David Parkes only once or twice at the Fall River home, which she found gloomy and depressing. Cousin David had traveled widely in the Middle East, India, South America, and other odd corners of the world, she could recall. Heart disease had limited his activities in the final decade of his life and he had died alone in the old Fall River house in 1956. The administrators sold everything on behalf of the cousins and she had no idea whatever of what kind of literary material might have been sold. She knew nothing whatever of any literary interests of her uncle, although she always considered him to be a queer old recluse. She was the most informative of the cousins, for none of the others had ever met David Parkes Boynton.

Further inquiry has turned up almost nothing. Despite his wide travels, David Parkes Boynton left only one published work, a thirty-two-page monograph on Lizzie Borden published at his own expense in 1929, two years after the death of Lizzie Borden herself. Boynton stoutly defended her innocence and attributed the crime to an unknown party X, regarding whose identity he promised further revelations. These revelations were never published, and today most scholars of the notorious crime dismiss Boynton's work as frivolous. One authority whom I consulted, Mrs. Hyman Vickers of Fall River, told me that David Parkes Boynton was reputed to have known Lizzie Borden personally. She told me there was a rumor he had at one time owned her home Maplecroft, but I have been unable to verify this. The house on Cowper Street proved uneconomical in twentieth-century Fall River. The sale price for the estate in 1956 was a mere $125,000; the house was ordered demolished in 1960, and today a light industrial development occupies its former site. I have been able to locate no modern photograph of it, although a book which I have on nineteenth-century Fall River has a plate of Ezekiel Boynton's mansion on Cowper Street.

Finally, I did just manage to ask August Derleth about David Parkes Boynton shortly before his death later in the summer of 1971. I reproduce his letter here in its entirety:

June 12, 1971

Dear Kenneth:

The extreme press of my writing and publishing activities have prevented me from replying to your letter of May 30 until now. I believe John Vetter stumbled across the same material by David Parkes Boynton several years ago, so I'll tell you now what I told him then. David Boynton was one of the original purchasers of *The Outsider and Others* at the pre-publication price of $3.50. I have his original ordering letter still, since it was so curious. "My friend Mrs. Ann Gamwell of Providence, Rhode Island, recommends to me your book of her nephew's stories scheduled for publication this fall. I am pleased to enclose my cheque in the amount of $3.50 for the same. Respectfully yours, David Parkes Boynton, 9 Cowper Street, Fall River, Massachusetts." I have just two other letters of interest from him. The first, dated January 5, 1940, sent us his praises of *The Outsider and Others* and asked to be informed of our future plans. I wrote him back on January 10, 1940, thanking him for his praise and asking him whether he had known Lovecraft as well as his still-surviving aunt. After some weeks, he wrote back on March 19, 1940, to state that his mother and Annie Garnwell had been schoolmates at a private school in Providence and that he had indeed met Howard Lovecraft on several occasions and had enjoyed his literary work in *Weird Tales*. He regretted that he had no letters from HPL to contribute to our *Selected Letters* project. Under the date of March 25, 1940, I thanked him and asked him to express my own and Don Wandrei's best wishes to Mrs. Gamwell when he saw her. That was the extent of my personal correspondence with David Parkes Boynton. He did faithfully order all our Lovecraft publications, the last correspondence I have in file being his order for *Something about Cats* dated October 29, 1949. It is from the same Cowper Street address in Fall River. Don Wandrei and I discussed him several times, I can recall, and wrote him off as a family friend with more than the usual amount of interest in HPL's writing. We meant to ask Mrs. Gamwell of him, even to visit him, but her poor health and death in 1941 prevented the former, while I did not personally return to the East coast again until 1954, many years after my correspondence with Boynton. I remember John Vetter telling me he had left some associational jottings—fiction in the Lovecraftian vein—but frankly I was and am too busy to look at it. I am glad, however, that you find your acquisition of interest and would be happy to have the précis you mention. I suspect Mr. Boynton had a moderately good Lovecraft collection, including many original magazine appearances and of course our early Arkham House volumes. I'll add the photocopy of the obituary which you sent to my file on him.

Cordially yours,
August Derleth

Before I could send Mr. Derleth the promised précis, he died on July 4, 1971. Over the ensuing years I became more excited each time I reread the Boynton manuscript. Finally, therefore, I have resolved to offer some extracts from it to the Lovecraftian reading public, in the hope that someone may be able to unravel the threads that still baffle and intrigue me.

COLLECTOR THE FIRST

Major Geoffrey Hopkinton-Smith (1857–1943)

October 2, 1943
Mexico, City, D.F.

Finally I find an opportunity to jot down some of the things I have seen and done in the months since I was last in Mexico City. It seems that I have been in the country for ages, and it's like coming back to a different world to experience the hustle and bustle of the capital city. Very soon there will not be much difference between Mexico City and New York, I believe. Yet in the background there is always the silent mystery of the native Mexican, proud blend of conquistador and Indian.

After my stay in the capital city in June, I first toured the Yucatán peninsula and saw the mighty pyramids where the Mayan priests offered human sacrifices to their gods. I find it difficult to comprehend how a civilization advanced enough to build such technical wonders as these temples could also embrace such savagery; then again, the state of our modern world hardly bespeaks much of a rise from savagery in our own times. The Yucatán is still very much off the beaten tourist path, and I found that my smattering of Spanish was nearly vital to get along in the native hotels where I stayed. Very many sites are hardly changed from the way they appeared to their discoverer Stephens in the 1840s. My guides told me that some temples that he discovered have once again disappeared among the lavish and all-conquering jungle growth.

From the Yucatán I swung up through the southern states of Mexico and along the rugged and treacherous Pacific coast, where bandits are still lurking in the mountains. For the last month I have spent my time wandering about the vast sun-drenched plains of the north. Visiting many places where Yankee travelers seldom tread, I feel that I have gotten a good feel for native Mexico and its way of life. The way of life of the common people appears to be little changed from the descriptions one reads in Calderón de la Barca of the life of a century ago. Here where birth and death are so much more starkly a part of life than they are in the United States today, where we seal them within antiseptic hospital walls, one gets a real feel for the true currents of life. The comfort of a well-functioning ceiling fan in one's hotel room to relieve the oppressive heat, the comfort of a good meal in a well-aerated restaurant with decent linen on the table—all these things which I can have one thousand times more conveniently in Fall River I find that I appreciate and relish a thousand times over here. I find myself getting down to basics, which is I suppose a part of visiting this place.

Nor have I been without an adventure of my own. When I was last in Mexico City, I recorded with delight my visit with young Barlow, whom I had met through John Howell the bookseller when I visited San Francisco in 1939. I had the joy there of reading his own letters from HPL, which he has always carried lovingly with him wherever he has gone; and these letters confirm in their every page my vision of the man and his environment. Barlow and I delighted in our personal recollections of the man, although of course his own memories are by far the closer and more comprehensive than my own. He had learned through August Derleth of the death of Annie Gamwell, but I was able to give him much more detail than he had hitherto had. He tells me that depending upon his circumstances he may have to dispose of much of his collection of Lovecraftiana and related material, so that I must make a note to visit him when I am in Mexico again.

It was in the northern city of Aguascalientes, however, that strangely enough I had a notable Lovecraftian adventure. I had originally planned a one-week stay in the city, where the comfortable accommodations of the Hotel Miraflores, the interesting markets and shops, and the temperate local climate provided welcome relief from what I had experienced in most of the rest of northern Mexico. I soon became acclimated to the universal noonday siesta, and generally did my exploring in the early morning hours when the shops and markets were bustling or in the evening hours when they reopened for several hours. There seemed to be no reason to extend my planned stay of one week until one evening, after the vast red globe of the sun had finally begun to sink below the horizon, I strolled out for a walk through a shopping district that I had not previously explored. This evening I did not stop in the open-air markets, but I did find a place to stop for a refreshing iced beverage, and shortly thereafter a turn of the corner revealed to me the shop window of the Biblioteca Rumor, the first book-store that I had encountered in the city. I had of course inquired earlier of Barlow whether Lovecraft had to his knowledge been printed in Mexico, and he had replied in the negative, but after a leisurely tour of the shelves of the Biblioteca Rumor, which seemed to specialize in volumes of history and belles lettres, I could not resist asking the clerk in my rudimentary Spanish if he knew anything of Lovecraft.

"Indeed," he said, "it is very curious that you should ask this question of me. Allow me to introduce myself. My name is Luis Rumor, the proprietor of this establishment, which my father, an immigrant from Italy, founded in 1921. I do believe we have the largest stock of history and literature north of Mexico City. Now why I say it is so strange that you ask of this Howard Lovecraft is that he is an author completely unknown, to date, to the Spanish-speaking world. But I know of him very well myself, through a curious coincidence. One of my customers here is Geoffrey Hopkinton-Smith, formerly a major in the Indian service under Queen Victoria. He is the patriarch of an estate some five miles north of the city, which he has owned and where he has resided since before the turn of the century. He was one of the first customers of any note of my father and he has been one of my own best customers as well. His principal interests have always been in the native races of Mexico, in which field I believe he has through our assistance assembled one of the finest collections in private hands in Mexico. However, he also buys sparingly in the field of literature, and this Howard Lovecraft is one of the authors I have been called upon to supply to him.

"Since my father's time we have been consigning copies of the *Weird Tales* magazine for Major Hopkinton-Smith through our agent in Laredo, Texas, not without some difficulty with the official censors here, I might add. The magazine, along with the other cheaper pulp fiction magazines, has never been readily available here, even from the foreign news distributors in Mexico City. In 1939 the Major noted with excitement the news of an omnibus of Lovecraft's fiction which appeared in the *Weird Tales* magazine, and I was able after some months to obtain for him a copy of the book, which was published by a small firm in Wisconsin. This would also likely have been delayed by our censors, but I am able to import a limited amount of material without their scrutiny. Just now, the Major and I are anxiously awaiting a second omnibus that has been promised from the same publishing firm. The first, I am told, has become a collector's item already since the appearance of Lovecraft's work in a new anthology of supernatural fiction that has just appeared from Bennett Cerf's Random House. I have several copies of the latter, which have just arrived from Mexico City. You will pardon me for saying so much about an author of whom I know so little, for Major Hopkinton-Smith has hardly allowed me to retain the Lovecraft volumes on my shelves for my own desultory browsing, but it fascinates me to find that one of the few American tourists I have had in my shop asks for the same obscure American author who is collected by our local English patriarch here." Here the garrulous bookseller at length paused, and looked for some response from me.

I decided to play my strongest card first. "Do you think, Señor," I inquired, "that the Major would be willing to see me? I have not much to recommend me beside our common interest in Lovecraft, although I do have to my advantage the fact that my family—I am from Fall River, Massachusetts, in New England—were friends of Lovecraft's family and that I myself met him personally on four or five occasions."

"Indeed!" replied Señor Rumor. He pulled his moustache and set his eyes upon me more intently than before. "I believe the Major would be delighted to converse with a fellow devotee. In fact, if I recall correctly, the Major himself either knew or corresponded with Mr. Lovecraft. I do not know that he has ever told me the precise circumstances, but I am sure he would be delighted to tell you. I have this evening to send my clerk to the Major's home to deliver several books that he has ordered from me—among them, the Cerf anthology—and I will enclose a note informing him of your presence, I presume, at the Hotel Miraflores. I am sure you will find him very happy to receive you."

Here I thanked Señor Rumor profusely and purchased of him the second of the three copies of Wise and Fraser's *Great Tales of Terror and the Supernatural* which he had behind his counter. I have packed it lovingly among the things I intend to take back from Mexico, and because of my adventure I am sure that I will always remember the curious circumstances whereby I purchased my copy of this anthology in a bookshop in Aguascalientes, Mexico. I retired to my hotel, where pleasant speculation regarding my possible interview with Major Hopkinton-Smith occupied my time until I lapsed into a peaceful sleep filled with dreams comprised of bits and snatches of my day.

I had not been long at my breakfast the following morning when the maitre d' pointed a small but neatly clad Mexican boy to my table.

"A letter for you, sir, from Major Hopkinton-Smith," he said in halting English. "The Major has asked that I stay for your reply."

The Major's note was brief, but nevertheless fulfilled my hopes.

Casa de Cualha
Aguascalientes
September 9, 1943

David P. Boynton, Esq.
c/o Hotel Miraflores
Aguascalientes

My dear Mr. Boynton:

I am pleased to receive an introduction to you from our mutual friend Señor Rumor. I did not think that I should ever have the privilege of greeting a fellow devotee of the work of my late friend Lovecraft in this part of the world, and I earnestly hope that you can accept my invitation to be my guest tomorrow for luncheon. If this suits your convenience, please inform the boy who shall bear this missive to you, and I shall arrange to have a carriage call for you at your hotel about ten o'clock in the morning.

Yours very truly,
Geoffrey Hopkinton-Smith

Without hesitation, I let the Major's boy know that I would be pleased to accept his master's invitation, and after finishing breakfast took a short walk through the neighboring streets to take advantage of the cool of the morning before the blistering midday sun rose to its height. I returned to my hotel room to freshen up for my visit with Major Hopkinton-Smith, when about a quarter to ten, Señor Gonzalez, the proprietor of the Hotel Miraflores, knocked at my door.

"Señor Boynton," he said with what seemed to me an undue note of gravity, "Suaran Singh has come to call for you."

"Who?" I asked in perplexity.

"Major Hopkinton-Smith's major-domo," he explained. "An Indian he has had with him since the days of his service in India before the turn of the century."

"Thank you," I responded. "Please tell Suaran Singh that I shall be down momentarily."

"Yes, sir," said Señor Gonzalez, with a nod of acquiescence. He turned and had taken half a step down the hallway, when he turned his head again and quite surprised me by half whispering in a confidential tone, "Sir, I hope you shall look carefully to your welfare when you visit Major Hopkinton-Smith. His home is very isolated and is not well thought of by the people here. He has lived in this part of the country nearly fifty years now, since before the turn of the century, but no traveler or neighbor has ever been invited inside his home, to the best of knowledge. I wonder how you have come to know him."

"Señor Rumor of Biblioteca Rumor introduced us," I said. "Major Hopkinton-Smith and I have a common interest in an American author, Howard P. Lovecraft."

"A curious name," said the proprietor, "but I know nothing of that. I only know that Major Hopkinton-Smith is very jealous of his privacy and has few friends hereabouts. I ask you to be careful of your safety."

"I certainly shall," said I, half tempted to engage the proprietor in further discussion concerning the Major. But the thought of Suaran Singh waiting below changed my mind, and I bade the proprietor tell him that I should be with him momentarily.

Outside the Hotel Miraflores, an ancient Victorian coach with two dappled gray horses awaited me. Suaran Singh proved to be a wizened Indian of indeterminate age, with a swarthy spotted skin that stood in marked contrast to the bleached white of his coat and turban. With his turban he must have stood seven feet tall altogether, and as he silently helped me into the coach, I could not repress an undercurrent of apprehension. I almost felt relief that he offered me no word of greeting, for I imagined that the hollow resonance of his utterance could hardly add to my comfort. As we pulled away from the main entrance of the Hotel Miraflores, Señor Gonzalez waved to me with a look of mild consternation on his face. Just as he disappeared from my sight around the first corner we turned, I saw him engaged in close conversation with several local men, and I could not repress the feeling that the subject of their conversation was myself.

With a determined effort, I dismissed these thoughts from my mind. I was hardly prepared to be a modern-day Jonathan Harker, borne by a mysterious coachman to a remote and ruinous castle deep in Transylvania. I was a traveler in contemporary Mexico, with an introduction to an interesting, if eccentric, fellow bookman. Still, it was strange how everything I had learned of Major Hopkinton-Smith reeked of the nineteenth century. The coach, with its faded velvet upholstery and its ancient squeaking springs, seemed something of an anomaly in modern-day Aguascalientes, where most of the propertied class owned their own automobiles. But perhaps, I pondered, Major Hopkinton-Smith was simply very much attached to his Victorian origins. Then a thought struck me that I must admit had not occurred to me before. If the Major had seen service in India under Queen Victoria before the turn of the century, he must be very old indeed. It was hard to imagine that he might be a man of less than seventy years. The same, of course, would apply to silent Suaran Singh. Then, too, I wondered how Major Hopkinton-Smith had come to know Howard P. Lovecraft. It seemed so terribly unlikely. Perhaps he had gone off the deep end with occultism and convinced himself that he possessed some manner of psychical linkage with the late author. I had met, I reflected, a few occultists who claimed that there existed a type of esoteric truth behind Lovecraft's work at which Lovecraft himself only dropped hints in his published writing. I reflected that dabbling in occultism might account for an evil reputation in credulous Mexico.

The dusty road along which Suaran Singh directed the carriage led north of the city. After we had ridden for nearly half an hour, canyons and arroyos began to make themselves evident. Presently, Suaran Singh turned our carriage into a rutted road that descended into one of the canyons lying to the west of the main road continuing north along the plain. Soon deep shadows succeeded the bright sunlight of the open road as we continued to descend deeper and deeper into the canyon. For another half-hour we followed the rutted road, which jogged back and forth across the floor of the canyon to avoid the worst of the obstacles, until finally we debouched into a small widening of the canyon floor that appeared to be situated at the very extremity of the canyon. Before us on three sides loomed the walls of the canyon, two hundred feet high and nearly perpendicular at this point, behind us the narrow canyon through which we had descended. Then in the deep shadows I perceived a white adobe mansion in the classic Spanish style clinging closely to the northern wall of the opening. A few stunted juniper trees decorated the road leading up to the doorway, but not even the trees and the traditional red tile roof could relieve the deep shadow that seemed to throw the entire residence into gloom.

Presently we came to a stop, and Suaran Singh debarked to open the carriage door for me. Here I expected him to utter at least several words, but he merely helped me to alight and then ushered me into the building. A fountain played in the shadowed central courtyard, and the playing of the water along with the greenery of the stunted plants that grew there relieved my feeling of discomfort and anxiety. We entered a book-lined room that appeared to be a study, and Suaran Singh motioned to me to take a seat with a movement of his hand. Then, silently, he departed.

A great desk decorated with curios of many kinds, most of apparently Indian origin, faced me, and behind it a wall of books shelved from floor to ceiling in glassed cases. I was about to rise to examine the titles, when a booming voice sounded behind me.

"Mr. David Parkes Boynton, I presume," said Major Hopkinton-Smith as he strode into the study. At least, I was relieved to find that the Major did not preserve his fondness for the past by dressing in his military uniform. He was dressed in a somewhat worn business suit that had a faded look of 1910 about it. A great mane of gray-black hair crowned his high forehead, and dark black eyes, a long Roman nose, high cheekbones, and a protruding jaw completed the picture of his features. I had somehow expected to see him tan and swarthy like his servant Suaran Singh, but his complexion was most distinctively pale, with a hint of unhealthy grayness. Nevertheless, he was trim and slender and looked not a day over fifty-five.

"You will pardon my servant Suaran Singh," he explained, striding through the room and motioning me to resume my seat before he seated himself at the huge desk. "There were times when it was not good for an Indian to be the servant of an Englishman in the late Indian campaign. Suaran Singh and I visited many strange places during our fifteen-year sojourn on the Indian subcontinent. It was his misfortune to lose his tongue and nearly his life in 1888 at Rangipore."

"I am sorry for the man," I interjected.

"I assure you, he is most capable of taking care of himself," the Major responded. "In fact," he continued, "he attends to most of my needs here. I am so removed from the populated district that I have difficulty obtaining any native help. A few boy runners whom Señor Rumor has introduced to my employ are able to supply us with most of the things we need. Suaran Singh will make an occasional trip into Aguascalientes when the situation requires it. Needless to say, he supplies me with an Indian curry that none of the native women for a thousand-mile radius could begin to conceive of. You might say, sir, that I have a good situation for an elderly and reclusive former member of Her Majesty's imperial hussars."

"Our mutual friend Señor Rumor tells me that you have lived here many, many years," I commented, hoping to get some feel for the Major's age.

"That is quite true," the Major responded. "When I took my retirement from Her Majesty's service in 1890, I traveled by military ship from Bombay to Cairo and then by commercial steamer and railway to London. After a few months of winding up my affairs in London, I set out for the United States, where I arrived in January of 1891. For several years I was engaged in mining interests in the western states. Having accumulated a small sum in this activity, I spent the years 1894 through 1897 in the city of San Francisco improving this sum through wise investments into an even more comfortable sum. During the good years of the late President Diaz, whom I had the fortune to meet personally on several occasions, I had the opportunity to secure firm title to this entire canyon from one of the old Spanish families of the locality, which had never improved it. Title had run in the same family since the days of the conquistadors, who had seized the land from the rude and primitive savages who then lived hereabouts. The isolated situation seemed to suit my needs for peace and quiet completely and this house was completed under my supervision in the year of Our Lord 1897. I may astound you, sir, if I say that I have not spent a night away from this dear homestead since that time. I have already seen several generations come and go."

"You must have been very young when you entered the Indian service," I ventured.

"The year was 1875, sir," Major Hopkinton-Smith replied, "and you are correct that I was a youth of but eighteen years, having just obtained my commission as a lieutenant. I had already buried all my close family, but for one sister," he continued, "and I had resolved to build a new life for myself in India."

"You hardly appear to be a man of eighty-six years," I said, attempting to be as complimentary as possible.

"I think my rugged and isolated existence has kept me in shape," he said. "The modern existence of the cities, with their luxury and evil influences, has deadened the faculties of our race and softened our bodies. I can tell you, I have seen it a thousand times over in India. The basest degradation of body and soul contrasted against the fullest and most rugged development of each."

I hoped the Major was not a physical culture devotee, for I feared from experience that an unwelcome monologue on this subject would inevitably ensue. Indeed, however, his appearance was very remarkable for a man of his age, and I so remarked again.

"I fully expect," he responded, "to live to see my one hundred tenth birthday, and healthy and hearty, too. India has much to teach the modern Englishman," he continued. "You will probably not believe me if I tell you Suaran Singh already numbers his years in three digits."

"I have no cause to doubt you," I replied. "He, too, has evidently seen much. But, Major," I said, "I should not tax you with narrating too much of your biography to me. Tell me, how came you to become familiar with the work of Mr. Lovecraft? This isolated location hardly seems to be a likely place to acquire the cheap American periodicals in which his work saw its only publication until very recently."

"You might be surprised at the breadth of my magazine readership in this isolated location," responded the Major. "In fact, the great fiction magazines of the last decade of the former century and the first several decades of this century were among my greatest loves as a reader. During the good days of President Diaz, it was perfectly simple for me to import whatever titles I wanted through my news agents in London and New York. You would be surprised to know that I had most of the issues within my hands within several months of their cover dates, as well. Radio and all the other incursions of twentieth-century civilization have I am afraid spelled the doom of the great storytellers of yesteryear. But I have here bound in my library quite a selection. Along those shelves," he said, pointing to his right, "you have nearly complete sets of *Blackwood's* and *Cornhill.* Here," he said, pointing behind him, "is a very beloved and treasured possession, a nearly complete set of the *Dublin University Magazine,* edited by Sheridan Le Fanu, and containing nearly all his rare, dark novels. I regret the decline in production values in the American magazines in the early decades of this century—the commencement of what I believe is called the pulp era—but nevertheless I have preserved ample shelves of the greatest of the American magazines—*Munsey's, Cavalier, All-Story, Adventure.* The lurid and juvenile titles one sees today are evidence of the decay of our culture. Even enjoyment has been vulgarized. I can tell you, my friend Lovecraft regretted deeply the kind of publication in which his work was presented to the public. In fact, most of *Weird Tales* magazine I considered so poor that I kept tearsheets only of those stories which interested me most.

"This," he said, pointing to a lower set of shelves to his left, "represents most of my collection of Lovecraftiana. Here is something of a prize," he said, pulling out a handsomely bound volume consisting of tearsheets of all Lovecraft's magazine appearances. "I had a bit of a struggle keeping my magazines up to date through the troubled decades that followed the resignation of President Diaz," he continued, "but Señor Rumor and a cooperative news agent in Laredo, Texas, were able to work wonders for me. You will see that very little has eluded me. Here is 'Cool Air' in its original appearance in *Tales of Magic and Mystery;* 'The Colour out of Space' from *Amazing Stories;* and *At the Mountains of Madness* and 'The Shadow out of Time' from *Astounding Stories.*"

Examining his unique volume with pleasure, I still felt bound to interject, "You have still not told me how you came to meet Mr. Lovecraft."

"I should qualify that statement to make clear that I never had the honor to meet him personally as you had. From what I have said about my continuous residence here from 1897 and the facts of Lovecraft's life as you know them, I am sure you could have deduced as much. However, I do have a claim to honor which you as a friend of his family do not possess. For I am a member of his family, his relative. That is how I came to know him through correspondence."

"Indeed!" said I. "That is most fascinating. Do you care to elaborate?"

"Willingly," said the Major, proffering me a cigar from the box on the desk, which I declined. After lighting his own cigar and drawing out the first puffs of smoke, he continued:

"There is not, however, all that much to tell. My own knowledge leads me to believe that a good deal of what Howard believed about his own paternal ancestry was fable. You see, I, like Howard's ancestors, hail from the vicinity of Newton-Abbot, in the county of Devonshire. My mother, who married my father Henry Walingford Hopkinton-Smith, was born Elizabeth Luckraft in the tiny hamlet of Diptford in 1828. She was the granddaughter of Thomas Luckcraft, who was a landowner in a small way in the Newton-Abbot region and predeceased Elizabeth by two years. Lovecraft's forebear Joseph Luckcraft, who emigrated to New York, was a grandson of the same Thomas. What Howard knew of this Thomas contained some elements of fantasy but was largely correct, I believe. We discussed this point quite thoroughly in our letters. Apparently, Thomas Luckcraft was addicted to the gaming table, and because of his gambling debts he lost most of his property shortly before his death. The Luckcrafts were thenceforth reduced to the classification of workingmen, although this brutal fact may have been resisted by the American line. Of the existence of this American line, my maternal aunt Maud Davies, in whose family I was raised, apprised me, although she could offer me no detail. Indeed, what the Luckcrafts preserved of their genealogy was very barebones indeed.

"When a Howard Lovecraft began to dominate the letter column of *Argosy* in the fall of 1914, I was astounded to notice the variant of my mother's own family name. Happily, Mr. Lovecraft answered my letter of inquiry according to his usual generous custom. There ensued, my dear sir, an exchange of letters that, although at times infrequent, continued to within several months of the death of my friend and kinsman. Of course, the letter exchange in *Argosy* is the story of how Howard came to be known to amateur journalism. But it is also the story of how I discovered the American branch of my mother's family.

"Lovecraft and I exchanged great gouts of information in the first burst of our enthusiasm. I believe we consumed veritable reams of paper. Yes, I have the entire correspondence in my safe here, and were you staying here longer as my guest I should certainly offer to allow you to read it. Certain things—call them harsh realities if you will—which I knew would hurt Howard I kept from him; but generally our exchange was factual and mutually enriching.

"Do you see the faded daguerreotype of a small eighteenth-century country mansion which sits here on my desk?" he asked, pointing to a gilt-framed photograph. "That is a daguerreotype of the former country home of Thomas Luckcraft which my mother's father John Luckcraft had made just before its demolition in 1848. A curious gesture for a man whose living was that of a carpenter and who I gather could barely write his own name. Nevertheless, when I was able in 1915 to have a copy made and sent it to Howard, he wrote to me that the ownership of this daguerreotype was a dearer thing for him than most of his actual acquaintances. We discovered with joy that we both owned books with the signature of that old reprobate, Thomas Luckcraft. We debated the spelling of the family name and its variants. We exchanged uncounted genealogical notes. Howard's mother, Sarah Lovecraft, was proud of her husband's English ancestry, and I have several letters from her pen which she sent me at Howard's suggestion. I even have some samples of the writing of his father which he sent to me in return for mementos that I had sent to him. Because of my own desire for privacy, we both agreed that the information we exchanged would be reserved to ourselves.

"As I have said," he continued, "I was able to inform Howard of several points on which he was in doubt. The American Lovecrafts had lost track of one small branch stemming from their line, so that Howard was left in doubt as to whether he had been left the sole survivor of his own name on the American continent with the death of his great-aunt Althea Lovecraft in Rochester in 1905. I was able to assure him that he was very probably the sole survivor bearing that name in North America, based upon my only previous encounter with the name here. You see, the year 1892 found me in a remote mining camp in Colorado. That year a miner was stabbed to death in a brawl there—not an uncommon occurrence in the rough life of a mining camp—and I discovered with shock at the inquest (these were publicly attended events in the camps) that his name had been George Lovecraft. No one knew another thing about him save that he had come to the camp several years before and that he had been a hard-drinking, hard-living man who generally kept to himself. The circumstances of his death were less than ennobling, and I spared Howard the more distasteful details; enough to say that there had already been enough tragedy in the American Lovecraft line without my compounding the matter.

"I am sure you can see," the Major continued, "that my correspondence with Howard was nearly unique. I am sure no other correspondence in existence contains the intimate family matters which ours embraces. I also have in letters a veritable thesis by Howard on the popular fiction of the great magazine era, composed over several decades of correspondence. Were the greatness of these magazines not so forgotten today, I should say that his writing on this subject richly deserved publication."

After a pause, the Major continued. "Howard was very busy making his living by writing, and I myself very busy with my own researches into the history and folklore of Mesoamerica, so that our correspondence became more infrequent as the decades progressed. Our monthly exchanges of the decade of the World War became quarterly and semiannual during the decade of the 1920s. By the advent of the 1930s. I must admit that we exchanged letters perhaps once or twice a year, generally around Christmas. By the way, by form of address we were to each other 'cousin.' Knowing you to be a friend of Howard and a collector of his work," he continued, "I have made a small present for you. Howard's response to my Christmas letter of 1936 was delayed, but in mid-February I finally received a postcard from him. I have been able to have my boy Manuel have this postcard reproduced by a local photographer in Aguascalientes just last evening, after I received Señor Rumor's introduction, and I am pleased to give you the reproduction."

Here the Major handed me a manila cardboard folder containing a carefully reproduced positive photographic print:

> 66 College St.,
> Providence, R.I.
> United States of America
> January 7, 1937

Dear Cousin,

    I regret that I am so late in replying to your welcome Yule missive, which Annie Gamwell shared with delight. It is so good to know that another branch of our line thrives in the heart of the Americas. My aunt is much recovered from her illness of last spring and sends her best wishes. I myself have been very ill with the grippe. I frankly fear matters may take a serious turn. I wish very much I could share the conversation of a congenial male relative here. I am happy to hear you have seen my latest scribblings, tho' I am displeased with them myself.

> With affection,
> Howard

Moved by such a personal note, I poured out some of my own memories of Howard and Annie Gamwell. Major Hopkinton-Smith appeared pleased to have the image conveyed by Howard's letters so vividly confirmed. He was eager to learn details of Howard's last home and his family life in later years. I confirmed his strong suspicion that Howard's description of Robert Blake's quarters in "The Haunter of the Dark" was nothing but pure autobiography. I told him of how I had received R. H. Barlow's special permission to read in the papers that he had deposited with Brown University's John Hay Library and delighted in the tenderness and love for family and homestead which Howard had shared with his aunts. "I feel," I said, "so much closer to him than the family acquaintance I actually was." I regretted that I had not thought to bring along to Mexico any of the photographs that I had made of Howard's homes and the places in Providence he had written about.

"You know," said the Major, waxing into a communicative mood, "I have loved my splendid isolation here. But of all places I have felt the desire to visit, Howard's Providence and our own common roots in Devon head the list. I shall die here, but I suppose I have visited them in spirit."

We talked for hours and several times sent Suaran Singh away with the request that he delay luncheon. We talked of the recent publication of Howard's work in book form and of the preservation of his most important papers in the Brown University Library.

"I am very glad his literary manuscripts have been preserved," the Major commented. "I am less sure his intimate letters to his aunts will be properly understood. The world is losing its concept of what it means to be a gentleman, of what it means to honor one's elders. No, I have given orders to Suaran Singh that my letters from Howard are to be burned after my death. There are things in them that scholars would find very enriching for the study of the man and his work, but they are ultimately family letters. They belong to my world and Howard's world and I do not care to share them. Your photographic copy of my last postcard from Howard shall be your evidence that Major Hopkinton-Smith did not fabricate all he told you."

"You know," I responded, "if I possessed intimate letters from Howard, I might feel the same way. As it is, my only mementos apart from Howard's published work are an inscribed copy of his book *The Shadow over Innsmouth* and a photograph of Howard that Annie Gamwell gave me after his death. I have had the opportunity to buy several letter files in New York, but I don't care to barter for such material. The recipient has to judge whether he or she wishes to share such stuff with posterity. Hopefully, the posterity will be a public collection and not the auction block," I added.

"Barlow has done a good turn in preserving the literary manuscripts," the Major noted. "If he were not so young, so liable to misunderstand my milieu, I think I should invite him here. From what you say of his studies, he and I share a deep common interest in the history and folklore of this land in which we both live. Even in his infrequent letters to me, Howard remarked upon the brilliance of this youth, and I cannot believe that Howard has misjudged his potential. Nevertheless, I am glad that a solid, practical man like Derleth has assumed the publication of Lovecraft's work. *The Outsider and Others* is a worthy tribute to his work. I am looking forward very much to *Beyond the Wall of Sleep*. The selected letters project you mention will be a massive one, but surely there are letters enough of literary interest to justify a thick volume. I hope the editors will be gentlemen, though, when it comes to the publishing of personal letters."

On and on we talked until finally the luncheon invitation became a dinner invitation. Finally, about eight o'clock, we adjourned to the dining room, where Suaran Singh silently served us with several varieties of curry. Explaining away my conservativeness by my New England upbringing, I restricted myself to the least fiery of Suaran Singh's creations. Finally, our meal concluded with sweet pastries and a fruit wine. A chill wind began to rattle the shutters of the house, and the Major called upon Suaran Singh to light a fire in the dining room fireplace. The fire started slowly as the logs crackled, but gradually the flames began to dance higher and cast moving shadows against the dining room wall.

By a glint of light reflected from the fire, I was attracted for the first time by a large jeweled ring that the Major wore on the index finger of his right hand.

"I suppose that is the former eye of some Hindoo idol and carries its own curse with it," I commented in an offhand manner.

Unexpectedly, the Major, who until then had been in an ebullient and talkative mood, whispered firmly: "Silence! You do not say such things with an Indian nearby. I assure you, Suaran Singh's tongue was torn out as a result of an indiscretion far less than your own. It is indeed an Indian ring, but the stone belongs properly to the ring in which it is set. The stone was set in this ring longer ago than you would believe, and has never belonged to any god or idol. In fact, if I may be bold enough to say so, the stone is a protection against certain gods and idols."

As he spoke, it seemed to me that the beams of light reflecting from the stone began almost to surpass the flames of our fire. As the darkness settled about the old mansion, the stone seemed to glow with a radiance of its own, as if it contained some internal sun or kernel of force.

"I must say it is an unusual and a dazzling gem," I commented, hoping to mend fences.

"It is a bastion against darkness, both temporal and spiritual," said the Major. "Just as the fixed realities and the personal relationships of our lives are bastions against darkness."

"Then there is some religious association with the ring?" I asked.

"I should not call it religious," the Major said. "The dark things against which it protects are hardly spiritual in nature. I can assure you that the spiritual darkness is in our own souls."

"Are you a religious man, then?" I asked. I had noticed not a single crucifix in the entire house.

"No," the Major replied, "I have simply tried to be true to my own nature and to face life and to face death. I have few points of agreement with Karl Marx, but my attitude toward organized religion is one."

"Well, at least you share that attitude with Howard," I said. "Although he had an abiding affection for the traditional observances that organized religion has preserved."

"I did not say organized religion was all bad, but merely that I do not believe it to be true," said the Major. "I believe in things that I have seen and experienced. I call that my religion. Howard wrote about my religion."

"How so?" I asked.

"Howard wrote a story for which I provided him the background," the Major explained.

"You must mean 'The Mound,' which Mrs. Bishop has so recently published in *Weird Tales!*" I exclaimed. "Barlow maintains that it is wholly the work of Lovecraft. I might have expected that you provided much of the background for that story."

"I fear," he said, "that I have neglected *Weird Tales* since the death of Howard. 'The Shunned House' completed the volume of tearsheets that you saw in my library. No, Howard wrote of this gleaming ring in a very early story, of which I have an autograph fair copy in my safe. I do not know whether copies of the story survive elsewhere. Howard was not pleased with the story and would not allow it to be published. It was based as I have said upon a background that I supplied him.

"As I mentioned," the Major continued as the fire began to reach its full maturity, "I worked as a mining engineer in the western United

States from 1891 until 1894. I saw many men meet tragic and violent ends. But none stranger than that of the poor Mexican miner—I believe a true native descendant of the original races of this part of the world—who wore this gleaming ring. He died, you see, because he lost it, at the moment its protection was most needed. No one believed my story, so that I kept very quiet when I later found the ring close to the spot where the miner had met his death.

"What I later learned about the miner confirmed for me the truth of some very terrible legends I had heard about the native races of Mexico—there are hints of these in the oldest Spanish accounts," he said, pointing to certain shelves visible through the doorway of his adjoining library. "In fact, the protection which the ring renders is a proof of the veracity of the legends to which I refer," he continued. "You see, I traced down the brother of the miner, a poor starving wretch who lived in the gutter in Mexico City and whom I and Suaran Singh nursed here until his death in 1908. Despite his degradation, he shared the noble features borne by his brother, the proud insignia of the oldest native races of the Americas. He confirmed for me the truth of the terrible things I had heard whispered. I visited the wretched place where those two brothers were born—not twenty kilometers from here—and excavated myself the terrible evidence of the powers this ring, fashioned so long ago, was made to protect against.

"All this I told to Lovecraft in circumstantial fashion," he continued. "Of course, he changed the names of the characters and the setting. But otherwise he set down the essential facts of my story."

"What was the name of his manuscript?" I asked.

"'The Transition of Juan Romero,'" Major Hopkinton-Smith replied.

Despite my researches in the John Hay Library, I had no knowledge of such a manuscript. But then, I reflected, I had not yet been able to examine all the boxes of material at the John Hay Library. By this time, however, Suaran Singh had appeared in the doorway of the dining room.

"If you wish to return to your hotel tonight," the Major said, "Suaran Singh indicates that you must depart now. There is little moonlight tonight and the way will be treacherous. I would offer you a bed, but I really haven't the facilities to put you up properly, and the comfortable rooms of the Miraflores will be much more congenial for you than the drafty corridors of my isolated home here."

If the truth had been told, I would have welcomed the offer of a humble cot in the face of the prospect of a long ride back to the city with the silent and ominous Suaran Singh. But no such invitation was forthcoming from the proverbially reclusive Major. I bade him farewell, all the while hoping for an invitation to return, which he did not offer. He seemed to be drawing back from his ebullient effusiveness of the afternoon and early evening. His words and aspect now were formal and severe. Perhaps the effect of the fruit wine was wearing off. In any case, Suaran Singh drove me home without incident. I noticed that Señor Gonzalez and his compardons had awaited my return on the balcony of the hotel. They and Suaran Singh exchanged evil looks as we drove up. For myself, I was too tired to do anything but to retire to my room for bed.

The next morning, Señor Gonzalez congratulated me upon my safe return. "An evil place you visited," he commented. "Nothing about it which belongs to Christ. My friends and I were prepared to intervene if you did not return within a short while."

"I assure you," I replied, "no such rescue was needed. The Major is a charming man. We had a delightful day of conversation. I suspect he cannot help the fact that his Indian companion is a mute, and a rather imposing one at that."

"The devil!" cried Señor Gonzalez. "I have nothing good to say about that Porfirian skunk and his Indian henchman." The proprietor turned away with an obvious indication that he did not wish to discuss the subject further. His reference to President Diaz made me wonder whether there was bad blood between the Major and the present town authorities. It seemed likely that some political or economic animosity was at the root of the more nebulous charges made by Señor Gonzalez.

The hoped-for invitation to return to visit Major Hopkinton-Smith again never came. Five days later, I departed to wend my way back to the capital city, where I am staying now in preparation for my return to the United States.

December 27, 1943
Fall River, Mass.

Winfield T. Scott has just published an excellent if occasionally inaccurate feature article on HPL in the Providence Sunday paper. How I wish Annie Gamwell had lived to see this article. I think a real swell of interest in Lovecraft's literary work is beginning now. I suspect I shall have much to collect in the coming years.

I finally heard from the bookseller Rumor in Aguascalientes. I had forwarded tearsheets of "The Mound" for him to send to Major Hopkinton-Smith. His letter was both very brief and very shocking:

December 14, 1943
Aguascalientes, Mexico

My dear friend Mr. Boynton:

Pardon my delay in responding to your package and my poor English.

"The Mound" arrived during the first week of November. I sent it out with Manuel the same day I received it. I saw Señor Hopkinton-Smith just once after forwarding "The Mound." He came to town to consult an old map in the provincial library. I asked whether I should acknowledge receipt of "The Mound."

As his words were the last he ever addressed to me, I remember them clearly: "No, something so important I shall acknowledge personally, if I am able." The last phrase was added almost as an afterthought.

On the night of December 1–2 we experienced a terrible storm, accompanied by a moderately strong earth tremor. On December 4 I sent Manuel with a delivery for Señor Hopkinton-Smith. Imagine his surprise to find that a landslide had totally buried the home of Señor Hopkinton-Smith in fifty feet of stone and rubble.

I pressed for an excavation, but the superstitious and fearful local authorities would have nothing to do with the suggestion. The coroner signed death certificates for Señor Hopkinton-Smith and his servant without so much as an investigation. I weep for the esteemed Señor and I also weep for the wealth in books and manuscripts that perished in his home. The Major was as you doubtless know the leading authority on the mysterious native races of this region of Mexico, and his collection of books and manuscripts—which I and my father helped him to assemble—reflected his stature as a scholar.

Perhaps someone will someday excavate his home and his collection. But it will require thousands of dollars.

The curious thing is that Manuel has Señor Hopkinton-Smith's ring. He will say only that he found it lying just beyond the pile of rubble which covered Señor Hopkinton-Smith's home. I do not know what this means, but I have decided to conclude in my own mind that the Señor misplaced this ring before the tragedy struck.

It is with regret that I inform you of these tragic circumstances.

Yours sincerely,

Luis Rumor

P.S. Yesterday I paid Manuel $50.00 US for the ring, and his parents tell me this morning he is missing. I fear he has run away to the capital city. I have placed the ring in my safe in case the firm conclusion of my mind in this matter proves to be untrue.

June 19, 1944
Fall River, Mass.

Marginalia arrived today from Arkham House. Derleth has published "The Transition of Juan Romero," dated September 16, 1919. I am left tingling with wonder and fear as to the fate of Juan Romero and of my friend Hopkinton-Smith. The Brown University Librarian informs me by telephone that the library does have a manuscript of this story. I must write to Barlow for permission to view it.

August 19, 1947
Aguascalientes, Mexico

Although I concealed my purpose from Barlow, I could not resist a visit here. I have, however, been frustrated in all directions in my inquiry. Señor Rumor died in 1945 of a heart attack and all his effects have been dispersed. There are no surviving relatives. No one knows what became of Manuel Rivera. He has never returned home. I did locate Manuel's parents. His father is a cobbler. He believes the Major was a wicked influence and corrupted his son. He did, however, consent to guide me back to the site of Casa de la Cuahla. Fifty feet of collapsed stone and rubble tell no story. Underneath it all, however, lie a man and a collection the like of which this continent no longer possesses. I have amply rewarded Señor Rivera for his kindness, expressed my sympathy, and leave tomorrow.

September 3, 1949
Fall River, Mass.

This summer I determined to breach the subject of Major Hopkinton-Smith to Barlow in a discreet manner. I simply mentioned to him that I had met the man in 1943 through a common interest in Lovecraft and inquired whether he had left any published works in Barlow's field.

I may as well quote Barlow's reply in full.

Azcapotzalco, D.F.
August 18, 1949

Dear Boynton:

I was certainly curious to learn that Major Hopkinton-Smith was an aficionado of HPL's work.

Hopkinton-Smith was the first to study the mysterious natives who originally inhabited the region around Aguascalientes. He was a self-made scholar and advocated a number of theories concerning the religion of this native race which professional Mexican scholars did not endorse. This native race, which he called the Cuahla, built a mysterious tunnel network under the present city of Aguascalientes, and it was the Major's theories concerning the construction and purpose of these tunnels which other scholars found the most controversial. By the time of the conquest, the Cuahla had descended to a state of semibarbarousness and fought ferociously against the Spanish conquerors. Most scholars believe that the race was completely obliterated in a savage battle in a canyon north of Aguascalientes, but the Major maintained that a few pure-blooded Cuahla survived. From these alleged survivors he gathered his entire corpus of Cuahla folklore and religious belief, with minimal support from the excavations that he conducted in the neighborhood of Aguascalientes for the better part of two decades under the protection of President Porfirio Diaz. His work on the Cuahla was published in Aguascalientes in 1912.

I had no idea that he had survived until 1943. He was an amateur researcher, but a pioneer in a still neglected field.

His interest in HPL's work, of course, meshes neatly with his love for the mysterious Cuahla of Aguascalientes. In retrospect, some of his Cuahla folklore reads like Lovecraftian fiction.

Sincerely yours,
R. H. Barlow

November 12, 1954
Fall River, Mass.

A trip to Cambridge yesterday. I finally discovered in the Widener Library a citation to Hopkinton-Smith's work on the Cuahla, published in Spanish in Aguascalientes (Imprense Rumor y Holguin!) in 1912. The Bancroft Library has a copy. I shall have to see whether I can obtain a copy of it. For a modern book, it appears to be devilishly rare. Perhaps Hopkinton-Smith's political enemies hindered its distribution. I wish I still had my friend Barlow to call upon for help in such matters.

Feeling poorly and plan several days of rest before doing anything.

COLLECTOR THE SECOND

Dean Alan Edgerton Noble (1876–1959)

December 12, 1929

Fall River, Mass. Visited HPL in his rooms at 10 Barnes Street in Providence and met his aunt Lillian D. Clark, widow of Dr. Franklin Chase Clark, for the first time. A charming and witty woman. HPL and I talked of many fascinating subjects, too numerous to record here, but I particularly questioned him about the source for his tale "The Dunwich Horror," published earlier this year by Farnsworth Wright in *WT*. "The principal source," said HPL, "is the scenery and legendry of the area around Wilbraham, Massachusetts, where I was the guest of an elderly amateur friend last summer. The home where she and her cousin live in retirement is a veritable treasure-trove of colonial antiques—many still used for the purposes for which they were originally constructed—and Mrs. Miniter and her cousin Miss Beebe are easily the best on anything appertaining to local history or tradition." The crying of the whippoorwills for souls at death a bona fide Wilbraham legend according to HPL.

Specifically asked HPL whether the drowned city of Dunwich on the Suffolk coast of England—famous in the lore of antiquaries—had anything to do with his inspiration. "Years ago," he said, "in my youth I encountered an illustrated article on Dunwich in one of the popular magazines of the time, of which I was a voracious reader. I can't recall now whether it was the *Review of Reviews* or *Harper's* or some other. It made a lasting impression, and I wish I had the tear sheets for my morgue of weird items. Unfortunately, I failed to cut the article out at the time; perhaps I read a library copy and hadn't the opportunity." (An aside: HPL is proud of his ability to cull learning from the public library. His repertoire at the Providence Public Library is astounding and includes the entire run of the *Providence Journal* from 1829 to date. "In my youth I was an indiscriminate accumulator of books—no idea of economy—but in my later years I have learned what may be achieved through judicious and economical use of a public library." A sensible attitude.)

HPL commented that the theme of ancient drowned cities has always fascinated him: in this connection, he particularly mentioned the legends of Ys off the coast of Brittany, Atlantis in the Atlantic, Mu in the Pacific, and Poe's famous poem "The City in the Sea." His principal fictional use of a drowned region so far—inspired mostly, he admits, by the flooding of several areas in western Massachusetts and Rhode Island for the construction of water reservoirs for Boston and Providence—occurred in his story "The Colour out of Space" in *Amazing Stories* in 1927, but he thinks that he has far from exhausted the fascination that the theme holds for him. Several early fantasies, including "Dagon," "The Temple," and "The Doom That Came to Sarnath," also bear upon the theme. Also the poem "The Nightmare Lake," echoing Poe's "The City in the Sea." "Cthutlu," of course, is a water entity, and he has also thought of a New England story involving commerce with his sunken regions. [Ed. Note: Here Boynton has added a one-word marginal note in a different ink: "Innsmouth."]

HPL admitted no special knowledge of Dunwich beyond the article that caught his attention years ago, but confessed a lively curiosity about the place. I told him he might consult a very rare history of the place at the Widener Library the next time he visited Cambridge and that I would send him my impressions if I managed to visit Dunwich on my spring tour of England. "I envy you. I don't know whether I would be able to return," he said. I was able to acquaint HPL with the fact that the port of Dunwich was the favorite resort of the poet Swinburne in the seventies and eighties of the last century and that the poet had celebrated its windswept desolation in several powerful poems. HPL evinced a lively interest and promised to look the poems up the next time he visited the public library. He hadn't an edition of Swinburne of his own. "Loveman adores Swinburne": HPL.

More family matters than previously. HPL showed me a photograph of his father, "whom I hardly knew." HPL reticent on the subject of his late marriage to Sonia H. Greene, whom he met through amateur journalism, but I gather it has been terminated. The entire family gifted artistically; I saw several paintings by the deceased mother and by aunt Lillian. The father wrote in a copperplate hand that HPL showed me. Bade HPL and Mrs. Clark a festive Yule before departing for Fall River.

April 11, 1930
London

Have been in England two weeks on antiquarian and bibliophilic tour. Am afraid the antiquary's lot is better than the bibliophile's— despite the world depression, everything seems to be as scarce and as expensive as usual. Sadleir's studies have quite bid up the once-unfashionable Gothic novels—they have simply disappeared, to be frank. I was able to make a joyous acquisition at Quaritch, however—a fine copy of Gardner's *An Historical Account of Dunwich, anciently a city, now a borough,* etc., etc., London, 1754, in the original binding for £200. I believe that there are only five copies recorded in public collections and less than that ever recorded for private sale. Several evenings of Gardner have quite whetted my appetite for visiting Dunwich in the near future. My friend Canon Weeks has given me a letter of introduction to the rural dean, one A. E. Noble, purportedly a scholar and antiquary in the legendry and lore of the place.

May 9, 1930
London

Only now do I find the time to pen some hasty recollections of my visit to Dunwich, which I wish to record before their vivid memory shall fail. I came in by hired motor on May 3 and took a simple room in the only inn and guest house in the place. The accommodations

were clean, the food decent, and the proprietor and his wife friendly
and helpful. Spent the first day just walking along the cliffs. I was
amazed by the desolation and desertion of the place—a street and perhaps thirty small houses, with one simple white church with octagonal
tower all that remains apart from a few ruins on the cliffs. To think,
this was a mighty seaport city a millennium ago, with brazen gates, its
own mint, several hospitals, and the greatest fishery industry in all England. All vanished today. The old parish church of All Saints and its
graveyard are tumbling into the sea, occasionally exposing the mortal
remains once interred there, while else there remains only the ruins of a
Franciscan monastery. The corporation is governed by its two bailiffs,
of whom my esteemed host is one and the other the local squire, Mr.
Barne of Sotterly Hall, something of an antiquary himself. (He excavated a tumulus in Greyfriars Wood south of the town some years
ago.) A hearty meal of English beef and ale at the inn refreshed me after a tiring day of exploring the coastline for several miles in each direction. A copy of Swinburne which I'd packed relaxed me in the
evening and summoned up the proper mood.

I sent my card over to Dean Noble (technically of the North
Dunwich deanery, I am informed) immediately upon my arrival, and he
responded with a cordial invitation to luncheon the following day. The
deanery proved to be just a few doors down from the guest house, a
bit of a ways from the simple white church that it served. Dean Noble,
a tall, graying man of perhaps fifty-five years, with close-cropped hair,
wrinkled brow, stern visage, and gnarled, veined hands, greeted me
with a firm handshake at the door of the deanery.

"Pleased to have another antiquary to talk to," he said by way of
introduction. "For all the fame of this place, I have few visitors. Mr.
Barne and I are virtually alone here as antiquaries and local historians.
By the way, I trust you are staying with us for a few days. Mr. Barne
has expressed an earnest desire of meeting you and has invited us both
to dinner two days hence at Sotterly Hall. And he proposes an exploration of the tumulus in Greyfriars Wood, too, before you leave. Oh, indeed, I hope you don't miss either. Sotterly Hall, you know, is a
veritable museum of local antiquity."

I assured the Dean of my willing acceptance.

"I am afraid I am rather a rank amateur, a mere enthusiast in these matters," I responded. "The most I claim is to have a proper appreciation of the work of the real workers in the field."

"Ah, we all have a bit of the enthusiast in us," replied the Dean, warming to the talk, as he motioned me to be seated in his book-lined study. The floorboards almost seemed to groan under the heavily-laden floor-to-ceiling bookcases. "I can assure you there is far more here than theology and antiquarianism—quite an accumulation of my varied interests over the years. You know the work of our late lamented folklorist, musicologist, novelist, and historian Sabine Baring-Gould? Ah, good. A dear friend of mine, I might add, a virtual mentor. I fear I am quite in his mold, although I shall never have one-hundredth of his productivity. Oh, I have my early indiscretion of a novel—*Ella Humphries,* published virtually without critical notice by Eveleigh Nash in 1911—but aside from that and some scattered poems in the press and magazines, I am afraid I have restricted myself to occasional articles in antiquarian publications. The Roman and early Saxon periods are my specialty."

"Much the most controversial period in the history of Dunwich," I ventured to add.

"Indeed, indeed," chimed in the Dean, "from Bishop Felix of Burgundy in the Year of Our Lord Six Hundred Thirty the way is rather clear. Ah, but the putative settlement of the ancient Britons, the Roman camp Sitomagus, the Saxon Dummoc-ceastre or Domnoc, the Seaham of the days of the heptarchy before Felix—that is all very far from clear. My friend Mr. Barne has thrown great light on the matter through his researches, which have progressed most notably since the Victoria History of Suffolk summarized them. It's only a pity so much remains unpublished. There's no doubt that Dunwich was indeed the site of the Roman encampment of Sitomagus—though, of course, the actual site of the main camp has been under the waves for centuries. The connection with the Romans is clearly established by archaeological remains. But, to tell you a secret, I believe Dunwich was a center of religion and commerce long before Felix and even the Romans. Those ancient Britons whose fabulous deeds you read in Holinshed and Geoffrey of Monmouth are another entire question. I fear the sea has indeed obliterated most of the traces we might have had of them here, but esoteric and occult traditions nevertheless run deep. And they have their bit to add to the story of Dunwich."

"I've read the local ghost story about the young lord of the manor who lost his heart to the servant girl and died of disappointment," I said.

"Yes, touching of its kind, and I assure you we also have our phantom hounds and a few other members of the traditional corps of spooks. The kind of thing that fascinated Sabine, but doesn't have the same hold on me. No, I speak of older, deeper traditions maintained by the esoteric societies that have flourished in these isles from the very dawn of their history—from the Druids of ancient times, whose knowledge I am convinced far surpassed anything we suspect today, to the lodges of the modern day."

"I noticed the Masonic symbol over your hearth," I ventured. "Isn't it rather unusual for a Church of England clergyman to belong to the Masons?"

"More civic good will than anything else in its outward form, I assure you," responded the Dean. "Two hundred years ago I would have been chaplain to the mariners' society or priest for the fishermen's guild. Today, I belong to the Masons and the Grange. I am proud to say the Church of England has never taken the narrow attitude toward these fraternal societies that the Roman Church has adopted. For the common man, they promote community interest and fellowship. But for the initiate, there is much in addition to offer."

"I once ventured to answer the Rosicrucians' newspaper advertisements," I said. "I wasn't very impressed with what I received in response."

"Nor is any worthwhile goal ever reached without many small steps," replied the Dean. "I assure you, Masonry has much to tell of Dunwich that is not recorded in your standard histories."

"And I thought that when I had the good fortune to acquire a copy of Gardner at Quaritch several weeks ago I had in my hands nearly the whole of her known history!" I said.

"So you are the lucky possessor of the Quaritch copy!" chortled the Dean. "Well, a good home it has, I am sure, though I am sorry to see another such treasure leave our shores. My friend Mr. Barne owns the only acknowledged local copy, though one or two others are rumored to be in the little-used collections of some of the aristocratic families of Suffolk. Perhaps it were well for another copy to go to America. One copy at the Widener is rather thin coverage. Your copy, by the way, is that of James Briggs Ponsonby, a London antiquary. Corresponded for years but never met. Ah, well . . . but, no, to return to our line of talk, Gardner recorded what the outer records of our society reveal about Dunwich, the once-great city. The Masons, whose pious members built the great city with its brazen gate, cathedral, and churches, record in their traditions much that is unwritten in the outer history."

"You don't say," I responded. "Do you regard their traditions as reliable?"

"Oh, yes, they meet the most crucial tests against modern fakery," said the Dean. "You see, I learned them from men with no business to suspect their correlation with recorded history. Simple townsmen and landsmen of the area, enjoying a convivial lodge evening, and recalling to their pastor what their parents and grandparents had whispered to them . . . which in turn a prior generation had whispered to the parents and grandparents . . . and so on going back who knows how long. I am convinced that Masonic traditions of a Druidic priesthood, embattled against the encroachment of the Christian religion, are correct. The great wood that once lay to the southeast of the city, now washed away for centuries, was one of their sacred woods, you know. The Druids, I mean."

"What's the evidence for that?" I queried.

"Tradition, tradition, only tradition. But I have come to respect tradition, Mr. Boynton. I believe we antiquaries in general only half suspect its real value."

"Then your Masonic traditions carry the history of Dunwich back beyond even Roman times?" I asked.

"Just so," said the Dean. "The city was a school and headquarters of the Druidic priesthood in pre-Roman times, dating to the second millennium before Christ. Masonic tradition speaks of the high science and technology attained by the Druidic priesthood, which guarded its secrets very closely. The Romans established a military encampment

nearby and tried to stamp the Druids out, but they held out in the fast-
ness of their great wood in the face of terror and torture. Only the
merits of Christianity gradually turned men from their savage practices,
which Masonic tradition firmly maintains involved human sacrifice at
various sacred times of the year. In fact, our Masonic traditions maintain that the Druidic priesthood persisted well into the Saxon period; I
think only the chaos and destruction of the Danish invasions in the
ninth century ended the outward Druidic priesthood. And some Masons will tell you the priesthood in an esoteric sense persisted far
longer, even unto the present day. A number of early hermetic lodges
of the Rosicrucians claimed descent from the Druidic priesthood,
some of them apparently with some validity. The Masons, you know,
have always maintained a strong Christian orientation—rest assured, I
would not associate with them if they did not—perhaps in this area descending from the Hospitalers who made their headquarters here in the
Middle Ages. The local tradition makes quite clear that the Masons and
our brothers the Hospitalers had need to fight the good battle against
the local forces of evil throughout the Middle Ages.

"Curious how the hermetic Druidic tradition—linked to the powers of nature represented by earth, wind, and water—battled the forces
of order and civic development here—represented by us Masons—just
as the town itself battled against the encroachments of wind and wave.
It is not, in fact, unheard of in the Masonic tradition to assert that conjurations were the source of some of the most devastating storms
which wrecked our fields and buildings. A murdered child, for instance, was found in Greyfriars Wood following the terrible storm of
1286. So recently as 1740 a young boy who lived at a good remove
from the shoreline wandered away before the terrible storm of that
year descended and was presumed drowned. But many local Masons
will tell you different. When Crowley, that archpriest and mage, came
to Suffolk to lecture in 1908, I'm proud to say the local men hooted
him from the podium. Yet, sad evidence of a cult of evil persists still."

"Are you saying that the Druids are still plaguing you?" I asked.

"Aye," responded the Dean, "many years as a pastor have convinced me that the evil in men's hearts will persist until the final judg-
ment, God have mercy on us. In a quiet community of less than two

hundred souls you would think that I would have an easy task. But I am convinced no one in lay life has any true idea of the cruelties of which the human heart is capable. Aye, we in Dunwich even today have those who would worship the raw powers of nature in opposition to the message of Christ's self-sacrificing way. It's mostly common evils I've stumbled upon—drunkenness, violence, adultery, the gamut of everyday vice—but here and there also I've uncovered a hint of a more organized kind of evil. I've seen the fires burn on May-Eve and Hallowmass and seen the leavings on the ritual stones when the night's doings are done. The devil's root persists here still. But men and church endure. Good men, like my churchmen and Masons."

"I am glad you have hope," I said.

"Aye," replied the Dean, "but you've not bargained for a lecture on morality. You must await your visit to Squire Barne to see a real museum of local antiquity. But I may show you just a few rarities of esoteric bent." Here the Dean went to his shelves and pulled from the lowest shelf a large folio volume bound in imitation leather. "Here I have put together just a few ephemera . . . probably the only collection of its kind . . . you may enjoy paging through it with me. If I thought it were of general interest, I should offer it for publication in the journal of our local antiquarian society. But I am afraid they are more interested in seventeenth-century mills and taxation rates." Here the Dean opened the volume, which proved to contain a number of documents and chapbooks, each enclosed in a protective sheath of transparent plastic.

"Here you have the charter of our Masonic Lodge here at Dunwich, granted by the Grand Lodge in London in the Year of Our Lord 1765. You'll note Squire Gardner's firm signature in the lower left-hand corner, so there is no doubt where he stood."

Noble turned the page.

"And here is a rare chapbook, *A Treatise on the Ancient Religion of the Britons,* by a fellow Mason, Hezekiah Wentworth, published in Northampton in 1792. Dreadfully rare, I'm afraid, but it was easily available to me through Masonic sources. On page twelve he mentions Greyfriars Wood near Dunwich as being one of the fastnesses in which the organized Druidic priesthood held out the longest. He claims that

Oderich the Dane finally burned the priests and their center in A.D. 832. But he also hints darkly of a persisting esoteric Druidic tradition 'which yet wreaketh havock among the brothers at Dunwiche.'"

Noble turned the page.

"And here's a reply in kindred, a chapbook dating to 1808, published anonymously and allegedly in Rotterdam, but we know it to be the work of an English author and printer. Titled *A Defence of the Right of the Ancient Druidical Priesthood of Britain,* it purports to show that the Druidic priesthood represents the two lost tribes of Israel and the only real claimant of Jehovah's covenant. A totally blasphemous work and a total cover-up of the true nature of the Druidic cult in my mind. But this copy is also special." Here the Dean carefully removed the fragile chapbook from its plastic sheath. He laid back the title page so that I could see the interior of the chapbook. There was an inserted sheet of notepaper with the following brief message in a spidery hand:

> Newton-Abbot
> 6 November 1806
>
> To the Brothers at Dunwich and Southwold, Greeting!
>
> It is to be hoped that the enclosed pamphlet shall be of some use in refuting the allegations of the Masons in your neighbourhood. In its pages I show the Druidic priesthood to be the only inheritor of the covenant of Jehovah; how in casting down our poles and molochs the ten tribes, now perished from the earth and consigned to gehenna, erred grievously against God's intent. Naturally, I have preserved our anonymity to guard us against the depredations of the ignorant.
>
> Yours in fraternity,
> Thos. Luckraft Grand Master, Alpha Lodge

"That rare name is borne by a literary friend of mine in America," I stated.

"That would be Howard Phillips, son of Winfield Scott," the Dean responded.

"Then you know my friend?" I asked.

"Of him," replied the Dean.

"I trust that no malicious Druid priest lurks under his rational exterior," I prodded.

"I trust so also, friend," responded the Dean.

"His life's work, you know, is the literature of supernatural dread."

"I know," said the Dean. "It happens to be an avocation of mine." Here he stepped to a distant bookcase and retrieved for me a familiar object.

"Why, it's the special edition of Paul Cook's *Recluse* with HPL's 'Supernatural Horror in Literature'!" I exclaimed.

"A friendly bookseller obtained this for me, after he noticed it in an American catalogue. I think it's by far the finest work of its kind, by far surpassing Birkhead, Railo, Yardley, or any of the others. It bespeaks a real connoisseur's interest."

"And the knowledge of a fine craftsman," I added. "Lovecraft has written some excellent supernatural fiction in his own right."

"Yes, excellent, but disturbing," replied the Dean. "I've had a devil of a time of it, but a couple of back-issue magazine suppliers in Chicago and New York have supplied me with enough copies of Lovecraft's pulp magazine appearances to assemble a fair sampling of his published work. I have bound the tearsheets up in a volume on the shelf over there," he said, pointing to the same distant shelf, from which he had retrieved his *Recluse*. "Masterful stuff, but hinting darkly of esoteric knowledge. Lovecraft's description of a sea-cult in 'The Call of Cthulhu' is particularly disturbing here on the edge of the sea at Dunwich."

"Yes, and he has more tales of the sea in mind, I believe," I added. "But, surely, Dean, you don't suspect my friend of dabbling in occultism. I assure you, he is the soul of the rational. Doesn't believe a jot in anything other than the mechanistic universe of classical physics. Quite an amateur astronomer."

"I am sorry to learn your friend is saddled with the burden of modern skepticism," the Dean replied, "but in response to your question, no, I am certain Lovecraft is no occultist. I believe, however, he may have inherited some rather scarce occult materials which he may be rather reluctant to acknowledge. I'll say this: his great-great-grandfather Thomas Lovecraft or Luckraft, the author of that blasphemous pamphlet we have just examined, was a libertine and a swindler, and a mage and a Druid priest. He went down to his death in the year 1826 unrepentant and burdened with his sins. His descendants here in England have struggled back from the penury in which his indiscretions left them to become honest men. Most still live in Devon, but some live in London as well. It was Thomas's younger son Joseph who carried his father's occult knowledge to America just a few years after the old man's death. I can tell you for a fact that the so-called Egyptian Lodge of Masonry in America represented this Druidic cult. The papers of Thomas Lovecraft, I am convinced, came down to your friend's father, Winfield Scott Lovecraft, who was in business in Boston at the time the Egyptian Masonic Lodge flourished there in the eighteen eighties and early nineties. It was dissolved swiftly, secretly, and permanently by the authorities after its excesses were uncovered in or around 1892. Just one year later, I believe, Winfield Scott Lovecraft was confined to the madhouse, where he died, the record states, on July 19, 1898."

"Howard the inheritor of occult papers?" I asked.

"I believe so . . . at least of fragmentary and suggestive notes that have been reflected from time to time in his fiction. The Egyptian Masons had a kind of perverse regard for the theosophical teachings of Mrs. Blavatsky, and you can find many curious interpretations of her work hinted at here and there in Lovecraft. Not the kind of thing a man totally unacquainted with occult tradition would come up with."

"Well, you know, Howard told me that he copied the conjurations in his story 'The Horror at Red Hook' directly out of the *Encyclopaedia Britannica* article on magic. That hardly bespeaks sophisticated occult knowledge."

"No," said the Dean, "as I said, I believe him to be no occultist. Lovecraft is a dreamer and an artist, a rationalist in his outward and everyday life. But I think he is susceptible to occult influences . . . through those Luckraft papers whose existence I suspect and perhaps even through psychic invasion of his dreams. . . . I trust you can appreciate the possibility of that . . . only read our Dion Fortune."

"Howard would scoff at your suggestions," I said.

"I know," said the Dean. "Look here." Here he turned the page of his scrapbook. There, bound in the next transparency, was a letter in HPL's distinctive hand:

10 Barnes St.,

Providence, R.I., U.S.A.

December 6, 1928

Dear Reverend Noble:—

I appreciate your compliment on my "Supernatural Horror in Literature." I didn't suspect that it had reached your shores, but then again Cook does cater to a select clientele.

To answer your question, I have read a few general volumes on magic and hermetic philosophy—I can recall wading through A. E. Waite at the Providence Public Library—but I've only used bits and snatches in my fiction—Mrs. Blavatsky's *Book of Dzyan,* etc. Some of the WT gang are far more astute in these matters than I.

I am interested to learn that you have discovered my great-great-grandfather Thos. Lovecraft as the author of a hermetic treatise, but I can only tell you I have inherited no copy of it. Of his books, I have just one, a geography dating to 1773.

Yes, I am aware of the English Dunwich; I used the name and only the name for my WT story. Years ago I read an illustrated article on the subject of your town in a popular magazine. The theme of ancient cities lost of the encroachments of the sea is one that continually recurs in my dreams.

Yours very truly,

H. P. Lovecraft

"You'll notice how guarded his statements were," said the Dean. "I believe your friend knows far more than he acknowledges; but he is a very discreet and reticent man in his personal life. And no mage. A middling to good writer, if you will permit me to criticize what I cannot hope to equal, but no mage. In fact, I am rather more concerned *for* your friend than *about* him. No true occultist would drop the kind of hints that he drops. I would give him warning after the fashion of Dion Fortune, but he, as a rationalist, would spurn it."

"I suppose we must all act upon our own view of the universe," I interjected.

"I wish more of us would confide our destinies to Church and God," replied the Dean. "But I promised no sermons. My scrapbook doesn't have many more leaves." And the Dean proceeded to show me the rest of his book. Next were the minutes of the Masonic Lodge of Dunwich for the year 1840. "You'll notice the reference to 'defending ourselves against those who would denigrate and oppose us,'" said the Dean. Turning to the next page, he continued, "Here's a very cheap and exceedingly rare pamphlet published by Winslow Corey, a member of a heretical Mormon sect, in Salt Lake City about 1889. He claims for the Egyptian Masons secret knowledge descending from the builders of the Pyramids and from the Druidic priesthood. Note that, like Thomas Lovecraft, he claims that the modern-day Egyptian Masons descend from the two lost tribes of Israel. Most startling, he maintains that ancient Atlantis was identical to fabled Ys off the coast of Brittany and propounds the thesis that 'the now-sunken port of Dunwich in ancient times was a center of Druidic communication with Atlantis, whose marvels we find so faintly echoed in Plato.'

"I will be frank," the Dean concluded. "I believe this man was a disciple of the same group in which Winfield Scott Lovecraft played a prominent role. You'll note he refers to the Master of his lodge as Tall Cedar. I think that might even be W.S.L. himself, but I don't know. Most startling is this drawing of a great hilltop city with astronomical temple on page 40. It is surrounded by forests. It bears the title 'Ancient Dunwich, Artist's Conception.' It is, I might note, signed WSL. Curiously, the pamphlet concluded with a diatribe accusing the Masons with involvement with ritual murder from the Middle Ages to the present. He claims these crimes, so often laid at the doorsteps of the Jews, have been perpetrated by the orthodox Masonic orders. That the ritual murders have been a conspiracy to discredit the true Egyptian Masons or Druids. In a curiously current note, he blames the 1888 Ripper murders on us Masons and cites the well-reported inscription 'the Juwes will not be blamed for nothing.'

"I think," remarked the Dean, "you can begin to appreciate the wickedness involved here."

"Nasty stuff," I agreed.

"I'll tell you, I think it was the Egyptian Masons themselves who dabbled in ritual murder. I think such a crime led to the dissolution of the Boston chapter in 1892. I think it unhinged the mind of our W.S.L."

"A well-woven theory," I commented.

"A disturbing one," the Dean echoed.

He turned the page.

"Here's a cutting from the *East Suffolk Advertiser* of 1908. Tells of traditions of modern witchcraft in the area—hill fires at sacred times, altar stones, Druid groves, the works. Anonymous, but penned by a late, lamented fellow Mason."

The Dean turned to the next page.

"Cutting, drowned boy, 1922. Hints of suppression of some of the facts by the authorities.

"Finally," he continued, turning to the next page, "a German pamphlet, dating to 1928. *The Occult Tradition of Ancient Thule and Its Modern Adherents,* by one Wilhelm Wolff, Stürmer Verlag, München. This fellow is associated with the Hitler of the Beer Hall affair of 1923. But it's the same glorification of Druidic nature-worship as representing an ancient tradition superior to our Christian tradition. And the same blasphemous attack on Church and law. I really do fear when I read this kind of thing. Again, the Thulites and Druids are the loyal lost tribes, and the pamphlet is almost savage in its wrath against the modern Hebrew of the Israelite race. I think the Nazis intend their extinction somehow or other should they ever come to power.

"But this were all a rather somber introduction to our shores," said the Dean. "Ancient and desolate though they be, they can still be hospitable. My sister keeps house for me, and should momentarily have a hearty Dunwich luncheon—sufficient for the fishermen of old time and more than sufficient for the pursuits of a sedentary clergyman—ready for us. Let's enjoy it and talk of more general matters. Do be circumspect in mentioning anything to your friend Lovecraft. He is a good man; I only wish he'd be a bit more careful. You might say that to him sometime, if you find the right moment."

"I may," I agreed, as we walked toward a memorable luncheon.

I spent most of the following evening and morning pondering all the things Dean Noble had told me. What a surprise to encounter mention of my friend Lovecraft here! And hints of a dark, esoteric tradition centered around the vanished city of Dunwich! Shortly after noontime repast the next day, Dean Noble sent a note around asking if I would join him and Squire Barne for a jaunt to the excavations in Greyfriars Wood that afternoon. I told the Dean's messenger boy that

I would be delighted to join the Dean and the Squire, and about one hour later they presented themselves in the lobby of the inn.

The Squire was a portly, balding man in his mid-fifties with faint eyebrows and receding chin. I daresay I would have expected a squire to look more like Dean Noble and a rural dean more like Squire Barne, but I've long ago learned not to put too much faith in outward appearances.

The Squire extended a hand. "Well, I daresay Dean Noble will have convinced you by now that ancient Dunwich was the spoor and spook capital of the world," he chuckled. "Today, I vow, I shall show you some solid archaeology which at least indicates that there were ancient inhabitation of the environs, long before the Romans arrived, I believe."

"I'll be delighted to join you and the Dean," I responded. "The Dean has certainly thrown out some dark possibilities about evil-doing in the environs," I continued, "but I should be the first to admit that he seems on far firmer ground than do most writers and commentators on occult matters. I daresay he has demonstrated that there is a long-standing hermetic tradition that Dunwich and the once-surrounding forests were a center of the ancient Druidic priesthood."

"Yes," said the Squire. "Though we find remains of Roman pottery and Roman coins in the vicinity, indicating a military encampment in the neighborhood, I believe the tumulus we will visit today is actually a burial place and site of worship of the ancient Britons. There's evidence of a pattern of standing stones on the perimeter of the open area—in fact, two separate geometric patterns of stones, long since removed, of course, perhaps by the Saxon general Ebusa when he finally suppressed the outward practice of the Druidic religion here in the sixth century. When you visit Sotterly Hall for dinner tomorrow evening, I'll show you the evidence which I believe clinches the argument—a star-shaped amulet, uncovered during my excavations in Greyfriars Wood, which has ancient markings very similar to others found at Druidic sites elsewhere in Britain.

"Yes, indeed, Mr. Boynton, I believe there's a good deal of archaeological evidence to back the esoteric traditions Mr. Noble cites. I believe Dunwich in ancient times was a great center of the Druidic priesthood, where they undertook the training of acolytes in their eso-teric sciences and practiced the ritual of their religion. Have you seen that sketch of Dunwich by W.S.L. in the Salt Lake City pamphlet Dean Noble has? You may have presumed those cottages the homes of me-dieval fisherfolk and townsmen; yes, I venture so. And the greater edi-fices the churches, hospitals, and mint of the city, am I not correct? If you look closer the next time you are at Dean Noble's, I think you'll agree that the architecture is nothing like the Middle Ages ever saw. No, to my eye, the larger buildings are clearly of Druidic origin and the scene depicted in the artist's imagination dates perhaps from the first millennium before Christ. I tell you, it is my belief that that illustration represents an uncannily likely portrait of Dunwich when it was the cen-ter of a great Druidic academy of esoteric knowledge. But come, let's have a hand at more solid stuff."

We motored two miles south of the town in the Squire's comfort-able sedan. Scraggly woods shortly overtook us. "The last of the once-great woods that surrounded Dunwich at one time," the Squire com-mented. Shortly we arrived in a windswept clearing. The faintest hint of a tumulus rose toward the center of the area. Posted signs warned passersby not to disturb the site because of an archaeological excava-tion. I noticed that there appeared to have been some vandalism, with one of the signs being upset and trash scattered about in its vicinity.

"It appears not everyone's as enthusiastic as yourself about these archaeological endeavors, Squire," I noted.

"Yes, I daresay," replied the Squire as he parked the sedan at the edge of the road. "Quite a bit of ignorance and superstition hereabout; there's a certain segment that doesn't want to see any of the ancient sites disturbed. I call such opposition mere backward superstition and ignorance, though I believe Dean Noble believes it may have its darker aspects."

"Squire," I ventured, "do you think there is a chance that preserv-ers of the ancient Druidic traditions still persist and may want to dis-rupt your excavation?"

"Oh, I don't think there's any question that most of the knowledge of the ancient Druid priests—look at the monuments they raised which still stand—has utterly perished. But the heart of man embraces shadow as easily as light, and men continually harken back to the darker corners of every age of human existence. We may wonder for instance about the existence of Satan, but there is no question that benighted human beings throughout history have seized upon the idea of Satan and constructed a framework for their wickedness around the idea of his existence. Likewise, we have very little idea of the Druids. Yet, the darker hints about them—their human sacrifice at appointed times of the year, their wicked necromancy, their glorification of the raw, untamed power of nature—remain to fascinate the darkness in the human heart. Oh, yes, I am sure there have been those who have called themselves Druids ever since the real Druids finally disappeared as a public priesthood at the time of the Saxon conquest. I think the Dean has a good case for organized activity in the forest surrounding Dunwich up through the suppression by the Danes in A.D. 832. Certainly, the Christianity brought by Felix the Burgundian was a great counterweight against the ancient folk belief, but I have no doubt that the cult of latter-day Druids, if you will, persisted for centuries after the planting of Christianity here.

"I don't know whether Dean Noble mentioned it to you or not, but John Dee, the magician, hermetic philosopher, and diplomatist who served Queen Bess, was very interested in Dunwich. Some correspondence of his on the subject is in the British Museum as well as encoded documents that may one day yield more information about the once-great vanished city. In my opinion there is too much that rings true in the otherwise insipid publications of these so-called Egyptian Masons to ignore the fact that they may preserve some hermetic traditions of the latter-day Druidic cults. Wherever the standing stones and sacred groves of the ancient Druids remain, seems to be a hotbed of these latter-day cults. Devon and the whole West Country were a particular center; I assume Dean Noble showed you the Luckraft pamphlet of 1806."

"That name's known to me as a contemporary American author and in fact a personal acquaintance of mine," I mentioned.

"Yes, Dean Noble has told me," replied the Squire, "and I have read some of the man's work. Rather too bizarre for my taste, but it oozes with hints of the Egyptian Masonic tradition. Everything leads me to believe your friend Lovecraft has somehow absorbed some of the occult legacy of his paternal line, albeit probably unwittingly. There is certainly every reason to suspect that his father—W. S. Lovecraft, I believe—was the W.S.L. of the Salt Lake City pamphlet and the guiding light of the Boston lodge of the Egyptian Masons.

"The last record the Dean and I have uncovered of outright Egyptian Masonic activity here in England occurs about 1916–1917 in London and involves Crowley and some of his friends; but we've unearthed dark hints that there is a connection with the Knights of the White Camelia and the Ku Klux Klan in the southern United States even up to the present day. A number of Klan publications maintain that the white Anglo-Saxon race is the true descendant of the lost tribes of Israel descended through the blond-haired heroes of ancient Thule; of course, their mission is to restore Thulian supremacy by wiping out the black and yellow races. And there are disturbing hints of Egyptian Masonic occultism behind the Hitler movement in Germany. Quite a thought, I'd say. I fear if the fellow ever obtains power. I rather imagine he'll make the depredations of the Klan look like Sunday-school gatherings. But let me show you a bit about the technical aspects of this excavation," he continued.

With this, the Squire led us on a half-hour technical exploration of the site. Midway through, I got the feeling of being spied upon and couldn't shake it. Nevertheless, I gleaned that there was solid evidence of ancient occupation. Squire Barne was striving to interest the authorities in further excavations, but obtaining the necessary funds had been very difficult. Finally, the chill of a still nippy late afternoon drove us back into the Squire's sedan. He drove us back to the town and had tea with us in the lobby of the inn.

"Did you notice that we were observed during our survey?" he asked, midway in the conversation. "Only a few of the locals ever evince any interest in my project, but I am constantly spied upon even in the most mundane undertakings at the site. Really gives me a bit of the willies, and my friend Noble here doesn't offer much consolation."

"A man delving into ancient traditions must needs be careful," commented the Dean. "Roots run deep. I wish your friend Lovecraft and all concerned would remember that."

With the expectation of an interesting evening at Sotterly Hall on the morrow, we parted, and I retired to rest and read before dinner. That evening, I put myself to sleep with the poetry of Swinburne that was inspired by this desolate region.

A veritable museum of antiquity awaited me the next evening at Sotterly Hall! The star-stone is certainly curious, and the Squire showed me plates of similar amulets found at Druidic sites. I get the impression the Squire is being hard-pressed economically, and I hope the reversals will not force him to sell Sotterly Hall. Again the curious feeling of being watched, of malevolent forces at work. The Squire's man Eldon drove me back to the inn very late, and I was very glad to be back. I think I have had about enough occultism for this trip and intend to expend the rest in sightseeing and book-buying. Did enjoy comparing notes on antiquarian volumes with Squire Barne. Struck a bargain with Dean Noble. For an excess copy of an older Suffolk topography in my collection, he will have photographic copies of the pamphlets made and sent to me. That will be a great aid to further investigation. Squire Barne promised some bits on the Dee material at the British Museum. We discussed Lovecraft's use of Dee in fiction—much discussion on the fabled *Necronomicon* which I am too weary to set down now. It does appear that Lovecraft must know more than he admits about an esoteric tradition. Someday, perhaps, I'll ask him.

November 5, 1930
Fall River, Mass.

Finally, a word from Dunwich. I thought Dean and all had finally dropped into the sea and the last bit of the place disappeared beneath the waves. But one thing has dropped into oblivion—my pamphlets. The originals have been lost en route to a London photographer. The mood of the Dean's postcard is dark and depressed. I am glad he has received the topography, though. I shall drop him a line advising him to keep it, though he wishes to return it.

May 4, 1934
Fall River, Mass.

A most curious letter from a Dr. Stanislaus Hinterstoisser of the Institute for Magical and Occult Research in Vienna, Austria. I quote it:

24 April 1934
Vienna

My dear Mr. Boynton:

My correspondent Dean Alan Noble of Dunwich, Suffolk, U.K., indicates that you may be able to help me in a serious and vital inquiry. I am deep in research on the Egyptian branch of Masonry and need several keys to pursue my research further.

(1) Can you tell me how I might reach the American writer Lovecraft? Is there an accessible edition of his work? Dean Noble tells me it may bear upon my subject.

(2) Has the famous murder of your city—the Borden case of 1892—ever been connected with occultists? Dean Noble tells me you are an authority on the case.

(3) Can you refer me to anything available on the Boston or Salt Lake City Lodges of the Egyptian Masons? Or of Masonic connections with the Knights of the White Camelia or the Ku Klux Klan?

Begging your pardon for so many inquiries but assuring you of their crucial importance, I remain,

Faithfully yours,
Hinterstoisser

Considering the obstinate silence of Noble despite several notes I've sent, I've decided to be compact in my reply:

1. I shall give the address of HPL.

2. I shall profess that I have never heard occultism mentioned in connection with the Borden case. My thesis is that the maid told the truth—there was a strange man involved—perhaps a lover who had gotten Lizzie pregnant. I shall send a copy of my chapbook of 1929.

3. I shall truthfully admit my ignorance of Egyptian Mason lodges in the U.S. or of any connection with southern irredentist groups.

I frankly have had enough of the topic, though why Lizzie should come up is disturbing. Perhaps Hinterstoisser believes W.S.L. was the mystery figure and that is why my thesis interests him. Why was Lizzie arrested in Providence in 1897 after acquittal on the charge of murder? The shoplifting story never held water as far as I was concerned. An attempted meeting with that madman W.S.L.? Dark thoughts.

November 23, 1935
Fall River, Mass.

Providence earlier today. First visit to HPL and Annie Gamwell in their home at 66 College Street. A heartening experience. I wish them both many happy years there. I insisted upon taking Howard out to the best Italian restaurant in town. Annie G. declined. A long and interesting conversation over an excellent dinner before I drove back to Fall River. (Though HPL would not even look at my squid!)

I finally summoned the courage to broach the subject of Hinterstoisser. Had HPL ever heard from him? He had written me asking about "Egyptian Masonry" in the U.S., at the same time making glancing reference to HPL's fiction.

"Why, yes," Howard began, somewhat hesitatingly, I thought, "that I did, several years ago. Now, cousin, you know my opinion of the whole of occultism and the so-called psychic sciences, so I'm sure you'll see why I gave the fellow a rather curt reply. I hate to accuse a man of charlatanism, but his field of research comes damned close to it. Naturally, I've a broad lay reading in the so-called classics of occultism. And I sprinkle my stories liberally with bits and pieces of real—if you want to call it that—occult claptrap to lend a little verisimilitude. But Egyptian Masonry?"

I muttered an apology.

"No, you were perfectly right to give the man my address, so that I might set him straight. You know, he had the effrontery to assert that my dear departed father—taken from me so early in my life because of his illness—was a practicing occultist from whom I inherited, 'albeit innocently,' in the words of Dr. Hinterstoisser, my bits and pieces of dark knowledge."

"I apologize again, profoundly," I said.

"Well, no need," said HPL. "You know my father, before his illness, was a successful businessman and he was a prominent Mason in Boston. But everyone with any sense knows that organization, whatever its origins in the misty past, is now a civic and fraternal one accommodating mostly the aspiring businessmen and politicians of each locality in which it is active."

"What I've always believed," I offered.

"Not that they haven't a hermetic tradition or two," HPL added. "I inherited a Masonic manual or two among my father's things and there's some fascinating mythological stuff involving the history and origins of the group. But to believe that these straitlaced politicians and businessmen are mages in disguise . . ."

"Incredible," I said. "Do any of their ancient traditions appertain to your city-in-the-sea, Dunwich?"

"Why do you ask?" queried HPL, visibly appearing to shift mental gears.

"When I was there in '30 the local Dean knew of your fiction and held basically the same beliefs as Hinterstoisser, I believe."

"Noble," said Lovecraft.

"Yes, he's the man I met," I replied. "And Squire Barne of Sotterly Hall."

"Barne of Sotterly," said HPL.

After a long silence, he began to speak. "My Grandpa Phillips was a Mason, too, you know. Same standard garden-variety as my father, as far as I know. In a way, Grandpa Phillips was my father, since my real father was completely incapacitated before my third birthday. I can barely remember him. Grandpa Phillips believed a bit in the idea that the Masons do originate from an ancient society of builders; and he saw the organization as continuing to do battle against evil and oppression in its own way. So maybe they did help to build that ancient city lost to the sea . . . the desolation written of by Swinburne seems so sad. Yes, maybe it was their mighty work and replaced an older order of things now hidden from us. That's just an idea. If that kind of idea occurs in my dreams and imagination, haven't I the right, as an artist, to seize upon it without being pestered to death by occultists?"

"Indeed, you have," I replied. "Had I known you'd be pestered . . ."

"I can't fault you for providing Hinterstoisser with my address," said HPL. "He's unfailingly polite and apologized himself for his unwarranted speculations about my father. But those speculations hurt deeply, nevertheless, cousin."

"I am sure your father was an upstanding man, HPL," I replied. "It's a pity illness took him so early."

"A right and proper Englishman," said HPL, "a proud scion of an ancient line. Some people, even some of my own distant relations, whisper things about him—about him, of whom I have only the barest tokens. Well, they're false. I resent their hinting. I went to the Vital Records Division at City Hall and with some difficulty viewed my father's death certificate. It says general paralysis; he never recovered from a series of apoplectic strokes, Boynton. I lost both mother and father to that sanitarium on the river, Boynton, and it hurts me very much when family or friend or especially an outsider drops insinuations—false insinuations—about them. Whatever you may hear my dear aunt say, or anyone else, my father and my mother and my wife are those I have loved most dearly."

"HPL," I muttered, "I've hurt you deeply. I apologize profoundly."

"No, you aided what you believed to be a proper inquiry," he replied. "Remember, cousin," he urged, "the dreams of dreamers leave their property once they have been set down on paper. They can easily become the common stock of charlatans who pretend that dreams are real. But life is real, not dreams. My parents are both dead and my wife and I, I fear, have permanently separated. She wanted a divorce, but a gentleman does not divorce his wife without cause. My dreams and the literary friends who share them are to a large extent my life today. Otherwise, I have only these familiar scenes, my home, and my aunt to relieve my loneliness. So, cousin, grant me liberty of my dreams. If lesser minds abuse them, pay it no need. It will always be so."

"Spoken with dignity, HPL," I said. "I promise to direct no more occultists to your door."

Gradually, the conversation returned to more congenial subjects, and we parted in brighter spirits.

Still, a disturbing conclusion to a day that began with such a pleasant reunion.

March 5, 1938
Fall River, Mass.

A letter from Hinterstoisser—the fourth or fifth in the past four years, without the encouragement of even one reply from me. He is frantic about the possibility of *Anschluss,* fears the Nazis with mortal fear. The man sounds wilder with each letter. He believes the Egyptian lodges engineered the slayings of the London prostitutes in 1888–1889 and the Fall River murder in 1892. The London murder, to stir hatred against the Jews, but why the Fall River slaying? Does he proclaim Lizzie a secret practitioner of Masonic sex-magic? Nonsense—I decline to reply.

May 22, 1940
Fall River, Mass.

Yet another letter from Hinterstoisser, mailed from Geneva. He *must* know how to reach HPL; mail addressed to 66 College has not been acknowledged. The world order—what there is left of it—depends upon his reaching HPL. More wild speculation about Nazis and Egyptian Masonry and Klansmen and W.S.L. et al.—some ten pages of it, written in an increasingly undecipherable longhand. I consider that a very brief reply may be helpful:

> My dear Hinterstoisser:
> Although I cannot see aught but madness in what you write, I think it may be helpful to inform you that Lovecraft passed away several years ago. I cannot help you further.
> Sincerely yours,
> D. P. Boynton

November 20, 1940
Fall River, Mass.

An hour-long visit with AEPG in a Newport sanitarium today. I fear she is failing, in much pain, and wonder what will become of 66 College Street if she dies.

Her tearful thanks for my small friendship with her nephew. Bemoaning HPL's misfortunes. She says W.S.L. led a profligate life and died as a madman as a result of his concupiscence. Infected his own wife, may have weakened HPL's constitution. Some dark, dark incident set off the final madness—terrible whispers. She believes Grandpa Phillips a broken man from that terrible day in 1893. I detect a note of resentment against HPL's wife. Even she abandoned HPL, according to AEPG. AEPG does not know where she lives or if she even knows that HPL is dead.

A terribly depressing visit. I hope AEPG will not suffer overmuch.

January 31, 1941
Fall River, Mass

AEPG has died, I see from the Providence paper. Have sent flowers for her funeral. No close relatives. I suppose the remainder of HPL's things will be broken up now. I must write to Derleth to urge intervention if possible.

March 12, 1943
Fall River, Mass.

Lizbeth research continues in desultory fashion. Letter today from Supt. of Butler Hospital in Providence:

> Dear Mr. Boynton:
> Butler Hospital cannot disclose the identity of any present or former patient without express leave of the patient or of his or her legal guardian. Medical information would be released only to a medical doctor and then only with the agreement of the patient or of his or her legal guardian, and then only for good reason with the agreement of the treating physician. There being no medical reason for its release, medical information on a deceased patient cannot be released and is generally destroyed after a period of time.
> I am sorry that I cannot confirm or deny that Lizbeth Borden was our patient in 1897.
> Sincerely yours,
> R. E. Tucker, M.D.
> Superintendent

April 1, 1944
Fall River, Mass.

By pressing very discreet inquiries through influential sources, I have learned that Lizbeth was confined at Butler in 1897. Self-committed. Records destroyed. Sexual mania?

June 22, 1945
Fall River, Mass.

A letter today from Derleth touching on the Lovecraft family. Paresis straight and simple as far as WSL was concerned. Curious not a scrap relating to the father survives among HPL's things, he comments. Did HPL destroy before his death? The former wife still living, according to Derleth.

September 1, 1953
Aldeburgh, Suffolk

Touched at Dunwich today, first time since 1930. More barren and lonely than before. Crumbling into the sea day by day. Innsmouth. Feeling too poorly to venture out to the tumulus. Noble still living, but retired and living in London. Barne family moved out. just as well. Very tired.

June 5, 1954
Fall River, Mass.

Hinterstoisser, after all these years! He thanks me effusively for my 1940 information. World saved for now from the Nazi-Egyptian Masons, but will they resurge from Argentina and Paraguay and Brazil, he wonders? Again asks for local help, but I see no reason to render it. I do not believe HPL owned John Dee's copy of the *Necronomicon.* I do not even believe in the reality of the book. I do not believe that W.S.L. slew those prostitutes in London or impregnated L.B. Too dark. No reply to Hinterstoisser. If he wishes to look for Tall Cedars, I should advise him to look in Lebanon, not Boston, U.S.A.

March 5, 1956
Fall River, Mass.

Hartzoll of Edinburgh announces he can supply the Thos. Luckraft chapbook for £55. My order dispatched today. None of the rest of the Noble pamphlets have I ever uncovered. Very poorly today, glycerin tablets twice.

[Ed. Note: Mr. Colin Wilson has described his own correspondence with Dr. Stanislaus Hinterstoisser (1896–1977) in the book *The Necronomicon* (London: Neville Spearman, 1978; London: Corgi Books, 1980). Inquiry has produced the information that Dean Alan Edgerton Noble died in London on October 7, 1959, aged 83.]

COLLECTOR THE THIRD

Charles Wilson Hodap (1842–1944)

Sept. 23, 1938

Attended a lecture today at the Providence Public Library—"Negro Entertainers of Old Providence" by Madeline Bavey, herself one of the leading Negro vocalists of the early years of this century.

Among her remarks (as closely as I can recall them): "Prestidigitation . . . although usually associated with foreign names . . . was another area to which the Negro entertainment community contributed. Not many now living will recall the Egyptian vogue of the eighteen-seventies . . . fifty years before King Tut and his curse fixed their hold upon the popular imagination . . . but a few of our older citizens will recall the famous Black or Nigger Hotep who held the audiences at Olney's Opera House spellbound with his Egyptian regalia and bizarre contraptions back in those days. How Charles Wilson Hodap became the Black Hotep is a story that I cannot relate to you, but his performances were a legend in local entertainment circles for decades after they graced the stage of Olney's Opera House. In the eighties I believe Charles Hodap had several eastern tours; but the change of vogue in the nineties left him sadly neglected. Even yet, there are those of us who remember his spellbinding performances from our childhood days. I have to admit, I have yet to see a magician perform who has fascinated me and frightened me as much as the old Black Hotep . . ."

I should like to have questioned Miss Bavey further on this topic, but I was unable to do so immediately following her lecture.

Jan. 10, 1939

Black Hotep is proving a tough nut to crack. None of the standard reference works on Providence theatres and entertainers contains any mention of him. Before I contemplate an exhaustive (and exhausting!) search through old newspaper files, I shall despatch the following inquiry to Miss Bavey:

Fall River 1/10/39

My Dear Miss Bavey:

I had the fortune to attend your lecture on the Negro entertainers of Old Providence some weeks past and wonder whether you can provide me with any further information concerning the Charles Wilson Hodap or Black Hotep mentioned in your lecture.

I have a deep interest in magic and have been unable to find any references to Mr. Hodap in the standard reference works on Providence entertainment and theatre.

My late friend Howard P. Lovecraft, whose first collection of supernatural fiction will shortly be published by two of his friends, wrote several stories involving a Black Hotep or Nyarla-Hotep, and I have been wondering, also, if he may have been inspired by a performance of the Charles Hodap whom you mentioned.

With my deepest appreciation in advance for any assistance you may be able to render me,

I remain, sincerely yours,

David Parkes Boynton

Miss Madeline Bavey
c/o Providence Public Library, Empire Street
Providence, Rhode Island

Jan. 18, 1939

A reply from Miss Bavey, written in a firm, distinctive hand on her personal stationery:

Providence
January 17, 1939

Dear Mr. Boynton:

My sincere thanks for your compliments on my lecture on the Negro entertainers of old Providence.

Charles Wilson Hodap is surely an obscure corner of the entertainment history of our city—I don't think you'll even find mention of Olney's "Opera House" in the standard reference works. I believe it was opened by Dexter Olney, Jr. at Pine and Friendship Streets about 1868. Charles Hodap was billed there at the height of his career in the early and mid-seventies. I believe he got his first start at Wilfred Enfanny's music hall on Africa Street about a decade earlier. For one reason or another, Hodap's career was waning by the eighties.

I believe Hodap joined Douglass's variety company during this period and toured with them up and down the east coast. I last recall a Providence performance with this company in Infantry Hall on South Main Street in the late 1890s.

So far as I know, Hodap's career had drawn to a close by the time I first entertained on the Providence stage in 1906.

I know Mr. Hodap's niece, Mary Ann Ellis, 46 Ventnor St. Undoubtedly, she can tell you far more of her uncle than I. If you would like an introduction, I will be happy to provide one.

I am not familiar with the work of your friend Mr. Lovecraft, but if he was growing up in the seventies, he may well have seen Black Hotep perform. He was quite a phenomenon in his day and strange things were whispered of him. If Mr. Lovecraft's *forte* was the strange and mysterious, Hotep would have been a natural for him.

I saw Hotep perform only once, at Infantry Hall long about 1894, and I recall a lot of mirrors and regalia and a shapely female assistant.

Thank you again for your kind words concerning my lecture.

Yours truly,

(Miss) Madeline Bavey

I send my profuse thanks and ask for the suggested introduction.

Feb. 2, 1939

Another letter from Miss Bavey:

Providence

January 31, 1939

Dear Mr. Boynton:

Thank you for your kind acknowledgment of my letter of January 17. I am glad that my information was of interest to you.

You will find Mrs. Ellis at 46 Ventnor St., Apt. 7. I have written to inform her of your interest in her uncle. I tried to telephone, but Mrs. Ellis apparently doesn't have a telephone.

I am afraid I cannot predict what success you may have in speaking to Mrs. Ellis. We have not met in seven or eight years, and when I last met her she was struggling with all the problems of a large family.

I hope, however, that she will be willing and able to provide you with something more.

Yours truly,

(Miss) Madeline Bavey

Feb. 12, 1939

I finally resigned myself to my task today and undertook a thorough search of two Providence newspaper files for mention of Charles Wilson Hodap, Black Hotep:

(1) The old *Inter-Ocean,* always strong on theatricals and the like, inter 1865–1880;

(2) The Providence *Vindicator* 1864–1869 and the Providence *American* 1873–1877, the principal Negro newspapers (each weekly) surviving from the period.

Fortunately, my friend A. E. Swandyck of the Historical Society opened his files to me and I had quite a comfortable afternoon of it.

Results most interesting.

Inter-Ocean, April 23, 1873, p. 5:

NEXT SUNDAY

OLNEY'S OPERA HOUSE
Cor., Pine & Friendship Sts.

ONE TIME
ONLY!

FROM THE DEPTHS OF SECRET
E G Y P T !

THE BLACK HOTEP

will regale
his audience
with feats and sight, unseen since the days
of
THE PHARAOHS OF ANCIENT EGYPT!

PERFORMANCE BEGINS PROMPTLY AT 8 P.M.
TICKETS AT THE DOOR

ADULTS/$1.00/75¢/50¢   CHILDREN UNDER 12/25¢
COME ONE!! COME ALL!!

Accompanying the advertisement was a line drawing of Hotep himself, sketched against a background of a fantastic array of mirrors and strange-looking apparatus. Naked from the waist up, Hotep's flesh was inked in the blackest ebony, forming a stark contrast with the white of the strange-looking turban that crowned his head and the loose, skirt-like garment that fell from his waist. From his features, so far as I could tell from the drawing, I judged him to be a Negro of the purest Nubian type.

A similar advertisement in the *Inter-Ocean* for Sept. 6, 1874, again advertising a performance for Olney's Opera House. Here, however, a few more bits:

SEE THE MYSTIC MOON-RISE OVER THE SEEKONK!! WATCH THE FLAMES DANCE ON THE MIRRORS OF MAGIC!!

Inspiration here for Howard, indeed! A pity these dated from 1873/74 rather than 1903/04.

In the *Inter-Ocean* I find as well four lesser advertisements for performances, all at Olney's Opera House, dating from 1871, 1872, 1873, and 1876. The 1871 advertisement advertises Hotep as part of Buck Henderson's Famous Negro Troupe. Apparently, Hotep began and ended his professional career as a part of a company. The Negro papers disclosed at least a dozen modest notices for Hotep performances inter 1868–1877. My real find, however, was a short column from the *Vindicator* of September 17, 1869:

> Your reporter viewed the show at Enfanny's on Africa St. given on the fifteenth inst., and among the performers we have to distinguish Miss Hadey Mount, who rendered both popular song and operatic theme with grace and skill, and the mysterious "Nigger Hotep" who has been holding forth from Enfanny's in recent months. There is much of skill and fascination in Hotep's demonstrations, but frankly we resent a bit the bugaboo of hoodoo and pharaonic mumbo-jumbo. If our Mr. Hotep will fascinate us with his contraptions and illusions, he will soon find he can dispense with the rest. Certainly, tho, we cannot deny that Hotep and his princess Amra el-Hazra know how to put on a show! E. J. M.

Princess el-Hazra! This begins to grow more fascinating by the minute.

Feb. 21, 1939

Alas, disappointment. Went to 46 Ventnor St. this morning about ten. A Negro working-class tenement district. Apt. 7 a third-floor walk-up. Rang the bell marked Ellis and was answered by a voice bidding me "c'mon up."

Met at the top of the stairs by a young Negro woman, aged I suppose eighteen or twenty.

"I'm looking for Mrs. Mary Ann Ellis," I said, politely.

"Whatchou want her for?" the girl asked me.

"Madeline Bavey sent Mrs. Ellis an introduction for me," I said. "I'm interested in Mrs. Ellis's uncle Charles Hodap."

"Grandma tell me she don't have nuffin' to say about great-grandpa," said the girl. "She say she can't help you."

"I am sorry," I said. "Do you think she would be willing to speak to me?"

"Grandma say tell you she don' have nuffin' to say," repeated the girl.

"Is your grandma in now?" I asked.

"No, Mister, she out, and I better get back to my chores or my ma's gonna be real sore," she said.

An ominous clang of pots and pans sounded from inside, along with the cries of a young child.

"Janie, whatchou doin'?" asked a loud voice from within.

"Mama, there's a man here wan's to see grandma," said the girl.

"Bill collector? Inspector man?" asked the voice from inside. "You tell him Grandma out."

"Ma, this man want to ask Grandma about great-grandpa," said the girl. With that a further stir inside. Aproned, a forty-five-year-old black woman came to the door.

"Listen, Mister," she said to me, "I got the man of the house comin' home hungry and six kids comin' home from school in an hour. And there ain' nothin' dun here yet. Hain't Janie tell you her Grandma is out?"

"Ma'am," I said, "did your mother mention to you a letter from Madeline Bavey about me? I am David Parkes Boynton and I'd like to see your mother about her uncle Charles Hodap."

"My ma didn't mention no letter from no one," said the woman. "Now how about you just git? Ma don't want to see no fancy gent about nothing. How about you just git?"

"I am sorry to have been a problem," I said, doffing my hat. With that, I turned and descended the steps. Before I had reached the first landing, I heard the door slam behind me. As I descended further, I could hear the blurred reports of an animated discussion within apartment 7. Before I departed 46 Ventnor St., I dropped my card in the box. When I looked at the front windows as I was about to enter my car, the drapery seemed aflutter, as if someone were watching my departure.

Disappointed, I am driven back to Fall River.

Mar. 4, 1939

My friend Stanton at the City Registrar's office has aided me again. Found the birth certificate for Charles Wilson Hodap, born June 5, 1842, 42 Elbow Street, Providence, son of Charles Hodap and Lizzie (Wilson) Hodap. He also finds for me the marriage certificate (Feb. 24, 1841) of Charles Hodap and Lizzie Wilson and the birth certificate (Sept. 9, 1845) of a sister, June Belle Hodap.

Mar. 8, 1939

The Historical Society. Charles Hodap is listed in the City Directories as a barrel-maker and general carpenter at 42 Elbow Street from 1829 through 1850. Lizzie Hodap, widow, is listed at 9 Ventnor St. from 1851 through 1873.

Mar. 12, 1939

Stanton strikes again! The death certificate of Charles Hodap, aged "about sixty-five," dated Sept. 26, 1850. Lizzie Hodap he finds for Oct. 2, 1895, aged "about eighty-five." The informants for Lizzie's certificate are Charles W. Hodap (son) and June B. Byerson (daughter).

Mar. 14, 1939

Stanton never fails to astound! June B. Hodap and Louis Nelson

Byerson are married in Providence, June 3, 1868. Charles Hodap and Arthur Byerson (brother of the groom) are witnesses. Seven children are born to the marriage, including Mary Ann Byerson, born Sept. 12, 1872. This is my grandma, I am sure. Mary Ann Byerson marries Benjamin Bickman, Apr. 19, 1894; divorced, Aug. 15, 1908. She marries Franklin Scott Ellis, Sept. 19, 1914. Five children are born to Mary Ann Byerson and Benjamin Bickman between the years 1895 and 1906; one child, Lee Cullen Ellis, is born to Mary Ann Byerson and Franklin Scott Ellis on Jan. 2, 1916.

Mar. 18, 1939

Stanton phones his final conclusions. Franklin Scott Ellis, employed as a die-maker at Holland & Clarke for thirty-five years, died of a heart attack, July 3, 1936, aged sixty-two. Informant is Leona Ellis (stepdaughter) and L. C. Ellis (son). The city housing survey from 1938 shows nine occupants for apartment 7 at 46 Ventnor Street: Leona Ellis, her mother Mary Ann, her six children, and her half-brother L. C. Ellis. Leona Ellis receives public assistance of $25 per month since her common-law husband, Wilfred Friday, deserted her in 1932.

I ask Stanton to have one last go at the death certificate for Charles Wilson Hodap.

Mar. 25, 1939

Stanton calls. He has found me the death certificates of June B. Byerson (Apr. 10, 1915, aged 70) and Louis Nelson Byerson (Oct. 12, 1909, aged 63). But no Charles W. Hodap!

Apr. 7, 1939

An afternoon at the directories. I pick up L. N. Byerson at 59 Africa St. in 1869 and trace him through his residences until his death in 1909. I find June Byerson (widow) in the directories for 1910 through 1915. I pick up F. S. Ellis at 26 Neighbor St. in 1914. I find him at 46 Ventnor St. (apt. 7) for the first time in 1928. For 1937, 1938, and 1939, the 46 Ventor St. listing is under the name L. C. Ellis, his son. But I fail utterly to find Charles Wilson Hodap in the directories, checking 1860 through 1930.

I fear I have taken this matter about as far as I will be able to.

July 7, 1940

An unexpected note from Madeline Bavey:

Providence
July 5, 1940

Dear Mr. Boynton:

I saw my old friend Mary Ann Ellis for the first time in many years just recently. She was sorry she could not see you when you visited several years ago, but she couldn't receive visitors for a multitude of reasons. I think she has much to say that would interest you very much. She and I would both like very much to meet you.

Can you meet us at my home at 2 P.M. on July 14th? I have invited Mrs. Ellis for that time.

Sincerely yours,

(Miss) Madeline Bavey

Miss Bavey appended her telephone number. I called and accepted her invitation.

July 14, 1940

I must record this before I forget a detail.

Driven to Providence by private car and lunched with my old associate A. at the Hope Club. Then off to Miss Bavey's at 1:30 P.M. She lives in a very well-kept home on the far south side of the city. I arrive promptly at two.

A very handsome black woman, aged about 55, greets me at the door. She introduces herself as Miss Bavey. She ushers me into a cluttered, but comfortable sitting room. A much older, heavier woman, hair completely grey, is sitting there.

"Mr. Boynton," said Miss Bavey, "I'd like you to meet my friend Mary Ann Ellis."

I motioned to Mrs. Ellis not to rise. I took her hand. "Delighted, I'm sure," I said.

Miss Bavey motioned me to sit down. "I hope you'll forgive all the clutter," she said. "It's hard to part with the mementos of one's life."

"Nor do I think you should," I said. "Frankly, I wish I had as many mementos to fill my own house."

"With many friends, the past does tend to preoccupy me," said Miss Bavey. "But Mr. Boynton, I don't want to preoccupy your conversation. I think you'd mainly like to talk to my friend Mrs. Ellis."

"Well, I am indeed grateful for the opportunity," I said. "I tried several years ago to visit Mrs. Ellis on your introduction, but was not able to do so."

"I'm sorry for that," said the elderly woman. "I didn't mean to be unfriendly. But there was just no way, with the problems in our house, that I could meet you there. I felt bad about it, so I asked Miss Bavey to arrange this meeting."

"I'm very grateful," I said. "I would very much like to ask you about your uncle, Charles Hodap."

"Brother of my mama June," said the elderly lady.

"Exactly," said I.

"Why are you interested in him?" she asked.

"Miss Bavey lectured to us several years ago about the black entertainers of yesteryear," I said. "She made some interesting remarks about your uncle's magic act. The motifs he used are starkly reminiscent of some stories by a friend of mine."

"Howard Phillips," said the elderly black woman.

"You are familiar with Howard Phillips Lovecraft?" I asked.

"Knew him personal," said the woman. "You see, Mr. Boynton, my mama, June Hodap, she married Mr. Byerson long about 1868. A good man, they stuck together until he died in 1909. I'm one of seven kids. Takes a heap of money to bring up a family of seven kids. So Mama went into service work. She first worked for Whip Phillips when he came to the west side of Providence in 1874. Big man down south in Greene before that, made a fortune in real estate and other business dealings. Whip Phillips built his mansion on the east side in 1881, and since the trolley service was good enough, Mama stayed on as a dayworker. When Whip Phillips died in 1904, his daughter Susie couldn't afford to keep Mama on. But Dr. Franklin Clark took Mama on and she worked for Dr. and Mrs. Clark right up through 1912 or so, when she became too ill to work. She died in 1915. My Mama, she knew the Phillipses real well. Even after she went by the Clarks, she did some work for Susie Phillips at 598 Angell. She knew Howard Phillips pretty well. Tell you the truth, I used to help her out a bit long abouts when Howard Phillips was a baby, before I married. That was a mighty handsome house Whip Phillips built himself on Elmgrove and Angell. I hear tell it's all cut up for doctors' offices now. Nothing like it was.

"Yes sir, if Howard Phillips wrote something about someone like Black Hotep, it's no coincidence. Whip Phillips always liked magic, Mama said, and he saw Black Hotep at the Infantry Hall around about 1895. Well, it came out that Black Hotep was Mama's brother. I remember now, Mrs. Phillips, Rhoby Place, died at the beginning of 1896. Howard Phillips, he was pretty well grief-stricken Began having bad dreams. So Whip Phillips figured to cheer his grandson up. He went and hired my Mama's brother for a special performance, long about August 1896 or so, Howard must have been six or seven. There was the Phillips family and seven or eight neighbor children and it was all done in the parlor of 454 Angell Street about eight o'clock of an evening. A pretty spooky show, you can bet. Mama and I, we came as well, by Whip Phillips's special invitation. Howard Phillips was so excited, he begged Whip, his grandpa, until Black Hotep came back several times to visit. Rather a liberal-minded man for his day, Whip Phillips, having a black man to entertain and to visit in his home. But Mama always said he was a very good man and his grandson a near-genius.

"You know, when Mama got too sick to work, it was her friend's daughter Hassie Murrow, a lady my age, who went to work for Dr. and Mrs. Clark. She cleaned for Lillian Clark right up through when Mrs. Clark died in 1932, and for a good number of those years she cleaned for Howard Phillips, too. I believe they both had rooms in a house up on Barnes Street on the east side. Hassie just died this past October, or there would be many a thing she could tell you about the Phillipses. Now, when the last sister Annie merged her household with Howard Phillips in 1933 or so, they decided they didn't need cleaning help. So that was that. But I was sorry to see Howard Phillips die so young. Must be three, four years ago already."

"So my friend Howard Phillips knew your uncle Mr. Hodap?" I asked.

"Yes, sir, like I said, Howard Phillips had Uncle Charles over several times by special request. Apparently, they hit it off, they did. I can recall uncle telling me little Howard Phillips became an Arab from the day of their first great confab. Now, Uncle Charles had as his assistant Lillie Darrow—she was called Princess Amra el-Hazra—and what do you know, but little Howard Phillips became Abdool el-Hazard. I don't think he ever did forget that performance Uncle Charles gave—Uncle Charles, 'with the golden pshent, from the ancient orient.' 'Moon-rise over the Seekonk' was his weirdest mirror trick, which he always saved to last. It would appear as if the whole town was tromping out to see the miraculously dried-up stream. No, I don't think Howard Phillips ever forgot Uncle Charles, the Black Hotep. I didn't know, though, that he put him into stories."

"Only very indirectly," I said. "Nyarlathotep—Black Hotep—was a name he used in several stories."

"I think Uncle Charles used that variation," said the elderly woman. "'Seer of the sentient void,' he called himself."

"Did your Uncle Charles meet Howard Phillips after his boyhood years?" I asked.

"I don't believe so," the elderly woman replied. "The years after the 1890s were difficult ones for Uncle Charles. Lillie Darrow was about fifteen years his junior and joined his act about 1874 or 1875. They were common-law husband and wife. They never had it easy. Uncle Charles was a full-time waiter and part-time magician up until about 1879, when he joined Douglass's touring company with Lillie. They traveled all up and down the coast till about 1885 or so, when Douglass folded. Then Lillie and Charles settled back to an apartment on Ship Street. Lillie worked in a used clothing store and Charles did odd jobs. Then Lillie died, aged only forty or so, in 1898. It just about broke Uncle Charles, and, frankly, he took pretty bad to drink. My Mama took her brother in just shortly after Lillie died. I took over for Mama when she became ill in 1912 (by then I was divorced from my first husband), and when I married Franklin Scott Ellis in 1914 he took all of us in—Mama, me, Uncle Charles, and my kids. A real godsend.

"No, I don't think Uncle Charles ever saw Howard Phillips after those meetings in 1896 or so, though he'd often ask about the Phillipses. As I said, he was pretty bad for several years after Lillie's death. About 1900 to 1910, he worked as bootblack in the railroad station— don't know, he might have seen Howard Phillips once or twice then.

From 1910 to 1925 or so, he did some grocery-clerking on the south side. Then he got too old to work—well into his eighties."

"I have to admit doing a little checking on your uncle, Mrs. Ellis," I said. "I found his birth certificate from 1842. But I couldn't find any death certificate."

"My uncle'll be glad to hear that, Mr. Boynton," she said. "He was just ninety-eight this past June 5, and said good-bye to me when I left the apartment this morning."

"Do you think I might meet your uncle?" I asked.

"As I told you, Mr. Boynton," said the elderly woman carefully, "I got problems to home. My daughter Leona's got a runaway husband, six kids of her own, and her daughter's little infant girl to look after. Not to mention my son Lee, Uncle Charles, and myself. I can't move Uncle Charles, he's just too old and feeble. Truth to tell, I think he'll be leaving us real soon now, probably. I don't know whether he can make another winter. Lemme tell you, though, his interest in that magic stuff mostly died off when his Princess el-Hazra died. Uncle Charles was what you might call a pretty cool dude back in his performing days—if he wasn't out drinking with his lodge buddies, he was off at some mystic séance, or giving Lillie the fits over some other woman. I think he feels a lot of sadness when he looks back at those years. He doesn't want to look back very much. I think it's been thirty years since he looked into his magic trunk that we've got down in the basement . . . I verily do.

"He's an old man, Mr. Boynton, who just wants to live out his days in peace. Everybody that he loved the most is long gone . . . not to say that he doesn't love us, but not like he loved his Lillie. Pity they never had any children. I hope you'll forgive me if I don't ask Uncle Charles to remember what he doesn't want to . . . but I tell you what. No one has asked about Black Hotep in twenty-five years. I didn't think anyone other than Miss Bavey here remembered Uncle Charles. His last public performance was at Infantry Hall on June 8, 1898, just a couple of months before Lillie died. And I can't remember when Uncle Charles did any magic for us privately. A card trick or two up until ten years ago, maybe. I tell you what, though. When Uncle Charles passes on, you'll have that trunk. I don't know what's all in it and I trust if it's anything of monetary value, you'll see that we get the price of it. But you're gonna have that trunk. That'll tell you more about Black Hotep than I or Uncle Charles ever could."

"Can you tell me a bit about the act, Mrs. Ellis?" I asked.

"I saw the full-fledged act six or seven times, Mr. Boynton," she said. "Uncle Charles would costume himself as a Nubian, Lillie as a princess. He had a lot of fancy machinery and mirrors. It was always done in semi-darkness, but sometimes you would see the strangest things in the mirrors. I think Uncle Charles once told us some of it was done with trick paintings. He used a pretty horrifying conclusion. The audience would see themselves pouring out of the theater and they'd all follow the shining moon over to the river, only to find it all dried up. Before you'd know it, it'd be all squirmy-like with tentacles and such, and as a red dawn rose in the east, the people would be fleeing back to their homes. 'Hotep, the audient chaos, the sentient void, beware ye!' Uncle Charles would cry. 'Princess el-Hazra, the rosa mystica, sybil aegyptica, etc., etc.,' he would cry. Then the gas jets would be turned up, and it would all be over except the bows. Mama says he would really wow his audience back at Olney's Opera House in the seventies. Egypt and hoodoo were much in vogue back then. Those were his high years."

"Miss Bavey, Mrs. Ellis, I can't thank you enough for your courtesy in seeing me. You have explained so much to me. You have my pledge that you will have a fair price for the contents of that trunk when I receive them. May it be a good many years yet. I should like to see your Uncle Charles, the famous Black Hotep, round out an even hundred years or so."

"The Lord willing, I'd be glad to see it," said Mrs. Ellis. "That's my dear Mama's brother. When she died in 1915, she especially asked me and Franklin to take care of Uncle Charles. Well, Franklin didn't live to see the task to completion, and maybe even I won't, but my son Lee is a good son, and he'll see Uncle Charles to rest if need be."

We spent some further minutes over Miss Bavey's mementos. And then we parted.

Aug. 21, 1944

A phone call from Miss Bavey. Charles Wilson Hodap passed away 9 P.M. August 20. Funeral August 23 at the African Evangelical Church with burial in the North Burial Ground. At Miss Bavey's advice, I am sending flowers to the family.

So Black Hotep made his 100 years and then some! A veritable Pepi!

Sept. 6, 1944

A letter today:

> 46 Ventnor St.
> Providence
> September 5, 1944
>
> Dear Mr. Boynton:
>   My family and I thank you for the flowers that you sent for Uncle Charles. He passed away in peace and is with his Lillie now.
>   Lee took the trunk to the express office today.
>   We are sending it to you collect.
>   Our thanks again for your sympathy. Our best wishes to you.
>   Sincerely yours,
>   (Mrs.) Mary Ann Ellis

Sept. 9, 1944

The Hodap trunk arrives. I pay $3.50 express charges. I have the staff place it in my parlor.

Sept. 12, 1944

I have finished my examination of the Hodap material. My reaction is a strange compound of different emotions. The costumes—the turban, the drapes, his wife's things—are all there. A whole stack of tarnished mirrors of various shapes and something like a magic lantern device, with eight windows arranged in octagonal fashion. I fear the slides—Seekonk and all that—must be lost. A lot of gold foil-covered cardboard—could this stuff covered with foil be the fabulous "golden pshent"? I am most disappointed, I suppose, by the lack of a photograph album or an album of cuttings or mementos. There is only what seems to be a primitive account book for the years 1877–1885. I have penned the following to Mrs. Ellis:

Fall River
September 11, 1944

Dear Mrs. Ellis:

I received the trunk of material which you sent on September 9. I found much of what I presume to have been the paraphernalia of your uncle's magic act, but, regrettably, no book of mementos or cuttings nor even any photograph. Regrettably, as well, any magic lantern slides appear to be lost.

I don't believe any of the material included is of any particular monetary value. Nevertheless, it is of significant interest to me and in appreciation of your kindness I am enclosing my cheque in the amount of $100.00.

Should you feel free to part with any other mementos of your Uncle Charles, I would be delighted to make sure that they find a good home at a fair price.

Cordially yours,
D. P. Boynton

Oct. 3, 1944

A note in today's mail:

46 Ventnor St.
Providence
October 1, 1944

Dear Mr. Boynton:

My family and I thank you for the $100.00 check. It will be a help to us.

I don't know of a single photograph of Uncle as the famous Black Hotep. Nor of Princess el-Hazra. I am sure many were taken in their day, but they have all vanished. Uncle Charles does appear in my Mama's bridal photograph from 1868, but that's an heirloom we can't part with. We also have him in a photograph taken at my husband's funeral in 1936, but there again we'd be pressed to part with it.

As I told you, I believe my uncle wanted to bury many parts of his past. I am sure he destroyed or gave away many things. When Uncle Charles moved here with us in 1928, that trunk and a bag of clothes were virtually all he owned. I guess the memory of common folks is pretty short.

I am sorry I can't help you more. Leona, Lee, and I thank you for your help.

Sincerely yours,

(Mrs.) Mary Ann Ellis

Oct. 15, 1944

Swandyck of the Historical Society is having photos taken of all the Hotep advertisements I managed to locate. The best one from the *Inter-Ocean* I am having specially enlarged in two copies. One shall go to Mrs. Ellis and her family.

Stanton of the Registrar's Office is going to provide me with official copies of the vital records pertaining to the family.

Nov. 4 , 1944

Photograph of *Inter-Ocean* advertisement sent to Mrs. Ellis.

Dec. 10, 1944

Note of thanks from Mrs. Ellis for photograph.

Mar. 15, 1946

Mrs. Franklin S. (Mary Ann) Ellis, wife of the late Franklin S., daughter of Louis N. and June B. Byerson, died Mar. 14, 1946 . . . *Evening Bulletin,* today.

Jan. 5, 1948

My "Black Hotep: An Early Providence Magician" is published in the *Sunday Journal.*

Jan. 8, 1948

Letter from Lee C. Ellis praising my article.

May 15, 1948

My article "Charles Wilson Hodap: An Early Providence Magician" published in the *Magic Quarterly.*

June 7, 1948

Providence dealer sells me original glass negative of 1880 photograph of Black Hotep and Princess Amra in full regalia. Price, $75.00. I have a reproduction made for Lee C. Ellis.

September 12, 1948

I lecture before the Providence Public Library Thursday Forum on "Black Hotep: An Early Providence Magician." Lee Ellis and two nieces attend.

Jan. 15, 1949

H. J. Ebenezer of Santa Rosa, California, writes me regarding my *Magic Quarterly* article on Hotep. Offers set of 12 magic lantern slides formerly belonging to Hotep for $500.00. I write letter of inquiry regarding the provenance of the slides.

May 5, 1949

Reply at last from H. J. Ebenezer. Came into possession of lantern slides in 1933 at death of Mrs. Hattie Batteson, his mother-in-law. She was a family friend of Hotep's family, according to her own statement.

May 10, 1949

Lee C. Ellis does not remember a Mrs. Batteson. I determine to offer $250.00 for the slides.

Dec. 14, 1950

At long last I hear from Mr. Ebenezer. He offers to reduce his price to $350.00 for the 12 slides.

Jan. 1, 1951

I mail Ebenezer my check for $350.00.

Mar. 29, 1951

After long delays, the lantern slides arrive intact.

Apr. 4, 1951

Slides projected. Seekonk scenes as described by Mrs. Ellis. If I just knew how all the mirrors linked up.

Sept. 22, 1951

My "Black Hotep's Magic Lantern Show" published in the *Magic Quarterly*.

Mar. 4, 1952

Mr. John A. Squires, a professional illusionist, visits me to examine the Hotep slides.

July 6, 1953

"New Light on the Hotep Magic Lantern Slides" by Mr. Squires and myself published in the *Magic Quarterly*. Illustrated with my 1880 photo of Hotep and Princess Amra and three reproductions, in black and white, of the slides themselves.

Jan. 7, 1955

My article "Lovecraft and Black Hotep" finished in draft.

May 31, 1955

I transfer my Hotep collection to the Providence Public Library to form a part of the Black Providence collection being assembled by Madeline Bavey for the library.

June 5, 1955

Madeline Bavey telephones me to tell me that Lee C. Ellis has donated the 1868 and 1936 portraits of Hotep to the library collection.

Sept. 10, 1955

Lee C. Ellis and I lecture on "Charles W. Hodap: 102 Years of Magic" at the Providence Public Library. With the assistance of the library staff, the Seekonk slides are presented while HPL's "Nyarlathotep" is read by Mr. Morton Hamilton of the staff.

Feb.17, 1956

I purchase an 1884 photograph of Hotep and Princess Amra for the Library collection. Price, $50.00.

Mar. 5, 1956

Letter from the Library acknowledging gift of photograph. "We have been offered what is purported to be a 35pp. holograph ms. on magic by Hotep," writes the librarian. I must urge him to investigate further.

Editor's Postscript

The materials donated by D. P. Boynton remain a part of the Black Providence Collection, now renamed the Madeline Bavey Memorial Collection, in the Special Collections Department of the Providence Public Library. The library records indicate that a private buyer outbid the library for the Hotep manuscript in 1956.

Miss Bavey died in 1969 aged 83 and Lee C. Ellis in 1975 aged 61. Leona Ellis and the remaining family removed from 46 Ventnor Street to public housing in 1978.

"Lovecraft and Black Hotep" by D. P. Boynton remains unpublished. The manuscript is held in the Madeline Bavey Memorial Collection. A photostatic copy of the manuscript is part of the H. P. Lovecraft Collection at Brown University.

The *Inter-Ocean* Hotep advertisement photographed and enlarged for D. P. Boynton formed part of an exhibition of the Madeline Bavey Memorial Collection mounted by the Special Collections Department of the Providence Public Library in the spring of 1980.

Collector and writer E. Burke Nelson announced in 1981 that he had acquired the 35pp. Hotep magic manuscript and that he intended to edit it for publication in a limited edition by Yuggoth Publishers. The price paid a New York dealer was reportedly $2,000.00.

On August 22, 1981, a memorial stone was placed on the previously unmarked grave of Charles W. Hodap in the North Burial Ground. It reads:

CHARLES WILSON HODAP
1842–1944
BLACK HOTEP

Funds for the marker were donated by members of the International Magicians' Guild and the *Magic Quarterly* magazine. The dedication was attended by Mrs. Leona Ellis, on behalf of the family, Mayor Vincent Cianci, on behalf of the city, and John A. Squires, on behalf of the International Magicians' Guild. The dedication was covered by the Providence newspapers and several of the wire services.

On September 7, 1981, *Evening Bulletin* reporter Dick Hennessey reported the discovery of the grave of Lillie Darrow, Princess Amra el-Hazra, in a pauper's section of the Field's Point Burial Ground. He proposed in his article that the Magicians raise a marker for Princess Amra:

LILLIAN MEELEY DARROW HODAP
1857–1898
AMRA EL HAZRA

On September 12, 1981, Providence magician Al E. Kroger wrote the *Bulletin* that a collection would be begun for a marker for Princess Amra. He also proposed removal of her grave to the North Burial Ground to join her husband.

COLLECTORS THE FOURTH AND FIFTH

David Parkes Boynton (1897–1956)
and Another Gentleman of the Hope Club

Sept. 19, 1939

An afternoon of scouting for antiques in and about Providence—a strange way to spend an afternoon so shortly after the outbreak of a conflagration that threatens to consume us all. Let us all hope that events do not pose quite so grave a threat as my sometime correspondent Hinterstoisser fears. In any case, life must go on—the book shops, the antique stores, the unmitigated junk shops—they and their proprietors continue their daily round, as do I, despite the happenings far across the sea in Europe.

A most curious find today—a woman's necklace with a locket containing a portrait of my departed friend HPL. I would say "bearing a strong resemblance to my departed friend HPL" but for the inscription:

C.B.

H.P.L.

3-12-10

I found this in a dusty shop in one of the small, twisted courts running off Atwell's Avenue on the crest of Federal Hill. "A. Alegria: Antiques and Curios" the sign read in Italian. Unfortunately, the proprietor was absent. Only a teenaged girl in attendance, who seemed most anxious that I should not depart without carrying the necklace away for $2.00. Really, the workmanship is exquisite, and I feel Signor Alegria has far undervalued his treasure. But the curiosity as to who this C.B. might be far outweighs the monetary value of my bargain. I am resolved to inquire about the origin of the necklace with Signor Alegria himself, if I am so fortunate as to meet him on my next visit to Providence.

Dec. 14, 1939

A Sunday afternoon's jaunt into Providence. By private car to the city center and thence by foot and trolley where I will. A lovely sunny day, dispelling the gloom that seems to have settled all around us. By design, I took my lunch in one of the pastry shops along Atwell's Avenue and then ventured to the further brow of the hill to watch all the vast crowds of worshippers emerging from church. Might my C.B. even now be among these throngs of the faithful, I wondered? From thence, I wandered among the narrow, twisted courts until I came to the shop of Signor Alegria. No signs of being open for business, but the door yielded to my nudge and I felt no doubt that the tinkling bell would summon someone to my attendance. After several moments of waiting, a stout, mustacchioed Italian gentleman wearing his Sunday vest and slippers emerged from the doorway behind the store counter, puffing domestically on his pipe.

"My I assist you, Signor?" he ventured. "In actuality, I am not open for trade today, but if there is some way that I may assist the Signor, I certainly shall do my best to do so."

"Don't fear, I am not a city inspector," I said.

"Grazie, Signor," he replied, awaiting my business.

I removed my prize from my overcoat pocket. "This necklace, Signor," I said, "I purchased it several weeks ago in your shop." I handed him the necklace. "I am particularly interested in the locket."

"The locket, Signor," he said cautiously. "I sell many necklaces and many lockets in the course of my business, Signor. Is something unsatisfactory?"

"No, quite the contrary," I said, trying to relieve his obvious concern. "I have no complaint. I feel it is a great bargain at the price at which I acquired it."

"I am gratified the Signor is pleased with his purchase," the proprietor responded. "But what can I do for the Signor?"

"I should like to know where you obtained this necklace and locket," I replied.

Signor Alegria gave me a look of concern and mistrust.

"Signor," he said, "as I have told you, I sell many pieces of jewelry in my business. There is no way I can remember them all. What I can tell you is that I buy only from reputable persons."

"Have no fear, my friend," said I. "Rest assured I represent neither the city inspectors nor the police. I come with no warrant. It so happens the portrait in the locket represents a dear old friend of mine. I was simply curious how such a curio came to be on sale in your shop."

Here Signor Alegria gave the locket another close look.

"It is very difficult, Signor," he said. "As I told you, I sell many pieces of jewelry. No matter how good or bad a man is, he wants something special for his lady on special occasions."

"A portrait locket is hardly the kind of thing that would do for that trade," I ventured.

"I think I bought the necklace and locket because of their inherent quality, Signor," the shopkeeper said. "Yes, yes, I remember distinctly, I bought that piece among a number of others from a lady simply because the quality appeared to be so fine. I believe this necklace with its locket was the last of the pieces I bought—as you say, a portrait locket is hardly in my trade. But I am gratified that you have found the piece, Signor. Perhaps you win even wish to return it to your friend. Who knows, a trinket of yesteryear, it may have some sentimental value."

"I regret to say that my friend has been dead these two and a half years. He was married only in middle age and thereafter separated from his wife, which is the reason this locket has roused my curiosity. Do you not think you might remember something more about it?"

"Well, Signor, I do not know that it is ethical for me to say from whom I buy."

"In this instance, you may be assured that the interest is solely a personal one. I have no financial interest in the transaction."

"Still, one can never tell when a disclosure might bring embarrassment. When a man or a woman sells a used article, they generally want its past history put to an end at the point of sale."

"In this case, I would be happy to offer you five dollars for whatever information you might be able to give me. Solely as a courtesy, a gratuity if you will. And you may rest assured that whatever information you may give will be handled by me with the greatest discretion. Here, here is my card. Should you encounter any difficulty or complaint as a result of anything you may disclose to me, I invite you to telephone me directly. I will do my best to see that any difficulty is resolved without cost or embarrassment to you."

"You are very kind, Signor," the shopkeeper replied. "I do not know, however, that the information that I have will be worth the gratuity you offer."

I laid a five-dollar note on the counter before Signor Alegria. "My friend, the gratuity is in return for your kindness in telling me what you know of the origin of this necklace and locket. As one gentleman speaking to another, I know that whatever information you provide me will be truthful and accurate. I can ask no more than that."

"Signor, you are very kind," he replied, lifting the note from the counter and depositing it in an inside pocket of his vest. Whereat, the shopkeeper took a long puff on his Sunday afternoon pipe. The noise of children playing in the street came in from outside the shop.

"Dora Berlucci sold me that jewelry," he said. "She is a young lady, about thirty, living with her aunt and uncle on the hill. A good, honest young woman," he added.

"Dora Berlucci?" I asked, for confirmation.

"Yes, Dora," he said. "I don't know what became of her mother. The jewelry belonged to her mother."

"What was her mother's name?" I asked.

"I do not know," said the shopkeeper. "I really should not tell the sorrows of other families. But you see, Dora was a love-child."

"Illegitimate?" I asked.

"Yes, Signor, as you say, illegitimate," the shopkeeper answered. "Dora's grandpa, Michael Berlucci, was one of the best-known building contractors on the hill back in those days. Put up many of the three-flats hereabout, Michael and his sons Joseph and Eduardo. His daughter—I think her name was Cristina, Signor—was the darling of the household. But when she became pregnant with Dora, her father, Michael, threw her out. Her mother's sister and brother-in-law took the girl in, and they brought up the daughter after she was born."

"Then, Cristina Berlucci is the name in this locket?" I asked.

"I venture to guess," said the shopkeeper.

"Can you describe Dora to me?"

"Signor, you must not think of approaching the child with this story."

"We speak gentleman to gentleman," I replied. "As I told you, you have my card and my word that I shall not misuse the information you give me."

"Dora, she's a good-looking girl, about thirty years old now, I believe. She clerks in her uncle's grocery store, Dora does, a good girl, you know. She was graduated from Classical High. Many the Federal Hill beau who wishes that he might have Dora cooking and tending house for him. But Dora, she's loyal to her aunt and uncle, who brought her up. Maybe she thinks her mommy caused them enough problems already. I don't know. Things have been tough. So maybe she's making ends meet by selling some of this old jewelry of her mother's. Maybe her aunt and uncle don't even know. Maybe it's just going to be a few more pennies in the till, you see, Signor."

"I see, Signor Alegria," I replied. "Dora Berlucci sounds like a very fine young woman. You have my assurance that I shall do nothing to embarrass her."

"That's good of you, Signor. I hope the story means something to you."

"Can you give me the names of the aunt and uncle?" I asked.

"Peter and Leona Buono, 7 Adelphi Street, Buono's Grocery Store," he replied. "Good folk. They've been good to Dora."

"I appreciate your help," I said, straightening my coat.

"Signor," said the shopkeeper, making a brief pause once he had spoken. "That friend of yours, he looks like a fancy gentleman. I don't think he did any favors for Cristina Berlucci, though. All that jewelry, maybe it made Cristina happy once upon a time. Now it's just a few more pennies in the coffer, a past the family would prefer to leave buried."

"His family as well as hers, I venture," I said.

"I knew you would see it that way," said the shopkeeper. "I can always tell a real gentleman. Understand, I mean nothing to insult your late friend. We can all understand such things. Signor, I send my best wishes with you and my hope that you may call again."

"I shall do so," I replied.

Returned to Fall River just before sunset.

Sept. 12, 1941

An evening with my friend A. at the Hope Club in Providence. This gentleman knew the Phillips family well and was intimately acquainted with its affairs. I record the high points of our conversation as best I can recall them.

"You know, David, young Howard was quite an extraordinary child . . . it bemuses me to hear him described as a recluse, although there was certainly an element of reserve in his character. I have never known a child to learn a city backwards and forwards as Howard learned Providence. Why, at age fifteen he could tell me the trolley routes from the Blackstone Valley to Narragansett Point—he had ridden them all. And where he couldn't penetrate on the trolley, he would go by bicycle. That young crowd of his, Slater Avenue grammar school kids, if I recall correctly, went all the way out to Rehoboth on their bicycles to build themselves a secret clubhouse. I recall those boys now, from the basement over at Addison Munroe's house, which was their city meeting place. Howard was their chief orator and the intellectual guiding light of the group. Someday, I must really introduce you to Addison. Albeit a Democrat, he's a wise man, and he knew your H.P.L. as well as anyone.

"You know, Howard took quite seriously this idea of one's duty to uplift the intellectual standards of the masses. He was quite a bit at the main public library as a young man—I think he began taking the trolley downtown well before his tenth birthday in 1900—and he befriended several young fellows there in the attempt to encourage them in their studies. After the remove from 454 Angell in 1904, of course, he brought fewer friends home. Howard's withdrawal from high school a few years later was a tragedy for the family. I never did learn the full story, although I gathered there was some form of nervous disorder. Those young adult years that should have seen his matriculation at Brown University were more or less lost. Private tutors were tried for awhile, but Howard apparently evinced little interest in studying subjects that did not appeal to him. He had a love of science, but while he could write excellent narratives and descriptions in almost classical prose, mathematics was a weakness. He never really mastered algebra and geometry. The family even toyed with correspondence courses, although they offered virtually no hope of advancement. At the time, I urged old Franklin Clark to put Howard into a clerkship in an office somewhere. That way, he'd either have resigned himself to the kind of life his credentials could support, or, hopefully, have resolved to do what had to be done to advance. Well, nothing happened. Maybe the nervous disorder was more serious than I realized. In any case, Dr. Clark and Howard's mother prescribed an additional dose of coddling and self-study. Exactly the opposite of what that boy needed to assure a happy adult life, so far as I was concerned."

"So that his blossoming out had to wait for his recruitment by amateur journalism?" I ventured.

"I don't know much about that," my friend replied. "Susie, his mother, was always quite leery about those people. I don't know how involved Howard became with the amateur journalists after Susie's death, but she restricted his involvement while she was living. I don't think Howard spent a night away from home to attend an amateur meeting until Susie entered Butler Hospital in March 1919. She particularly mistrusted Paul Cook. But then, I think Susie was more protective of her son as an adult than she was of him as a child. Howard's attempts to enlist in the Rhode Island National Guard and the army in 1917 nearly drove Susie over the brink. Her eventual institutionalization in 1919 was a blessing for her son's sanity."

"Can you suggest any reason why Susie was so protective of her son as an adult?" I asked.

"Let me see," my friend pondered. "Our dear friend Aunt Annie Gamwell is dead these eight months, so I don't see that I can do any harm by telling you this now. Howard had a disastrous involvement with the evening classes at the old Central High School downtown. It was a seven-year disaster, and I believe it contributed to his mother's decline and final institutionalization."

"I have a number of items produced by the Providence Amateur Press Club, which consisted of evening high school students under Howard's leadership," I said.

"That was the final phase," said my friend.

"Can you tell me the beginning?" I asked.

"I just know the sketch of it," said my friend. "I must ask you to keep it confidential. Howard met a youth named, I believe, Fredlund. Son of a Swedish immigrant, living somewhere down on Eddy Street. This bright boy was working as a shelver at the Providence Public Library during the daytime and attending evening school at the Old Central High after work. He met Howard at the library and they found some mutual interests. Several trips over to 598 Angell Street and before you know it Howard wanted to be enrolled in evening classes as well. Well, Ed Phillips and Frank Clark apparently decided it was worth the attempt, and Susie cast no veto, so Howard was enrolled.

"Well, the upshot was that he dropped Fredlund pretty quickly. I don't know what the difficulty was. Susie always claimed that Fredlund 'corrupted' Howard. But Howard met a girl. A bright, young Italian girl from Federal Hill with a fairly prosperous daddy who was attending evening school through some unique suffragè negotiated with her parents. I don't know how long things went on, but suddenly there was a crisis. Both the girl and Howard were out of evening classes for the term. There was even talk that she was pregnant and that her support would have to be arranged. To be frank with you, I pitied the boy in that 598 Angell Street household ever after this incident. As you know, Susie's husband had died from paresis, which he contracted from prostitutes. Can you imagine Susie's reaction to the involvement of her son with a young Italian girl from Federal Hill? Somehow, however, things were smoothed over. If Ed Phillips and Frank Clark weren't dead these twenty-five years, they could undoubtedly tell you a story.

"Howard, apparently, actually fought the decision to separate him and his lover. He never formally reenrolled in evening classes, but he maintained some connections at the school. There was an instructor who knew of his problems and who befriended him, I believe. In any case, he kept up the club stuff there for years—I am sure there are several middle-aged persons in our city today who owe most of their educations to Howard. He was, you know, a rigid conservative politically, and I think Susie eventually induced him to break off his connection with the evening school because of the radical views of some of his fellow club members. I believe at least one of them was arrested for resisting the draft. Susie used to rail about Howard's amateur friends, 'Why aren't they in the army?' even though friends like Paul Cook were middle-aged and married. Howard and the draft . . . that's another story of its own. His enlistment attempts in 1917 were probably the final blows to Susie's feeble hold on mental normality. But I must say Howard had spunk; he acted out of patriotism, not out of any desire to hurt his mother.

"You know, for him his intelligence was in many ways a misfortune, I think that it provided Susie with an additional ground for the abnormal upbringing that she gave him. Psychologically, I believe he was very close to normal. I can't help but feel that the abandonment of normal schooling was principally caused by the abnormal environment in which he lived. Can you imagine this young man—his childhood friends growing up before his eyes as he festered in the hothouse environment of 598 Angell Street? The Munroes were both active boys, and the rest of the Slater Avenue gang equally so. While they began their careers, courted their sweethearts, and established their adult lives, Howard remained imprisoned at 598 Angell Street. I wonder whether you are I would have had the strength to retain our sanity under the regime Howard underwent from 1904 until 1919. No wonder he broke out . . ."

"I have something I wish to show you," I said. Here I removed the locket from my carrying-case and showed it to my friend. "I bought this on Federal Hill several years ago. I found out that a young girl had sold these things, which had formerly belonged to her mother. I promised the storekeeper that I would be discreet with the information he eave me. It would appear that Howard and that Italian girl did have a child, and that she is still living with her aunt and uncle on Federal Hill."

"I wouldn't take this any further," said my friend. "Feelings run deep over there on the Hill, and pride is just as strong as it is with the Browns and the Tillinghasts over here. You don't know who is still living . . ."

"The information I obtained was on pledge of discretion."

"So then the boy did leave a child?" my friend pondered.

"Yes," I said. "Several years ago, she was working for her aunt and uncle in their Federal Hill grocery store. My source—the shopkeeper who sold me the locket—didn't know what became of the mother."

"You have names?"

"Oh, yes," I said.

"You know, David," my friend said, "I have ways of learning things that I need to know here in the city. If you will promise to let this lie fallow, I will find out what I can for you."

"I shall do so," I said. "What you promise is more than I have a right to expect."

"Agreed, then," said my friend. I quickly gave him the information Signor Alegria had given me regarding Dora Berlucci and her family.

By private coach to Fall River, late at night.

Apr. 26, 1942

At the Hope Club with my friend.

"David, on that matter regarding Howard," he said, "what I have is just the sketchiest."

"More than I might have expected," I said.

"Cristina Berlucci died in the Brooklyn Tuberculosis Hospital on April 2, 1933. She had been born in Providence on May 25, 1892, to Michael and Santina Berlucci. She died in her forty-first year. Her occupation at the time of her death was cleaning lady and her residence apartment C, 35 Gower Street, Brooklyn. She had been hospitalized several times, as a ward of the state, before her death, and entered the hospital for the last time on March 23, 1933. Her death certificate lists her as unmarried, and the informant was a neighbor. She had a police record for public drunkenness and disorderly conduct, with a final conviction in 1927. After that point, she apparently lived within the framework of her job and her illness."

"Your New York informants have been active—a tragic story," I said.

"Nor have I allowed Providence to lie fallow," my friend replied.

"Dora Berlucci was born in Providence on October 7, 1910, the child of Cristina Berlucci. The father is listed in the public records as unknown. She was baptized in the Roman Catholic faith at St. Procopius Church on November 12, 1910, with her uncle and aunt Michael and Leona Buono standing as godparents. You will be pleased to know that Dora was graduated *cum laude* from Classical High School on June 17, 1928, and that she worked as a bookkeeper at the downtown offices of Rhode Island Bell Telephone Company from March 5, 1940, until September 7, 1941. Two days later, on September 9, 1941, she was married to Joseph Isagria in St. Anthony Church, Father Domenico Gappi presiding. Less happily, I learn Mr. Isagria was summoned to military service this past March, leaving his expectant bride in the care of her uncle and aunt, Michael and Leona Buono, in the house at 7 Adelphi Street."

"My friend, you have exceeded all my expectations," I said.

"I have more," he replied. "Michael Berlucci, the father of Cristina, died on the scaffold at a construction worksite on June 29, 1936, aged sixty-six years—heart attack. His will, filed for probate on October 13, 1936, specifically disinherited his granddaughter, Dora Berlucci. He left his widow Santina a life tenancy in the family home at 17 Geneva Street, 'provided she shall give no assistance or shelter to Dora Berlucci or any of her descendants.' His sons Joseph and Eduardo divided the remainder of the estate equally. I am told, David, that old man Berlucci never once looked upon his daughter after he was informed that she was pregnant. He allowed her to be buried in a pauper's grave in New York City when she died there in 1933. He never acknowledged Dora Berlucci as his granddaughter or spoke to her, despite being invited to her graduation from Classical High in 1928. It's a common Federal Hill story that Michael Berlucci threatened to kill the young man who 'dishonored his daughter.' In fact, they tell the story that the young man himself, of a prominent East Side family, wanted to marry the young girl, to do the honorable thing, but that his family interposed to prevent the marriage. In that regard, I have discovered some interesting documents."

"Go on," I urged.

"My friend in the diocesan chancery here in Providence has uncovered some very enlightening documents. They tell a dramatic story almost day-to-day. There is first of all the marriage intention of Howard Phillips Lovecraft and Cristina Berlucci, dated at Providence on August 17, 1910, and witnessed by Father Vignelli, since deceased, of St. Procopius Church. Dated the same date, we have the marital promises of the proposed groom that he will bring any children up in the Roman Catholic Faith. The bride being a minor, parental agreement to the proposed marriage was necessary. The parental permission form, signed by Michael and Santina Berlucci and witnessed by the same Father Vignelli, is dated at Providence on August 22, 1910. The records of the diocese indicate that the banns of marriage were publicly proclaimed at St. Procopius Church on Sunday, August 27, 1910, and Sunday, September 3, 1910. They were not, however, proclaimed the third and final time on September 10, 1910, and the marriage, which had been scheduled for Saturday, September 16, 1910, in the parish rectory of St. Procopius, never took place. Instead, the diocesan files contain a letter dated September 5, 1910, from the City Registrar of the City and Town of Providence, the Honorable Willis A. Johnston. The letter advises his excellency the bishop that the City and Town of Providence has denied the application of Howard P. Lovecraft and Cristina Berlucci for a marriage license on the grounds of 'the minority of the said Howard P. Lovecraft and medical conditions which those responsible for his welfare have brought to the attention of the City Registrar.' I was told confidentially that there was a heated meeting at the diocesan chancery with Father Vignelli, Michael Berlucci, and Albert A. Baker, Howard's guardian and the family attorney, in attendance, in addition to diocesan officials.

"The final act in this drama is the record of a lawsuit for breach of promise and support brought by Michael Berlucci on behalf of his daughter in the Providence Superior Court on September 12, 1910. The suit was privately settled and removed from the court docket on December 8, 1910. I am told that the settlement was an annuity of $50 per month, which was payable to Michael and Leona Buono during the minority of Dora Berlucci. The insurance company paid this annuity beginning on January 7, 1911, and continuing until October 7, 1931, to Michael and Leona Buono, as guardians of Dora Berlucci. The purchaser was Noel G. Conrad, Esq., on behalf of Edwin E. Phillips, Howard's uncle. The probate court appointed Michael and Leona Buono as guardians of the child on December 19, 1910, the grounds being abandonment by the mother, who was, of course, virtually driven from Providence by her father.

"That's the bare paper record. So far, I haven't been able to flesh it out any more. I was given the name of the priest who mediated the conference that took place in the diocesan chancery on September 8, 1910, but I discovered that he had died in retirement in Florida. Thus, the official record will probably have to stand as the full one. As I told you, pride still runs strong among the farrdlies of Federal Hill. I cannot urge you strongly enough to allow this matter to rest."

"And so I surely shall, my friend," I replied. "I am deeply indebted to you for satisfying my curiosity. But I'd be grateful to know what you make of all this."

"I am deeply troubled by what I have discovered," my friend replied. "The signature of that young man on those declarations of his intention to marry Cristina Berlucci is heartening, though. I wonder what might have been his life and her life had he succeeded in his determination. Obviously, the family intervened. The cost of that annuity, by the way, was $7,793.28, which must have been about the final blow to the waning fortunes of the Phillips family. From the involvement of Edwin E. Phillips, never very close to Howard, I think that Susie made an effort, perhaps successful, to conceal the matter from her sisters Lillian and Annie. Probably Susie determined that Edwin had not concluded the negotiations in a satisfactory manner, and this was the cause of their subsequent estrangement. As for Howard, I doubt whether any marriageable young girl was allowed within the precincts of 598 Angell Street during the remainder of his joint residence there with his mother, 1910–1919."

"Do you think the boy might have tried to meet his sweetheart again?"

"I doubt whether Howard ever saw Cristina again after September 1910. She was gone from Providence within a week of the birth of her daughter at Providence Lying-In Hospital on October 7, 1910, and I have no evidence she ever returned. We all have limitations to our courage. Perhaps Howard was actually made to believe he had done wrong—obviously, he was possessed of a high sense of morality. Not to say that he did not do wrong by impregnating that young girl outside of marriage—but far worse wrongs are certainly done every day and the scraps of paper that survive tell us that he had resolved to marry Cristina and to raise their child. Frankly, I shudder to think how much money $7,793.28 represented in 1910. It might have launched young Howard into his own household with a clerkship in some respected firm. Instead, it was used to buy off Michael Berlucci. And the money never really aided Cristina. She was driven from her home. To my knowledge, she had no family or friends in New York; or if she had, Michael made every effort to make sure they did not help her. Howard was left more a prisoner of 598 Angell Street and his mother than before. I suspect that the result was a nervous breakdown, far worse than the 1907–1908 troubles that forced the end of his formal education. Lovecraft virtually disappeared for the period 1910–1912, and I suspect much of the time was spent recovering from the blow this incident dealt him."

"And the girl?"

"As I told you, I have only been able to trace the barest outlines. That she led a rather 'fast' life for some time is certainly apparent. A friend of mine recalls Annie Gamwell mentioning a hope that Howard wouldn't be bothered upon his marriage to Sonia Greene and removal to New York City—perhaps she did know of the incident after all and feared that Cristina Berlucci would try to locate HPL. It would have been typical for Susie to conceal the incident for as long as she was able, but with the death of Edwin in 1918 and her own commitment in March 1919, perhaps she felt the need to confide in Annie. I can only speculate. As far as I know, Cristina Berlucci never knew that Howard resided in Brooklyn from 1924 until 1926. Cristina had a long succession of employers until after her final arrest for disorderly conduct in 1927. Her employer from 1928 until she became too ill to work in early 1933 was Berkowitz & Company, garment makers, and Mr. Johnson, a supervisor there, remembered only her struggle with illness.

"But we cannot hope to mend all life's tragedies. Cristina must have been a very bright and talented girl to attract Howard's attention.

She did get good grades in evening high school classes in 1909–1910. It is only a shame that that $7,793.28 was not used to launch her and Howard into a life together. I think the Phillipses and the Berluccis made a tragic mistake in agreeing to that settlement on the child. To buy off Howard's responsibility for the child and to send the girl an outcast to a strange city—the very worst thing in the world for all concerned. Michael Berlucci lost a daughter and a granddaughter. Howard lost perhaps his best chance at a more normal and happy life. The solution adopted left a legacy of hatred and deprivation that has still not been lived down. So my friend, I beg you, leave this matter he where it is. Lives have yet to be lived. We have been shown a secret episode in history. Perhaps in a hundred years it might be made known without hurting anybody. But let us leave it to history."

I agreed. Late car back to Fall River.

June 14, 1944

PFC Joseph Isagria, 25, killed in the Pacific Theater. Leaves a widow, Dora Isagria, 7 Adelphi Street, and child, Berenice, aged 2, never seen. *Providence Evening News,* today.

Oct. 4, 1949

Santina Berlucci, 88, lying at rest in Conti Funeral Home . . . mother of Joseph and Eduardo Berlucci, grandmother of . . . No mention of Dora Berlucci Isagria. *Providence Journal,* today.

July 23, 1952

Saw my old friend at the Hope Club. He looks all his 82 years. It must be eight years since we last had dinner here, sometime during the war.

Dora Isagria returned to work for the Rhode Island Bell Telephone Company in 1945. She was promoted to supervisor in 1948. She married Joseph Nito in 1949 and they now live in Barrington. He is a successful plumbing contractor. She has two children by Joseph Nito in addition to her Berenice, now ten. Michael Buono, her uncle, died in 1950. His widow Leona is still at 7 Adelphi Street, where the Nitos visit frequently.

My friend gives me a copy of the Rhode Island Bell personnel photograph of Dora Isagria Nito. A handsome young woman, soft eyes, strong, firm jaw. A bit of Phillips for certain.

July 19, 1955

To Providence, though feeling far from well. Sakovitz Resale Shop, Elbow Street. For $5.00 I buy the following locket on key-chain:

C.B.

H.P.L.
3-12-10

The enameled photograph is of a beautiful young woman. I know it is Cristina Berlucci. Abe Sakovitz says he thinks he bought this in a lot from another dealer five or six years ago. I would guess it was among the items at 66 College Street dispersed after the death of Annie Gamwell in January 1941.

Now I have a pair.

Nov. 14, 1955

My friend of the Hope Club dead at 85. He leaves me copies of all the 1910 HPL/CB papers he collected for me.

Jan. 4, 1956

Talking on the telephone to the librarian in the Brown University Special Collections. Yes, they have a sealed packet of HPL material that is not to be opened until March 15, 2037. It was given not by Barlow in 1937 but by the attorney for the estate of Mrs. Gamwell, Ralph Greenlaw, in 1941. I ask if Brown will accept an addition to this material.

Jan. 9, 1956

Brown says yes.

Jan. 13, 1956

Two lockets and a slim packet of papers to Brown, all that exists about HPL and Cristina Berlucci, so far as I know. "Do Not Open Until March 15, 2037."

Jan. 20, 1956

Letter of acknowledgment received from Brown. "As I shall be the last person to look upon this material for another eighty years, allow me to express my gratitude that you have elected to leave this extremely personal material regarding our late Providence author to posterity. I am sure the scholars of the next century will find it endlessly fascinating."—Brown librarian.

Mar. 7, 1956

Leona Buono, 77, lying at rest at Girraldo Funeral Home . . . funeral mass March 10 St. Procopius Church . . . burial following. *Providence Evening Bulletin,* today.

Mar. 10, 1956

I attend the funeral mass. Sign as a friend of the family. Shake hands with Mr. and Mrs. Nito and see their family, now consisting of Berenice, 14, and four other children. So much sadness, yet so much strength. The rarefied blood that flows in my Old New England veins must be thin indeed compared with the lifeblood of these people. I feel my friend Howard would be happy today. His natural daughter seems to have a happy and normal life.

Mar. 17, 1956

I am disturbed over these notes. What will happen to them. I pray they not be misused, yet I cannot destroy them. They are the journal of my life in my friend's life.

Postscript

The Special Collections
Brown University
August 17, 1977

Dear Sir:

This is to inform you that no part of the collection of material donated to the Brown University Library by Robert H. Barlow in 1937–1943, relating to the life and work of Howard Phillips Lovecraft, is restricted. The entire collection has been catalogued and is available for examination by qualified scholars.

Insofar as we are aware, there are no items such as you describe in the Lovecraft Collection.

The University Library has in the past from time to time been the recipient of restricted deposits from various individuals. It is possible that some such deposits may contain material relating to Howard Phillips Lovecraft. Any such material would certainly be considered for inclusion in the Lovecraft Collection at the time it becomes available for public use, provided the terms of the gift permitted.

It is not our policy to confirm or deny the existence of restricted deposits. Therefore, we cannot confirm or deny the existence of restricted deposits made by David Parkes Boynton or by the executor of the estate of Annie E. Phillips Gamwell. However, you may rest assured that if deposits of this material did exist, they would be evaluated for inclusion in the Lovecraft Collection at the time they become available for public inspection.

Very truly yours,

Special Collections Librarian

COLLECTORS THE SIXTH AND SEVENTH

Miss Susan M. Rounds (1780–1878) and
James N. Arnold (1844–1927)

(From the Journal of David Parkes Boynton)

December 3, 1926.

I've just returned from a most interesting interview with James Newell Arnold, dean of Rhode Island genealogists since the death of John Osborne Austin in 1918. The old man is as sharp as ever, but it is painfully evident that his health has begun to fail. He remains adamant in his break with the Historical Society, and the latest codicil to his will specifies that his genealogical records go to the Providence Public Library, which I understand has agreed to maintain them in their own room at the Knight Memorial Library in Elmwood. It is indeed an irreplaceable

collection—only partially published in the *Vital Record* in 1891–1912—
and it is good, at least, to know that it will not be dispersed.

I'll be honest enough to say that HPL has irritated me considerably
with his paternal genealogical fantasies based on the published lines of
virtually every surname his own records link up to. On the subject of
his maternal ancestry he's always been more circumspect, at least in
conversation with me, perhaps because he's aware I have more than a
beginner's knowledge in this field. For many years, HP maintained,
based on information from Dr. Clark, that his Phillipses came to western RI from England in the late seventeenth century. But in recent
years he's apparently decided that he descends from Michael Phillips of
Newport, through his son James, who died in Smithfield. That, com-
bined with a somewhat confused assertion that James and his son lie
buried far to the south of the section of western RI where the Phillipses flourished in the eighteenth century (Scituate, later Foster), determined me to broach the subject of HP's Phillipses with Mr. Arnold. I
hardly expected a narrative as extensive as that which I received from
Mr. Arnold. I shall set it down here before my memory fades.

"Oh, yes, I recall meeting Lovecraft," Arnold began. "In those days,
John Austin, Frank Clark, Sid Rider, and I would meet infrequently to
trade genealogical notes. I had completed the *Vital Record*—or as far as it
was practical to complete it in print—but we, the wizened sages of the
Rhode Island genealogical scene, would meet every other month or so,
at our residences, to trade stories. Many a one we could tell of town records rescued from the latrine or family burial grounds from the
farmer's plow. But that's neither here nor there. I remember well meeting young Lovecraft at one of our meetings held at the home of Dr. and
Mrs. Clark on Barnes Street. It must have been 1912 or 1913. Dr. Clark
was failing badly. All of us could see it, though none of us could tell him
so. We could see that his wife, Lillie Phillips, whom he married late in
life, was worried about him. By the way, Boynton, is Lillie still living?"

"Oh, yes," I replied, "she lives in a rooming house on Barnes
Street with her nephew Lovecraft on the floor below. She has rather
bad arthritis and doesn't get out much anymore. Her nephew cares for
her quite tenderly."

"I should think he ought," replied Arnold. "Many a time Frank and

Lillie welcomed that young fellow into their home and introduced him to their friends. I saw Howard at a lecture at Brown University this past year and was pleasantly surprised that he nodded in greeting. He was a highly nervous young man when I first met him in 1912 or 1913 at Dr. Clark's home. But he did sit attentively through our meeting and even offered some intelligent observations. Dr. Clark had some thought of obtaining a library post for his nephew. But it came out that he hadn't even a high school diploma, and that was the end of the matter. I was surprised to see him at the Brown University lecture, for I had heard that he had married and removed to New York City."

"He had only returned this spring," I replied. "The marriage failed, and Lillie and Annie invited Howard back to Providence. He has, I ought to note, for several years supported himself independently on his writing."

"Well and good," said Arnold, "for I should hate to think of him as a burden on the small fortunes that Whipple Phillips was able to leave his daughters. Lovecraft's mother, I know, is deceased, but Lillie and Annie need no burdens."

"No," I replied, "Annie has been separated from her husband for over a decade, and both of their children died young. I suspect Lillie's means must be very narrow."

"Regrettably," replied Arnold, "Frank Clark left her no great estate. He was always too generous with his work, too willing to accept a promise to pay in lieu of actual payment. His knowledge of Rhode Island history and Rhode Island families was profound, and it is not without reason that I acknowledged his help in the very first volume of *Vital Record*. In the '80s and '90s we often shared expeditions in search of forgotten family records and burial grounds. Let me be honest— without Frank's horse and buggy, there are many places I would never have been able to visit, particularly considering my game leg. Frank left Lillie no great competence, but he gave her all his love, which was the greatest thing he could do."

"I think she has found a happy setting in the Barnes Street rooming house, with her nephew Howard nearby to look after her. I understand he spends several hours most evenings in Lillie's room, reading to his aunt."

"Frank would be proud of him," Arnold replied. "In my Clark file I have a cutting of the memorial poem dedicated to his uncle which Lovecraft published in the *News* just after Frank's death. A very fine work of its kind. But I am glad to learn that Lillie and Howard prosper, after their way."

"Which brings me to the point of my inquiry," I said. "Howard has the most grandiose notions about his paternal ancestry, based on some notes supposedly left by a great-aunt and any surname he can hook them up to in the published genealogies at the Historical Society. He always seemed more realistic about his maternal, Rhode Island forbears. For years he let it out, on the authority of Dr. Clark, that his Phillipses came to western Rhode Island—Scituate, later Foster—from Lincolnshire in the second half of the seventeenth century. But of late he's been claiming descent from Michael and Barbara Phillips of Newport, through their son James. I wondered if you had any thoughts on the matter."

"Now that you mention it," replied Arnold, "I believe we must have touched on that matter at the meeting of our little society that Howard attended at Dr. Clark's house on Barnes Street in 1912 or 1913. I seem to remember his interjecting Dr. Clark's opinion and asking the assembled elders what they thought of it. An interesting topic, for I knew more than a little about the background of Dr. Clark's opinion. And I was in possession of a distinguished dissenting opinion as well. I must have laid it out, at least in summary fashion, at our meeting. I remember Austin's commenting that the Phillipses were one of the most difficult families to trace, with branches of the Michael and Barbara Phillips descent scattered all over Rhode Island. And of course branches from entirely different trees invading from across the borders. Sid Rider usually did not speak unless he had a definitive utterance, and he had none on this subject. By the time he'd gotten more interested in the Indians than in the colonists. But perhaps his long political conflicts—over clean water and the like—had wearied him. He was the elder of our group and we lost him next after Dr. Clark, in 1917. Old Austin's going in 1918 has left me alone with my records.

"But to return to Lovecraft's Phillipses. Well, of course, there is no difficulty up through Asa or Aseph, his great-grandfather. He went to the Foster town clerk's office and recorded all the vital statistics concerning his family in 1811, motivated, perhaps by the marriages of his daughter Waite to Richard Fry and of his son Benoni to Richard's sister Lucy. (I believe it was a 'double' wedding.) Asa and his wife Esther Whipple—who came from a fine old line—had a family of four boys and four girls, all of whom lived to adulthood, an unusual feat for that time. He farmed on a small scale on Howard Hill in Foster. The old homestead, I understand, burned a few years ago, but the pear tree planted by Asa still bears and stands along the road. You can't miss it. It makes a lovely walk on a summer's day, with well-maintained family cemeteries all along the way. Asa and Esther lie in the Phillips-Cole plot just to the south off Briggs Road. Several sons and their wives—I believe Benoni and Captain Jeremiah—lie there as well. Asa's and Esther's youngest daughter married a Cole—Israel, I believe—and brought in that connection.

"Asa was a classic Rhode Island hill farmer and perhaps just barely prosperous enough to leave a will. His widow Esther survived him for many a year. Their sons and daughters led divers lives—I am familiar with only some of them—one of them. James, had early marital problems, served under Simon Bolivar in South America, and amassed a fortune in land and cattle in Illinois late in life. Captain Jeremiah, the youngest son, inherited Asa's farm upon his death and purchased, a few years later, the Blanchard grist mill on the Moosup River. He lost his wife Roby Rathbun in the summer of 1848 and was himself killed in the gears of his mill that same fall. The farm and mill had to be sold to pay his debts, and that was the end of that branch of the Phillipses as yeoman farmers in Rhode Island. Well, one son James did farm on a small scale on Johnson Road through the end of the century, but the other son Whipple was interested in real estate, lumber, and other businesses. I hear tell he made and lost fortunes several times over, the last one in irrigation interests in the west. That left his daughters with a very modest inheritance. Whipple's son Edwin never really had a head for business except on a very small scale.

"Now, these are the Phillipses you mean? An old man can go astray from time to time. Well, there is no doubt that Asa was of James, but of whom came this James, there's the rub. I don't believe he

is either James Sr. or James Jr. of the Middletown vital records, although Lovecraft may have confuted him with the latter."

"He's taken lately to giving his descent as Howard, of Susan, of
Whipple, of Jeremiah, of Asa, of James, of James, of Michael. He and
his younger aunt Annie paid a visit to the Moosup Valley region earlier
this fall and hope to visit Howard Hill before too long."

"I am sure they'd be very welcome," Arnold replied. "They must
be sure to call at the home of the new proprietor of the Asa Phillips
homestead. He's erected a fine new home in the colonial mold and is
quite cordial. If Howard and Annie call during the bearing season, I am
sure they will go away with some pears from Asa's tree. And the Phillips-Cole family burial lot is virtually in the backyard."

"I'll pass the information along to Howard," I replied. "But what
do you think of his lineage as he gives it?"

"I think he's right back through James but dead wrong thereafter,"
replied Arnold. "I can give you quite a bit of background on Dr.
Clark's position. But let me first tell you the opposing side. Do you
know Henry Byron Phillips of San Francisco? Born right here in the
South Country, but out west for many years now. The Michael and
Barbara Phillips family tree is his own, and he's interested in all its
branches. He wrote me about Asa many years ago; it's in my vertical
correspondence file. I wrote to tell him that Pardon T. Howard was
and is the authority on the Foster families of Asa's era. A substantial
man of business as well as a schoolteacher. His son Isaac Howard published the standard Howard genealogy, which you've probably seen.
Well, Pardon would have it that Asa's father James was of Gloucester's
'Great Jeremiah' (d. 1779), himself of Joseph (d. 1719) of Michael (d.
ca. 1676). James, who apparently died between 1800 and 1810, married,
according to Pardon, Anne Phillips of John of Richard of the selfsame
Michael, so you can see how these lines get tangled. 'Great Jeremiah'
himself married a first cousin. That 'Great Jeremiah' had a son James
the Gloucester records leave no doubt, but it's the identification of that
son with Asa's father James that is the point in question. We need a
will or other document linking 'Great Jeremiah' to his reputed grandson Asa (or, for that matter, Asa's sisters Alice, Nancy, and Freelove,

who married, respectively, a Smith, a Rathbun, and a Battey, if my memory does not fail me).

"As I recall our conversation in 1912 or 1913, Mr. Austin opined that there was much to be said for lineage as given by Mr. Howard, although Asa's father James remained the vital unproven link. You wouldn't expect it, but the late eighteenth century, at least up until the federal census of 1790 but even after, is a very difficult time for family history. It was still the exception, rather than the rule, to register births, deaths, and marriages at the town hall. Some even considered it irreligious to do so. And of course everyone was suspicious of taxation. One can still find one's way around the families of seventeenth- and even early eighteenth-century Rhode Island and make correct inferences almost without fail. But the population had grown more numerous in the wake of the Revolution. The late eighteenth century and even the early nineteenth century can be very difficult.

"But let me tell my story. I don't recall how much of it I told, in how much detail, that evening in 1912–1913 in the Clark home, but I doubt not that Dr. Clark imparted it several times over to Lovecraft. It all took place many years ago. Because of my disability, you know, I could not fight in the War of the Rebellion. So I formed the habit of tracing our old Rhode Island family lines while so many of our finest men were away at the front. I shouldn't admit it, but many were kind to me because of my disability. I was admitted to view records and to visit private family burial grounds that I probably wouldn't otherwise have seen. Between gentlemen I can admit that I even had a few offers from lonely wives and widows to relieve their loneliness, but I never accepted. Many the time I slept in the open after a long trudge in search of forgotten records and burials and breakfasted on the humble loaf in my knapsack. Sid Rider would appreciate the fact that I could drink clear water from the rural brooks back then. Many have since been fouled. An issue he cared deeply about. A lot of city children nowadays have no idea what it is to drink cool water from a sylvan brook. Or even what a rural landscape is like in summer. I don't know how they can read poetry. Perhaps they don't.

"I began my habits as a very young man with the indulgence of my parents. By 1880 I had formed a fulltime enterprise to record the vital record of my beloved state, but in the 1860s and 1870s it was still a hobby, although one over which I spent many laborious hours. My tramps in search of forgotten burials with trowel and shears and sketch-pad and compass became famous all over Rhode Island, and I was usually welcome wherever I went. I had birdshot in my posterior only once in a long career long about 1877—I was always careful to ask permission to enter private property and thought I had the necessary permission, which the tenant believed I had not. Records were another matter—a minority of town clerks considered me an unwelcome pest—but it was a distinct minority who mistreated or neglected their records.

"My daybook would give the exact date, but I can place it to 1872 or thereabouts without any problem. It was midsummer, and I had started out my day in Exeter if I recall correctly—that is, the tiny hamlet that is the town center. Heavily wooded, wild country then—still is largely so. I wanted to explore the back roads bearing westward toward the New London Turnpike that had been cut in the second decade of the century. The old Ten Rod Road was the principal route, but I didn't spend much of my time on it. I can recall I lunched along Pardon Joslin Road, a beautiful idyllic scene—I hope not changed much from when I saw it last. Thereafter I plunged south of the Ten Rod Road into unmarked rural lanes with only the help of my survey map and compass. I got myself rather lost, but I don't believe I was more than a mile from the Turnpike by late afternoon. I later discovered that I ended on an unmarked lane that debouched into what is today called Gardner Road.

"I noted many burials along the way and recorded them all on my survey map without undertaking the effort to take any detailed censuses of the occupants. I regretted these habits later, when in the 1880s I took up my hobby in earnest and found that many of the family burial grounds that I had recorded earlier had vanished entirely in the face of advancing development. In any case, I was weary from the heat and my long tramp by late afternoon. A hillside cottage shaded by ancient trees offered an attractive well, and I strode up to the door to ask permission to partake of its waters.

"The most sprightly little old lady came to the door, and I knew instantly that I must be in the presence of the local sibyl, one Susan M.

Rounds, a spinster of some ninety-two years who, I had been assured by all the neighbors, knew everyone and anyone who had lived thereabouts for the last couple of centuries or so. At one time, every Rhode Island village had such a sibyl, and one could learn a lot by listening devoutly to her oracles.

"Miss Rounds didn't miss a beat and knew all about who I was. After inquiring about my relations—including some distant ones I was surprised she knew about—she insisted that I come into her parlor to enjoy the root beer her great-nephew, then doing chores about the place, had put up that spring. Mr. Boynton, I can still recall that as the most refreshing, most delicious drink I ever drank. I even accepted seconds and several cuts from Miss Rounds's loaf. Before I knew it, I had accepted the offer of the hayloft in the barn behind her home for the night and an invitation for johnnycakes and coffee the next morning. They were good, too.

"I have always had a greater propensity for talking to old ladies than to young ladies. Perhaps that is why I have always remained unmarried, although I was not without offers through the years. Miss Rounds did indeed know the locale for the last century, having been born in the year of our lord 1780 in the very farmhouse she still occupied. Her memory of the century prior to that was admittedly based on verbal tradition. 'If I had my legs of but ten years ago,' I remember her telling me, 'there is many a burial lot I could show you where no man or woman has been for half a century and the markers are crumbling into ruin.' Sad words, but truer words never said, for a man in my line of work, vital records.

"We must have talked for hours and hours, well beyond the setting of the midsummer sun. There wasn't a family whose members had inhabited the locality that we probably didn't cover. She got out her spectacles and marked for me places where I might find hidden burials on my survey maps. 'Mind that was nearly covered with ivy and overgrown twenty-five years ago,' she would say; or 'You'll need to ask Farmer Brown if he has plowed the Porters under.' And suchlike until my hand grew weary from taking notes.

"I had a standard list of difficult family names—in terms of Rhode Island names—that I always went over with well-versed informants, and Phillips was high among this list. It must have been under flickering candlelight, however, that Miss Rounds and I reached the topic of this family.

"'A numerous family,' she said.

"'Aye,' I replied, 'but I'd be interested in any local branches, whether descended from Michael and Barbara of Newport or not.'

"'Many likes to claim it, but not all is,' she said succinctly.

"'Many up north in Scituate and Foster and Gloucester speak of southern Rhode Island roots, albeit,' I offered.

"'Some true, some 'tain't,' she said. 'Not eight hundred feet from here, north side of the hill, lived a Phillips family I could tell you all about. Son moved north, and from what I hear they now trace their ancestry to Michael and Barbara of Newport. But 'twasn't so when I was a young woman, if you believe I was ever such.'

"I could well believe it, but deferred any observation.

"Miss Rounds began her narration without further prompting. 'It was Othniel Phillips and his wife Rebecca Moore who occupied that homestead, which is now but a cellar hole. It was one of the oldest homes hereabouts and was erected by Othniel Phillips and his wife when they came here longabouts 1725 or so. He lived a long life, Othniel Phillips, born 1696 somewhere in western Massachusetts, and didn't die until 1788, aged ninety-two, my own age now. I can just recall him and his wife Rebecca, who herself lived from 1703 until 1786. An aged and well-loved couple, although in considerable poverty in their later years. After their deaths the homestead went out of the family and wasn't lived in properly after 1825 or so. So many of our lovely hill farms went to ruin in that era. In the height of the harvest season, some of our hands would sleep there in the 1830s, but by 1850 the house was falling into its cellar. Must have fallen in entire sometime that decade. The little burial plot was just above the house near the brow of the hill—the markers are now totally obliterated, although you can still see the stone footings around the tiny plot. As far as I know, only Othniel Phillips, his wife Rebecca Moore, and their son James and his wife Anna were ever buried there. If my legs are up to it, I'll show it to you tomorrow morning before you go.

"'But I think I promised a story about these Phillipses. Their only son James—I think there may have been a daughter but I never heard of her—was an ambitious man and sought his fortune up north, Scituate way. I was told he married an Anna Phillips of the real Michael Phillips line. Story was told here he was confuted with a son James Phillips of Great Jeremiah Phillips of Gloucester and didn't deny the attribution. James and Anna had a son Asa and three daughters, Alice, Nancy, and Freelove. A beautiful name, that last, so sadly neglected now. I won't tell you what a gentleman told me the name now connotes. In another era one would not even have entertained any such thought. Of those daughters I knew Alice best; it was she and her husband Daniel Smith who wound up the affairs of the Phillips family hereabouts after Othniel and his wife died. But I remember James Phillips, his wife Anna, and their son Asa at the funeral of old Othniel Phillips as well. He had been a freethinker all his life and never affiliated proper with any local church. Nevertheless, the Baptist preacher rode all the way from Nooseneck to say some words over him. He was well thought of hereabouts. I can just barely remember the funeral supper—served by James's daughters, with the help of the local women.

"'Sad to think how one loses track of folk. I think I saw two of James's daughters at a harvest home in Coventry sometime in the 1820s. They told me Asa was still farming on Howard Hill at that time, although his health was beginning to give way. I read in the paper that Asa died in 1829 of a stroke. In the 1830s—you won't remember, but I do well—there was an upsurge of revivalism hereabouts, and I attended revivals preached by Baptist preachers several times in Hopkins Hollow. It was 'long about 1840 that I met Esther Phillips, Asa's widow, there. She was then an old woman, near her end. She told me of Asa's final years, of his sisters, and of their own eight children, four boys and four girls. All eight of them were then living, and many may still be for all I know. Only one I ever knew was Benoni, the first son, who married Lucy Fry. Benoni was a blacksmith in Providence for most of his life but had a lot of filial piety and returned home whenever he could. He and his wife Lucy had eleven children of their own, one of whom was a boy named Asa named in honor his grandfather. This son Asa also became a blacksmith—powerful men, he and his father Benoni. I remember Benoni and Lucy well, for they had accompanied their mother Esther to that revival at Hopkins Hollow. It was summertime and warm as it is now. Esther—she was a Whipple, you know, of the same line as old Commodore Abraham Whipple—told me of the beautiful family lot where her husband Asa was buried, and I told her of the burial lot just behind my home where his grandfather Othniel and his father James and their wives were buried. I can remember well how Esther's son Benoni asked me for directions and promised that he would bring his family to see this family burial ground as soon as he could manage.

"'In fact, he was as good as his word, although I waited nearly another decade to see him. One fall day of 1849 a wizened figure strode up to my door and announced himself as Benoni Phillips. I recognized him right away and saw that he had his wife Lucy and nine or ten of his children—all adults or teenagers—in the wagon down the hillside a bit. I invited them all in, but Benoni and Lucy insisted that the children remain outside and refresh themselves at the well. They had brought their own food, he said.

"'Well, I led them all across the hill to where the Phillips home of 1725 was in the final stages of falling into its cellar. Two of the hale and hearty boys removed a few planks as souvenirs, but we dasn't venture inside for fear of falling into the cellar. Benoni kept his composure until I led the family group to the small burial ground near the brow of the hill. Here only field stones remained, but I could identify for Benoni which belonged to Othniel and his wife Rebecca, and which to their son James and his wife Anna. It surprised me to see that big brawny man of sixty years shed copious tears, but he did, unashamedly. He lectured the boys especially and enjoined them to remember from whence they came. He asked about the land, and I could only tell him it now belonged to the neighboring farmer. That was then Nathan Evans, and he later told me that Benoni had stopped at his farm on the way home and asked that the burial ground be protected.

"'I never saw any of the family again. Benoni, I was told, died the next year in Providence, at his forge, and the children scattered to the winds soon after that. I still have his memorial card, which his widow Lucy Fry Phillips sent me. I wonder whether she is still living. She would be a woman nearly as old as I by now. As I said, I'll be happy to show you the field stones in the morning. I am afraid there is less and less to see. As far as I can recall, you'll be the first to be shown it by me since Benoni Phillips and his family visited me in 1849 or thereabouts.'

"At this, Miss Rounds rose, and I thought our interview was at an end, for that evening. 'Now be patient for a minute,' she said, however, as she rustled through a nearby drawer. 'There, I have it. I was a bit interested in your hobby even as a young woman, allowing that young women seldom have much time for such hobbies. Perhaps it was just a bit of filial piety. But I would record bits and pieces from old family Bibles and the like. Well, when the body of James Phillips was returned here for burial, I asked his daughter Freelove Battey if there was any family record. She had with her an extremely ragged Bible that she said had been her father's. She let me examine it and copy a few family entries. James Phillips, born 1741, married Anna Phillips, born 1738, A.D. 1762. Children, Asa, Alice, Nancy, Freelove. Anna died 1805, which must put the death of James himself a few years later; her death entry is in the shaky hand of old age. Othniel Phillips, born 1696, died 1788, married Rebecca Moore, born 1703, died 1786. I gathered that their marriage occurred before they left Massachusetts for Rhode Island 'longabouts 1725. All the entries were in one hand, I suspect that of James. They showed no other children of Othniel and his wife Rebecca than James. What went before got even sketchier: Jeroboam Phillips 1671–1718 married Faith Milsap 1675–1713; Eleazar Phillips 1645–1710 married Dorcas Mowry 1643–1724; Absalom Phillips 1608–1673 married Tabitha Sampson 1611–1647; Jeremiah Phillips (Lincoln, England) 1564–1630 married Hope Cocroft.

"'I can remember Freelove Battey—she was a lovely woman, befitting her name—telling me just a bit more after her father was buried here. Her Phillipses were nonconformists, and Absalom Phillips had to flee England after the restoration of King Charles in 1660. Imagine having to pull up stakes at his age! His wife Tabitha had died in childbirth during the time of troubles. His son Eleazar Phillips was a yeoman farmer in western Massachusetts; if Freelove Battey told me where, I have now forgotten. Perhaps it is in your power to find out where. Jeroboam Phillips was the last of the Massachusetts line, and according to common repute his wife Faith Milsap was a 'praying Indian' who took the name of a local family. According Freelove Battey, Jeroboam Phillips had been hanged for horse theft in 1718, an event that spelled the end of the Phillips connection with western Massachusetts. Jeroboam's son Othniel came to Exeter, Rhode Island, as a young man with his bride.

"'Now James, for all I heard, was an ambitious man, and I saw him only occasionally during his lifetime, the last time when his wife Anna was buried here in 1805. According to his daughter Freelove, he was tender-sensitive on the subject of his lineage and especially with respect to what had happened to his grandfather Jeroboam Phillips. So when he married a Phillips girl up north it was perhaps only natural that he 'adopted' her lineage. Right enough, however, he came back to his roots to be buried. I don't know that his children ever returned here after he was laid to rest. I got the feeling he was a troubled soul in many ways, although I heard he was a Revolutionary soldier with a good record and some success as a farmer up north in Scituate. A man of roots who never could reconcile himself to his own. When I saw her in the 1820s Freelove asked about the old homestead but told me her father James had told his son Asa and daughters Alice, Nancy, and Freelove to be buried near their adopted homes. And so they were.'

"But then it was truly getting late, and Miss Rounds asked to adjourn our discussions to the next day. I had an excellent rest in the hayloft, and true to her word, Miss Rounds made johnnycakes and coffee for me the following morning. She allowed as she felt rather spry that morning, and after breakfast she took hold of her gnarled cane and told me that it was time to visit the Phillips homestead and family burial lot.

"In truth, it was but a brief walk from her home. An old oak shaded the brow of the hill, and just below it, one could make out the boundary stones of an old family lot. It was all overgrown, and despite some handy work with my shears I could not discover any of the field stones. 'Like as not, this will be forgotten within a few years to come,' I remember Miss Rounds opining. She took me down the hill just a little bit to the homesite, where indeed the remains of the house had long ago fallen completely into the cellar. 'These cellar holes pose a danger according to some hereabout,' my guide said. 'I suspect they are also a reminder of better times some would like to forget.' I've not forgotten her words over these many years. She showed me a bit more local scenery, pointed across the hills to where she believed another family burial ground lay, and then led me with firm step back to her own home, where at her insistence I again partook of the hand's fine spring root beer before bidding her adieu. What I'll do is find my notes from 1872 and lend them to you so you can correct the errors of my recollection.

"There is not much more to tell. I suspect I first told the story of Othniel Phillips and his son to Frank Clark sometime during the 1890s; he was interested in all Rhode Island families. Well, when in 1902 he married into the family of Whipple Phillips (son of Captain Jeremiah E. Phillips who was killed in his mill in 1848), the matter became one of filial urgency. It must have been that very summer—I can recall attending Frank's and Lillie's beautiful wedding in April of that year—that Frank, Lillie, and I set out in Frank's buggy to find what might remain of the homestead of Othniel Phillips and his wife. We would have wandered quite a bit, but I had the foresight to stop in Exeter town, where the local antiquary John E. Munro knew all about Miss Susan Rounds, who it turned out had died in 1878 at the matriarchal age of ninety-eight. Her home, dating to 1775 or so, was still well-kept by local folk, and it would not do until we accepted Mr. Munro's kind offer to accompany us there—for I knew it would be the key to finding the remains of the Phillips homestead and burial ground.

"The occupant, a local tenant farmer, was good enough to let us see the parlor where Miss Rounds had received me in 1872. She is buried in the Rounds family lot at several miles' distance. Neither the farmer nor his wife knew of any local Phillips plot or homesite, but he said that Mr. Luther Cobb, the landowner, who lived just up Gardner Road, would have no objection to our seeking for them. So I strode out with Frank and Lillie and Mr. Munro to try to recall the lay of the land from my visit some thirty years before. A line of fence that I didn't remember passed just behind the barn whose hayloft I remembered so well. Beyond, if you will believe it, was a field of berries, in nice, neat rows extending all the way to the brow of the hill. When we reached the brow of the hill, we saw that the berry plantings extended all the way down the other side of the hill. We walked carefully, for fear of disturbing the plantings of the delicate fruit. We saw Mr. Cobb working in a nearby pasture, and he motioned us to a meeting at the picket fence which divided the berry plantings and the pasture.

"'Kin I help you folk?' I recall his asking when we met. We introduced ourselves, and Mr. Cobb acknowledged hearing of me and of Mr. Munro. 'If I kin help you I will,' he said. 'I come of old Rhode Island stock myself.' We explained our errand, and Mr. Cobb look chagrined. 'I never knew of any such thing,' he said, with some concern. 'I bought this berry field from the Nathan Evans estate in 1888, soon after I bought my first land hereabouts. He had it in beans, but I thought it would be just the thing for berries, which the nurseries and seed merchants were promoting heavily for local farmers at the time. Nate had left an old dead oak near the brow of the hill amid wild grass, but I didn't want to lose it for my berries, so I and my boys cut down the old dead tree—it must have been a hundred years old—burned out the stump, and plowed over the land. I don't recall even hitting rock. If I had known there was a burial lot there, I can assure you, Mr. Arnold, I would never have disturbed the graves.'

"I put the man's mind at rest. He said he had never seen a cellar hole in the vicinity, and Mr. Evans himself must have filled it in, just as Miss Rounds had predicted. 'I wish I could help you more,' he bemoaned. I reminded him then of the very fine root beer I had sampled at Miss Rounds's home. 'Oh, that was the brew of old James Hutchinson, who helped Miss Rounds with her 'farm' toward the end of her life. He also worked for me, but then he retired to Windsor Falls across the state line some ten years ago. Perhaps they're still enjoying his brew over there.' But farmer Cobb did direct us to an excellent lunchroom in tiny Austin, where Frank, Lillie, and I mulled over our discovery.

"For the life of me, I don't remember just how much of this detail Frank and I got into in the course of that meeting at his house in 1912–1913 when his nephew Lovecraft attended. I think it must have been a pretty professional and objective discussion. I don't think I would have gone into the more 'colorful' aspects of Miss Rounds's tale—Jeroboam Phillips's execution or his Indian wife, for instance. Perhaps James Phillips would be pleased with what Lovecraft abstracted from that conversation. It's pleasant to think that the family, as represented by him, retains some memory of a familial farmhouse crumbling to ruin far to the south of the western Rhode Island region where James Phillips and his son Asa settled. Of course, the Plainfield Pike is an error for the New London Pike, but Lovecraft will know that if he ever undertakes to investigate the matter. Perhaps it is just as well that he believes James and his putative father James of Michael sleep in that unknown spot. Actually, James of Michael probably sleeps somewhere near the Smithfield homestead where he died in advanced old age during the winter of 1746–1747. As for finding the grave of Michael Phillips himself, I can assure you the matter is hopeless. But I am an old man. I don't want to put the damper on a younger man's genealogical ambitions. I think Lovecraft's heart is in the right place. There is a tension between what Frank and Lillie have told him and what he wants to believe about his descent from Michael Phillips."

"He has said to me once or twice that Michael is a youngest son of Reverend George Phillips of Watertown," I added.

"I have heard other Rhode Island Phillipses claim that," Arnold replied. "That, however, he has not had from Frank Clark. There is nothing to support that claim. Tradition, according to Henry Byron Phillips, has it that Michael Phillips was one of three Welsh brothers who emigrated during the Great Migration of the 1630s. But in truth his ancestry is at present unknown. He was certainly no son of the Reverend George Phillips of Watertown."

"Maybe Howard ought to know of Othniel Phillips and his ancestors," I ventured.

"Oh, I will leave that to you," replied Arnold. "As I said, I will loan you my daybook from 1872 with my notes based on Miss Rounds's narrative. You be the judge. For years, to be frank, I've been on the lookout for that Phillips Bible, and I have even hunted among Phillipses and Smiths and Rathbuns and Batteys for it, with no luck. Not that I doubt Miss Rounds, but it would take the actual Bible itself to convince an Austin or a Rider that the authority of the Phillips ancestry as given by Pardon T. Howard should be overthrown. But then my friends Austin and Rider and Clark are all gone, so who's to convince? It's just an octogenarian's tale, based on notes he copied from a ninety-two-year-old spinster half a century ago. I feel the truth of it may be as lost as those graves under the berry field out in Exeter."

December 14, 1926

The long-expected parcel from Mr. Arnold, larger than I expected, has arrived. The precious daybook entries are contained in a cardboard folder, but what surprises me is what is contained in a larger interior box. An ancient set of worn shears. Attached is a tag in Mr. Arnold's hand: "Miss Susan Rounds presented me with these in 1872 in the hope they would help me find more old family burials. And indeed they did. They had belonged, she said, to Mr. Othniel Phillips, Exeter, R.I., 1696–1788. Given by me to my friend David P. Boynton, December 13, 1926, J.N.A."

December 18, 1926

I have had photostatic copies made of the Arnold daybook entries from 1872 and have gratefully returned the originals to their author, with thanks for the ancient shears.

I write to Arnold as follows: "I don't know whether I shall ever present this evidence to Howard or not. I shall see how his researches and his feelings emerge. However, I can assure you these shears have touched my life, for Othniel Phillips proves to be my distant kinsman as well."

September 19, 1927

I note with deep regret that James N. Arnold has died. Rhode Island has lost an institution. It is sad to think that all but Lillie Phillips and Howard Lovecraft have now passed from that group which met at Dr. Clark's house in 1912–1913.

November 18, 1929

Howard and Annie have been to Howard Hill and seen the graves of Asa and Esther Phillips, as he had long desired. Upon inquiry, he is stronger than ever about the descent from Michael and Barbara Phillips and the claim that Michael was a youngest son of George Phillips of Watertown. James Jr. and James Sr. are buried "far to the south, on an abandoned stretch on the Plainfield Pike." There, at least, is some shard of the truth coming out. Lillie had never had any great head for such matters and apparently she is increasingly incapacitated. One year soon, Howard will lose her. Annie, like her father Whipple, seems more forward-looking. I doubt she, or her father, ever gave the matter a thought. Maybe vague recollections of things Whipple's uncles once discussed. At least the doughty blacksmith Benoni and his children knew the truth. I wonder if that Bible passed into the hands of one of them.

July 5, 1932

Frank's widow Lillie has died. I send Howard my note. Funeral private.

March 17, 1940

Now that Howard is dead, I am passing the 1872 Arnold daybook entries along to my genealogist friend A.M. I'd like to see what he can discover of the Massachusetts side of this matter.

September 26, 1941

A.M. reports he has found a 1665 — land transfer from Absalom Phillips to his son Eleazar Phillips, with witnesses George Roberts, Henry Daugherty, and Samuel Anson. No other record found so far.

August 10, 1948

A.M. reports that he has searched the town court records for all western Massachusetts without success for my Phillipses. He asks my permission for a discreet *Transcript* inquiry, which I authorize. With Annie Gamwell dead since 1941, no one will be offended.

February 19, 1949

The *Transcript* advertisement runs in A.M.'s name: "PHILLIPS. Exeter-Scituate-Foster (RI), western (MA). Family record shows James of Othniel (d. 1788) of Jeroboam (d. 1718) of Eleazar (d. 1710) of Absalom (d. 1673) of Jeremiah (d. 1630, Lincolnshire, England). Seek families claiming descent and contemporary records substantiating descent. c/o A.M. [address]."

July 26, 1953

An unexpected letter from A.M. regarding "a long-delayed communication in response to our *Transcript* advertisement, which I enclose."

Braintree, Massachusetts
July 21, 1953

Dear Mr. M.:

A niece of mine has just pointed me to your advertisement concerning the Phillips family in the Boston *Transcript* for February 19, 1949. I hope this reply will still be of some interest.

Most of my family claims descent from Michael and Barbara Phillips of Newport, R.I. My grandfather, James Wheaton Phillips, of Foster, R.I., however, used to tell a different story.

He said our line of Phillipses were Massachusetts refugees and that one of our Phillipses was hanged there by the Massachusetts elders. He said that the first Massachusetts Phillips had to flee England when Charles II was restored. He said that one Othniel Phillips was the first of our line to settle in Rhode Island, in what is now Exeter, ca. 1725.

He said he was told this by his uncle Benoni, a Providence blacksmith, before the latter died. Benoni showed him an old Bible that had some entries supporting this lineage. It had belonged to his aunt Freelove Phillips Battey. Benoni told him he visited the Exeter homestead to find it falling into the cellar and the graves gone.

According to my grandfather, Benoni's eleven children scattered across the country after he died in 1850. His widow Lucy, however, died at an advanced age in Providence in 1884. Benoni and his widow are buried with my great-grandfather Captain Jeremiah Phillips in a Foster cemetery that I have visited. My own grandfather and father lie in another family plot near the juncture of Moosup Valley and Johnson roads.

I have always wondered whether there was any truth to these stories. Your advertisement is the first I have ever seen regarding this line. I would value any further communication that you may be able to send.

Yours sincerely,
Elston C. Phillips

August 4, 1953

I authorize A.M. to lay the matter before Elston C. Phillips in its entirety.

September 25, 1953

I have a letter from Elston C. Phillips as follows:

Braintree, Massachusetts
September 23, 1953

Dear Mr. Boynton:

I am grateful to you for allowing Mr. M. to share with me the Arnold records concerning the Othniel Phillips line. It certainly conforms to what my grandfather told me in 1898 or 1899 when I visited him on his farm in Foster, R.I.

I think my grandfather was under the impression that one of the children of Benoni and Lucy Phillips inherited that family Bible. Harley was the one boy who stayed in Providence. My grandfather told me he'd asked Harley about it, but Harley had no idea of where it was.

I don't know where the other children of Benoni and Lucy Phillips settled, save for a general notion that some went to Illinois (where Benoni's brother James had settled) and others to California. My late cousin Annie Phillips Gamwell was in correspondence with a Nina Phillips Kimmler of Santa Fe, Illinois.

Should I discover anything more, I'll let you know and I trust you will reciprocate.

Sincerely yours,
Elston Corey Phillips

November 22, 1954

Cutting back my roses with those old Othniel Phillips shears that James Arnold presented to me a quarter century ago. Many memories flood back. I've never been to visit the Phillips homesite and burial ground in the Exeter berry field, nor have I searched very hard for that James Phillips Bible. But we are all circumscribed by the circumstances of our own lives. I wonder if Howard has met Othniel Phillips in the hereafter (in which he always disbelieved) and if so what the two have made of each other. I leave to future researchers the discovery of what bare records this earth may still contain of H.P.L.'s real ancestry. A friend of mine says that electronic computing devices now contain the information that once required rows and rows of shelves in business endeavors like insurance companies. Perhaps family as well as business information will one day benefit from storage and access on such equipment. It will not be my destiny to live to see this development, but I can always dream of what the future may hold.

———————————

LIFE AND DEATH

By H. P. Lovecraft*

For many years Menelaus and his friend Dydion dove for pearls in the bright blue waters off their native town. And the swarthy traders from the city would come and give Menelaus and Dydion money for the pearls which they had found, money which enabled them to buy the coarse bread and the simple ale of their town and to put a roof over their heads. Nor did Menelaus and Dydion care for the money as did the traders, who always bargained for the lowest price for the pearls which they bought; for Menelaus and Dydion lived for the joy of diving into the sea and harvesting pearls from its sandy bottom. Though the swarthy traders spoke often of the beautiful jewellery which the silversmiths of the city wrought with the pearls that Menelaus and Dydion found, little did the two youths care for such things. For their joy in life was diving into the warm sea from the sunny cliffs of the coastline, swimming with their lank tanned limbs through the blue and green-litten waters past the shadows of the little creatures of the deep, searching for pearls along the sandy bottom until their lungs, almost bursting, sent them quickly to the surface for exhilarating gulps of air. And though their hard work left them with little energy for other pleasures, and there were often days and even weeks when the sea did not reward their search and their landlord pressed them for room and board, Menelaus and Dydion loved the life they led and had no thought of abandoning it.

One evening the people of the town saw Menelaus treading the streets toward his landlord's home with his head hung low and sadness

*Actually by the author.

129

written in his expression; and, since they were used to seeing him treading the same route in the happy company of Dydion, they asked him what had befallen his companion.

"Alas," cried the youth, "this morning, as the sun climbed toward its height, we dove into the waters off the point as usual, and I saw my friend surface several times. But after one quarter hour's time, I missed him, and when I could not find him after frantically diving many times, I called the fishermen to my aid. They spoke of a treacherous tide which sometimes swept their ships toward the rocks more than one mile off the point, and said that I might well never see my friend again. So saying, they refused to help me in my search; and though I swam even to the rocks they spoke of and exhausted myself in the search for my friend Dydion all afternoon, I could find nothing. I fear he is lost as the fishermen said." And having said so much, Menelaus broke down weeping; and the people helped him toward the landlord's house and comforted him as best they could.

Though Menelaus returned to the sea within a week of the loss of his friend Dydion, no more could he rejoice in the sunny surface of the water; no more in the shadowed depths of the sea; no more in the sandy bottom which held the pearls he and his friend had sought for. And seeing his dejection when next they visited his town, the chief of the swarthy traders said to him: "Seeing as thou hast lost thy friend Dydion to the sea, Menelaus, and the sea is no longer a friend to thee, come thou with us to the city. The pearls which thou hast shewed us will pay for thy passage, and we have need of a clever youth such as thou to shew us the best places to set other youths to work diving for pearls for our jewellery. Mayhap the diversions of the city will take thy mind off thy friend Dydion and lift some of thy grief."

And although he hesitated to leave the familiar surroundings and faces of his town, Menelaus was so stricken with grief at the loss of his friend Dydion that he agreed to go with the traders to the city.

Next morning, the landlord bid Menelaus a gruff farewell, and his wife handed him a small packet of food for his journey. And then Menelaus commenced his journey with the traders. Two days' journey over the hills brought them to the walls of the city, where the traders exclaimed, "Now, Menelaus, thou shalt know some of the joys of life and reap the reward of thy hard work in the treacherous sea." And with this they swaggered into the public houses near the gates of the city, dragging Menelaus along with them. Jangling the gold in their pockets, they ordered the tavernkeeper to lay their table with the best his stores could provide; and soon Menelaus, used to the coarse bread and the simple ale of his native town, found his head swimming with the amber wine and smoking joints of meat which the tavernkeeper produced. Stranger and stranger did the faces in the room become, making Menelaus recall the simple, friendly faces of the townsfolk and the beautiful face of his friend Dydion; and soon the room dissolved into loud cries and oaths as dusky dancing girls plied their charms among the customers. Seeking to escape from the suffocating heat of the room, Menelaus excused himself from the company of the traders, who were now too inebriated to object to his absence, and walked out into the cool of the evening.

All along the dark street the sound of riotous laughter and carousing rose from the taverns. While in the street with Menelaus wandered the poor and haggard, chilled to the bone by the evening air but refused entrance at all the taverns. And as Menelaus watched, these poor dejected ones would alternately whine for pity and attack those equally lost in hope of plunder. For everything in the city was for sale for money; nor was anything to be had in the city save by money.

Fleeing from the street of the taverns, Menelaus came to the city's bustling marketplace where even late into the night all the staples and luxuries of life were haggled over. With shock he passed the slaughter-houses where hung dozens of carcasses above the blood-stained floors; and Menelaus reflected that in his native town a family might slaughter perhaps one sheep each year in thanksgiving for the simple bounty of the gods. Here in the city the only god which the people worshipped was gold. And in the street of the merchants Menelaus saw the bright furnaces of the silversmiths and the shops of the jewellers wherein were displayed fabulous tiaras, necklaces, bracelets, and armbands fashioned with pearls like unto those he and Dydion had collected. And here the rich and powerful, clad in fine clothes, bargained for these beautiful things with the smiths and the jewellers, while outside in the city the cruel struggle of life and death went on.

Exhausted by his wanderings, Menelaus came in the early morning hours to the stream which flowed through the city and followed it out through the city walls into the hills. As his head began to recover from the effects of the wine and meat, he determined that he wished to see no more of the life of the city, and steered his course over the hills toward his native town, foraging for food as he went. And when he arrived in the streets of the town several days later, the people welcomed him, but still Menelaus had no heart for his joyous life of old. "What peace Dydion has now," he said to his landlord.

Several weeks later the traders came again to the town and reproached Menelaus loudly for his strange disappearance; finding him uninterested in resuming his former business, they contracted with the young boy Xeno to do their pearl-harvesting along the coastline. And lacking money to pay for his room and board, Menelaus began to spend the warm summer nights in the hills surrounding the town, foraging for food in the mornings and spending his afternoons in wandering along the coastline where he had lost his friend Dydion. After some weeks, the townspeople and Xeno no longer saw Menelaus and assumed he had wandered off into the hills in his loneliness. Then one day the cries of Xeno brought the fishermen scurrying down to the point. There along the rocks had washed ashore the bodies of Menelaus and Dydion, united in death as they had been in life. [March 24, 1919]

THE SQUIRREL POND

Behind the great stone walls lie the legions of the city's dead.

Outside, the teenagers roar past in their jalopies on a hot Sunday afternoon. The elevated rattles by carrying the diminished crowds who find it necessary to traverse the city from end to end on a Sunday. Down bears the sun on man and woman alike on a hot summer afternoon.

But inside the walls, in the city of the dead, all is quiet. The hot-rodders on the streets outside, the elevated trains, are a distant, almost unreal rumble.

For inside the walls is the city of the dead. Men say the dead tell no tales; and although the stone monuments give their names and dates, there seems imposed upon the entire city of the dead an eternal hush that gives all the noise and activity of the outside world a sense of unreality.

Indeed, knowing as surely as we all do that this circumscribed city or another like it will be our final destination, perhaps it is worthwhile to reflect that the hush of the city or of others like it is the reality that will correspond to our reality for most of our days on this planet until we are dissolved into utter dust scattered among the planetary orbs; the hush that excludes all the noise and bustle of the outside takes on a greater reality when one allows one's thoughts to turn in these directions.

But it was the intention to take an architectural and antiquarian tour that brought me within the great walls of this city on a summer's Sunday afternoon. Ordinarily, I might have spent the afternoon reading and writing in the comfort of my study, in my own special isolation from the hustle and bustle of the outside, but the riches reputedly enclosed within the silent walls of the great cemetery lured me outside my comfortable cocoon into the midst of the hustle and bustle of the

133

city. My wife, knowing the city better than I and having in fact several times visited the great cemetery before, volunteered to accompany me. So, with trepidation, keeping our distance from the hot-rodders and their jalopies, we slowly made our way from our suburban residence through the crowded and teeming streets of the city, busy with traffic and bustling with humanity even at the height of a Sunday afternoon in summer.

At last, we cut across the relentless traffic through the great iron gates and into the city of the dead. A modern cemetery office where we were provided with a map of the grounds was the only intrusion into the massed legion of past glories. We left our automobile parked by the cemetery office and proceeded to explore the grounds on foot.

It is not my purpose here to tell you about all the wonders of that vast city. I could hardly begin to do so within the space of my narrative. The stately Roman tombs and the eccentric Egyptian pyramids of the prominent men and women who once walked the streets of the city, now forgotten entirely apart from their names. How sad to reflect that only four or five generations at most may actually "touch" our lives—that a dim, faded daguerreotype, as it were, is the most we can expect of the more distant past. How ephemeral the beat of a human heart! How lost to human memory is one hundred years ago! The hush of the great city of the dead! How profound! The dead have nothing to say to us!

We wandered down an avenue where the wealthy had raised their marble vaults above the level of the common ground burials.

Alas, the power of death and of time cannot be stayed. Here a magnificent bronze door was sadly rusted. Here a windowed door protected by grillwork revealed a dusty and cobwebbed interior. How profoundly sad to find even the great residing so terribly silent in their coffins! Eternity on a ledge! Amidst the universal desuetude and neglect. Not even for wealth and prominence is there rescue from the oblivion that overtakes those hearts that have ceased to beat and which now reside in these precincts. Making the circle of the lagoon and the great tombs of the most prominent—most of them sensibly entombed below ground and not beledged in a dusty room—we strolled thereafter through the more distant reaches of the cemetery, finally emerging into a low valley among the banks of hillside tombs where, preserved from the common eye, were burial vaults built into the sides of the valley walls, vaults of utter desolation and horror. Here a proud family name was obliterated; here sheet metal and bolts replaced what must once have been a fine ornamental door. Here moss, decay, and neglect appeared to have conquered all. On the hillside tombs outside the walls of this terrible valley, the sun shone on an orderly array of stone memorials with a pleasing effect of light and shadow; if one were dead, perhaps, one might even enjoy such a scene were not the cold of death so chill in the veins. But here in this valley, where desolation and neglect conquered all, it seemed the sun never shone. Triumphant over all was the conqueror worm.

We hastened through this morbid memorial of our mortality and looped back slightly to see several of the more prominent memorials that we had neglected. Soon a landscaped plaza with an ornamental pool, all quite modern in appearance, rose up before us. A welcome relief after the valley of despair. Here, indeed, preserved better than any others against the ravages of time and neglect, was one of the greatest and most prominent families of the city's past and present, prominent socially, culturally and economically, and preserving, it seemed, a proud dignity, care, and good order even among their dead.

Imagine, then, as we crossed the grass plaza in which the tombs lay, our horror, upon coming to the beautiful ornamental pool, to find floating on its surface—marred otherwise only by grass clippings—five or six floating bodies, not human, but the poor bloated carcasses of dead squirrels, far gone in decay, animals apparently killed by poisons intended for rats and other vermin, poisons that produce a wild and ravening thirst—poor creatures who had come here to slake that terrible thirst and end their miserable sufferings in convulsions and drowning. We both recoiled in shock. Surely the fine staff that kept this hushed city so reserved unto its own would not tolerate such an open breach of etiquette. I think as a result we ended our tour far more abruptly than we might otherwise have done.

It was a question whether we should make a stop at the office before leaving, but, after wavering, we finally decided to do so.

The young man in his early twenties who had furnished us our maps at the beginning of our tour was still reading his paperback novel behind the glass window that sealed the office from the lobby.

"We thought you'd like to know they're lots of dead squirrels in the pond at the F—— tomb," I said to him.

The young man looked at me blearily through his thick glasses.

"That's easy," he said. "Grishkin's been ill all this week. Custodian for that area. Knows all about the problem. Ought to be back on the job next week."

"Couldn't someone else take care of this while he's away?" I pursued.

Thick glasses and bleary eyes looked at me with positive resentment. "Grishkin wouldn't like it. Each of the principal custodians has his own area. He'd think we were trying to put him out of a job. Besides, he's here most every day anyhow. He lives above that drug store just outside the gates. Don't see how he stands all the noise and weirdos, but he's here on the grounds nearly every day, working or not. We'll tell him when we see him. Since you're so concerned, why don't you tell him yourself? Name's Emil Grishkin, just across the street above the drug store."

It seemed to me like a good time to pile back into our car and head back to the suburbs. I didn't want to get into any kind of trouble between the cemetery and an incompetent—or so I felt—custodian.

But my wife settled it all. "Thank you, we will," she chimed. "Those squirrels are disgusting."

With this, bleary eyes and thick glasses fell silent.

I looked at my watch and found we still had forty minutes until closing time.

"You really want to?" I asked my wife.

"Yes, c'mon," she said, taking my hand, as we negotiated our way across the busy street.

At the far end of the drugstore building on the cross street was the apartment entrance, unlocked.

Wife and I found Grishkin's name on one of the battered and faded mailboxes—small protection they might offer for any important mail—but his button failed to summon any response after five or six rings.

"Guess he's out," I contributed, hoping, I must admit, to back out of the entire interview.

But just then a big black man came out on the first-story landing.

"Who you folks looking for?" he asked, in a friendly enough fashion.

"Emil Grishkin," said my wife. "We're from the cemetery. We want to talk to him about something there."

"I don't think Mr. Grishkin is feeling so good," said the black man. "I ain't seen him for a couple of days. But he's third floor right, you go up and see him. He'll be glad to see you. No one ever comes to see Grishkin." With this, he went back inside his apartment.

Again I looked at my wife. Again I received my answer. We began to mount the well-worn stairway.

The door of third floor right stood halfway open.

"Mr. Grishkin!" I called.

"Oh, Mr. Grishkin," called my wife.

"Grishkin! Oh, Grishkin!"

Several times over.

"He may be in trouble," said my wife. "Let's look inside."

"Maybe his neighbor would help?" I ventured.

"C'mon. He's busy."

So we went into the apartment of Emil Grishkin.

The light admitted through the bleary windows of the third-floor apartment showed us a picture of poverty and isolation. One faded and torn sofa looked toward a dusty portable television, evidently very much out of order. Parlor and kitchen were common, and an ancient refrigerator and kitchen table with one chair only filled the room. The door leading to what was evidently the bedroom and bath was very nearly closed.

"I'm not so sure we should . . ."

"C'mon," said my wife. "Grishkin! Oh, Mr. Grishkin!"

I pushed open the door. Shabby curtains drawn across the bedroom windows—looking out into what must be the bleak alley behind the drug store—would have thrown the room into total obscurity had it not been for one bare bulb burning forlornly overhead, hanging unadorned by a short wire from the ceiling fixture. Everything in the room appeared to have a cover of dirt and filth. The bedcover and sheets were rumpled, but the bed was unoccupied. Only a battered easy chair and an old floor lamp with a study table at its side relieved the air of total abandonment that seemed to have settled upon the room.

"Now see," I said to my wife. "Grishkin's out, probably fishing the blasted squirrels out of the pond now, and here we are trespassing in his room. Let's go."

"What's all that, Ken?" asked my wife, pointing to an array of what must have been nearly a hundred small bottles residing on the study table.

I went over to the table and examined. "Looks like powders and chemicals to me," I said. "They're labeled with scientific and technical names. Here's a pile of books on the floor—one on 'Poisons and Antidotes' and a lot of plastic dishes—the kind you get to store leftovers. What looks like a bag of seed, too. Say! I think this old goat is poisoning those squirrels himself. That's what all this points to!"

"Yuck!"—finally came a positive response from my wife. Or so I felt. "I've a good mind to tell the cemetery," she added.

"Let's get out of here," I suggested again.

Finally, acquiescence.

I don't know what made me do it, but I swung open the door of the john as we were leaving. Bare bulb burning there, too.

My wife screamed.

I screamed.

There was Grishkin. He must have been lean, spare, and athletic in his better days. A very efficient person, I should think. Not a man easily crossed. For some reason, I imagined that his uniforms must be as neatly stacked in his closet as his poisons on his study table.

But Grishkin was not so intimidating the day we met him.

In fact, it seemed remorse had finally caught up with him.

There he was floating in the bathtub, bloated, terribly swollen, obviously several days dead. A broken water glass lay on the floor.

"He took his own stuff! Gave himself what he fed to the squirrels!" I cried.

Now wife ran out of the room.

I caught up with her on the landing.

We were out of the building before I could gasp, "They'll know we've been here—the man on the landing . . ."

"C'mon," said my wife, as we negotiated the flux of hot-rods.

We marched straight to the cemetery office. Old bleary eyes and thick glasses was obviously not happy to see us again.

"Grishkin give you satisfaction on those squirrels?" he inquired, with an obvious lack of interest.

"We found Grishkin dead in that apartment," said my wife. "Call the cops."

Finally a reaction from old bleary eyes. His jaw dropped.

Wife also did not hesitate. Within two minutes we were headed northward and homeward.

I kept an eye on the obituary column for several days afterward. No notice of Emil Grishkin. Now, I'm a pretty lonely fellow, without too many friends, but my wife has a relative at city hall. So I told Jimmy a story about our trying to get in touch with one of the custodians at G—— Cemetery named—you guessed it—Emil Grishkin. Unable to do so. We'd heard he might be sick. The cemetery office wouldn't help. So could Jimmy check this out for us?

Unusual, but OK, said cousin Jimmy, who had never even been able to oblige his cousin (my wife) with a traffic ticket before.

Couple of nights later, a call.

"Heh, lucky you didn't come across that Grishkin fellow. Police got an anonymous tip to check his apartment last Sunday. Floating in the tub. Poisoned himself. But that ain't the worst of it. This guy had all kinds of poison. Apparently he had been poisoning animals in the cemetery for decades. Gotten worse in recent years. Cemetery office asked the city to hush it all up. Not a relative in the world, apparently. Poisoned 'em all, maybe. My source said the cops may be looking at some kind of diary or notebook he kept. Strange thing, they took him to the county morgue and you can bet he was destined for the charity lot in the county cemetery until they did the inventory of his apartment. Aside from a good collection of poisons and lots of apparently useable grass seed, he left just two things besides his clothes and some wretched furniture. First was a deed to a lot in G——, paid in full for perpetual care, and second was a will, all done up properly by a local attorney and directing that he be buried in that plot. So it looks like that's what's going to happen to him. Lucky you and Carol didn't actually try to look this guy up. You didn't, did you? Cops said he was a real loner and probably a psycho."

"I guess we were lucky, Jimmy," I said. "And thanks as always."

"Nothing to it, kid," chimed cousin.

I do not think we are going to G—— Cemetery again. If we do, we shall very definitely not look up the Grishkin tomb.

Innsmouth 1984

Statement of Dudley M. Spurgeon, Rowley Police Station, 9/9/84

My name is Dudley Matthew Spurgeon. I am 35 years of age. I live in Toledo, Ohio. By profession I am a die-maker. My wife Marilyn and I have been motor-touring in New England for the past seven days. It was the first vacation since our honeymoon two years ago. I have been driving a blue 1976 Chevrolet Nova, Ohio license plate number CB 3383.

We spent the evening of September 7 in the Sea-View Inn in Salem. We had spent the day seeing the sights in that city. Early the next morning, we started to drive farther up the coast along 1-A. We spent most of the morning exploring Marblehead, and decided to spend the afternoon in Gloucester. We stopped for lunch in Ipswich, where Marilyn did a bit of antiquing. We were intrigued by the low marshlands around Ipswich and the seemingly endless twisting streams which ran silently through the banks of reeds. Leaving Ipswich, the road began to climb toward Rowley. About two miles out, a gravel road veered to the east, following what appeared to be a headland. We still had plenty of light, so Marilyn suggested we try it. We've had luck in the past finding interesting things by veering off the major roads. So we turned on the unmarked road.

The road, which proved to be in poor repair, skirted the edge of the marsh for a mile and a half or so. No sign of human habitation. We emerged at last on a rocky headland. To our surprise, a small cluster of buildings appeared to be nestled in the inlet on the other side of the ridge whose backbone ran out to the headland. A confluence of the twisting marsh streams appeared to join to flow into the inlet just below the town, whose outlines we could see climbing a rather steep slope above the inlet.

I asked Marilyn if she thought we ought to chance a look at the town. We couldn't find it marked on our maps. We decided, however, that the road had to rejoin 1-A somewhere to the north of the town. So we decided to give it a shot. The road twisting around the north side of the promontory was no better than that on the south. About midway to the town, we passed what looked to be a boarded store, with rusting gas pumps in front. Fortunately, we had left Salem with a full tank in the morning, so I had little concern on that score. The road was twisted and in poor repair. We had to cross several wooden bridges over the marsh streams, and we negotiated them and the rutted roadway with care.

It must have taken us a full thirty minutes of driving to reach our destination. There was little sign of life was we rolled into the public square. Curiously, we could find no sign announcing the identity of the town and street signs seemed also to be completely absent. What appeared once to have been the town hall seemed to have been converted into a movie theater. The carelessly lettered marquee indicated only "X-RATED WED PM $2," which surprised us. Another building on the main square seemed to have all the hallmarks of having once been a hotel—solid red brick, but now in a sorry state of disrepair with all the windows above the first floor boarded. What must have once been the main entrance of the hotel was padlocked—lettered in blackened stone just above the doorway we could barely read "Gilman House"— but impromptu panelboard advertisements seemed to indicate a corner grocery open. We found a pick-up and a couple motorcycles outside, and decided that we might at least find out where we were.

As you know, it has been unseasonably warm. The screen door of the store was standing half open. It took us several moments for our eyes to adjust to the dim interior. A couple of very sparsely stocked shelves—mostly canned goods—along with a service counter occupied the front of the store. The counter was unattended. In the rear was a row of nine or ten battered-looking "electronic games". Two youths with greasy hair and leather jackets were busy over one of the games. No one else was in evidence. I tried to inquire politely as to our whereabouts and what there might be worth seeing.

"Fuck off, man," the elder boy replied, turning back to his game. I considered whether I ought to teach the young punk a thing or two about courtesy, but decided just to let the matter ride with Marilyn along. You never know when someone is going to be carrying a knife or a gun. So we beat a rapid retreat out of the dingy store.

Marilyn noticed that someone had in the meantime occupied the ticket booth in the converted town hall across the street. The marquee lights had been turned on. Although we definitely had no intention of being customers, we thought we might at least get a more civil response to our inquiries than we had received at the store. When we got close enough, we saw that the occupant of the ticket booth was an elderly man, frail and weathered-looking and dressed in a pale sweater despite the heat.

"Two dollars, gent," he said. "Lady's free."

"We didn't want to see the show," I explained.

"Then what DO you want?" he asked, with an air of suspicion.

"We cut off 1-A between Ipswich and Rowley and followed the gravel road around the headland," I said. "We'd just like to find out where we are."

"Why'd you do a thing like that?" asked the old man. "Ain't nothing here."

"Just to see where the road might lead."

"To hell, as far as I'm concerned," he said. "When I came to work in this here town in 1926–27, the refinery was going strong and the jewelry business was prospering. Well, when the feds came and cracked down in 1927–28, there wasn't much left. The tax men took over the refinery for delinquent taxes and closed it down. Destroyed a lot of warehouses and seized the contents. Just a few of us outsiders stayed on. The old families, though, rounds-about here they're clannish to the extreme. The feds thought they got most of that brood, but some of us thinks they mostly just went underground."

"I hope those two young punks at the store aren't representative of your local gentry," I said. "They cursed me out just for asking where we were."

"Those'll be the Soames boys," said the old fellow in the ticket booth. "Probably be over here to plunk down their admission before you know it," he said. "They come most Wednesdays."

"You work here every day?" I asked.

"Just Wednesdays. Them who wants to see 'em, comes to see 'em on Wednesday. When old man Gore first started showing this stuff in '75 there was a bit of a ruckus—Reverend Hoadley and the Free-Will Baptists 'an all—but that died down. There's a steady trade here now in wickedness. I'll get maybe fifty folks between noon and midnite on a Wednesday."

"What's the name of this place?" I asked.

"Took away our post office, they did, long ago as 1927–28," the old fellow continued. "The Marshes had to pull a few strings in Boston to stop 'em from clearing the whole place out back then. Nowadays, we get the mail addressed Rural Route 5, out of Rowley," he continued. "Not much in the way of mail, though. Seth takes it at the store."

"We didn't see anyone there but the punks," I said.

"Well, Seth's pretty far gone," said the old man. "He'll let the Soames boys play the machines while he sneaks down the street to take a nip. Tell you the truth, I think those boys got Seth a bit intimidated. I think he's afraid they'll smash up his store one of these days."

"Anything left worth seeing?" I asked.

"I'd advise you to head back the way you came from. No road north. Fed's destroyed it back in 1927–28, along with the railway connection. They wanted to clear the whole place out, and close what passes for a road on the south, too. Marshes pulled a few strings to prevent that. No siree, the only way out's the way you came in, and I'd advise you to take it."

"What you got playing?" I asked.

"Nothing to take a lady to see," he replied. But he motioned for us to come inside. "Take a look for yourselves," he said, stepping from the ticket booth into the darkened lobby. A flyspecked ceiling fixture provided the only light. To one side, were booths for quarter-a-play loops. Several of them seemed to be occupied. The dusty concession stand appeared to have been closed for many years. The display counter was empty.

"Look for yourself what suits the local taste," said the old man, opening the door into the theater itself.

We stood for a moment just below the projection booth.

There must have been four or five slouched figures scattered around the theater. The beam of light from the projection booth projected a grainy picture on the screen. The smell of unswept aisles and unwashed bodies assaulted our noses.

The image on the screen was black and white. It seemed to depict a foreign police station. A man and a woman had been stripped naked and were being tortured by the policemen, who were using electrical prods. It was very rough stuff. I could see that Marilyn wanted to leave.

"Didn't want you to waste your two bits," said the old man.

"Thanks," I said to him. "But you could lose your job for giving us a peek without paying."

"Well, time's long past I should 'ev gone back to Salem—that's where I was born, back in May 1910, you know. Son of immigrants working in the mills. Might well take up a dishwashing job and a room at the Y back Salem way to provide security for my declining years. Just never did have the gumption to get out. Old Marsh went to prison for five years after 1927–28 for tax evasion, but he came out meaner than ever. Lots of drugs and booze run through this place during the depression and war years. Even a bawdy house or two for sailors coming north from Boston. Worked for the Marshes all that time, keeping the official books for the feds to look at. The official books warn't never one-tenth of the action. Old Marsh died in 1950—must have been pushing ninety—and things have been going way downhill ever since. His boys—three of 'em—were all just drunken perverts. Eb Gore married Old Marsh's one girl—his son Zach owns this here theater and the bar down the street for that matter. One of the Marsh boys got killed when the mob decided to show who was the boss, and nother died of syphilis in the county loony bin. Lem Marsh, the youngest son, though he must be well into his seventies today, he's still living, up the hill on the old Marsh estate, but god knows what kind of hell hole that is now. But Lecia—Old Marsh's daughter—she had the brains of the Marsh siblings. Her two boys—Zach and Will—pretty much run things here now. Me and Seth kind of keep downtown—if you can call it that—together for 'em and keep the local police well paid-off. Why, Zach and Will they even got Hoadley of the First Baptists to shut up after the big fuss about the sex films. You live here, you better pay attention to what Zach and Will Gore say."

"I think we better leave," I said. "We've appreciated your kindness to us."

"Might as well do something decent once in awhile," said the old man. "I never killed no one, but I got a lot of other Marsh sins on my conscience."

"Would you like a ride out?" I asked.

"No, they'd kill me if I just up and away. They got friends—or maybe I better say connections—all the way to Boston and back. Still a few minor league hoods running contraband in here, you see. Where do you think we get the shit they're showing right here, for instance?"

"Well, we'll be going if you're sure we can't give you a lift."

"That's OK. Real soon now, I'm going to be getting sick. They'll let me go to the Rowley Infirmary, and from there I'll just slip away when their guard is down. I got a cousin out in the Midwest, and I've saved up enough for a bus ticket if there's too much heat in Salem."

"We wish you luck."

"Thanks, I'll need it. And from now on, you folks watch where you go. That road's not marked for a reason. Hasn't been marked since 1927–28. And there's still folks in the know who'd like that road blasted into nonexistence."

"We still haven't found out what this place is called," Marilyn complained.

"Ain't called nuthin' now, ma'am," the old fellow answered. "If you're interested in the story, though, I'll tell you something. There was a fellow—some years after the 1927–28 raids—who made a study of the whole town. Cast it in the form of fiction. Had it printed by a young fellow—must've been a teenager—who lived in Pennsylvania. Died right after that—the author I mean. Always wondered if Old Marsh had a hand in that. I do know that Old Marsh arranged to have most of the books destroyed after the young fellow struck out west to make his fortune. Well, I wouldn't have ever seen the book, but I knew Zad Allen, who'd done some talking to the author. Zad went to his reward at the age of ninety-six just shortly after talking to this fellow, and it was well known in town that his passing wasn't natural. At the time, surveying what meagre post came into town was part of my duties with the Marshes—a small part. Long about February 1937 comes this parcel—

unheard of—for the late Zad Allen. Looked interesting, so I smuggled it out. Tell truth, I been keepin' it looking for a way to get it out.

"Now, missy, you just take this in your purse, and then when you've read it, you'll know more than you'll ever want to about where you folks have been." The old man handed Marilyn a small parcel neatly wrapped in brown paper.

"I really couldn't, it's your only copy," said Marilyn.

"No good to me, dear. Cost me my life if certain people—at least them as could read—found it on me. Might've cost the author his life, and I know for a fact his young publisher would have come to grief if he hadn't cleared out. Old Marsh thought he had destroyed about every copy, but he was livid when a bowdlerized version appeared in a popular magazine back in the war years. Had some of his thugs go up and burn every copy they could find on the newsstands in Salem and Boston. No, missy, now you just put that book in your purse like I said, and you'll find your answers when you get home."

Looking out the theater door, I noticed the Soames boys approaching from across the street.

"Well, look at the fancy-dancies come all this way just to see the fuck films," said the elder boy with a sneer. "'Course, maybe the gent ain't got such fine stuff back where he comes from," he continued.

"Now, don't talk like that, Ez," said the old man. "They just got lost and were asking for directions."

"Got to go in to get directions?" sneered Ez.

"I was just showing them a map," said the old man.

"Like hell," said Ez. "Zach Gore's gonna know you been talkin' with outsiders."

"Then tell him," said the old man. "'Tain't no harm in giving directions out."

"Well, now that you know how to go, why don't you git, shithead," said the young punk to me. His younger companion leered at Marilyn with an idiot look. "Maybe Ike and I'll entertain your young lady as our date while you get the hell out of here," continued the elder boy. "Maybe you won't find the locals so inhospitable after you've been doin' it with Ike and me down in the passion pit," he said, turning to Marilyn.

Just then, the younger boy, Ike, made a move for his pocket. I must've acted of pure instinct. I dashed against Ez and shoved him into Ike. Ike had pulled a knife. The old man staggered between us.

"Now, you let them alone!" he cried. At nearly the same instant, Ike's knife plunged into the old man's chest. The old fellow let out a scream, and fell to the floor with an expanding red stain on his chest.

Marilyn and I were out the door in an instant. The stabbing seemed to have raised a hub-bub in the theater. We saw Ez and Ike, Ike holding the blade, standing over the old man, apparently gaping at him, but several shadowy figures seemed to emerge from the quarter-a-play booths and the projection room. Fortunately, the town square was deserted. We had just started the car when a group of several men—it may or may not have included Ez and Ike—started toward us from the theater. The ignition hit, the tires squealed, and we were on our way out. I was concerned about pursuit, but tried not to drive recklessly. We were fearful the locals might try to cut us off before we regained 1-A. Thankfully, we made it. We drove right here to the police station in Rowley to give this statement.

Notes by Officer McClennan, Rowley police Department, Case 17-293A, Reported Stabbing Incident, Rural Route 5, Rowley

Mr. & Mrs. Spurgeon unhurt. Escorted to Sea-View in Salem by Officer Lynch, 6:30 P.M. Advised to remain until contacted.

Officer Homer investigated in person same day. Found X-Way Theater closed but rounded up the Soames boys and brought them in for questioning. Seth Akins says Ed Barnes (the ticket taker who was allegedly stabbed) left without explanation a few days ago, but Seth looks cowed. Says X-Way has been closed since. Same story from other locals. Zach Gore came and bailed the Soarnes boys for $2,500 each 9 P.M.

Advised Spurgeons of contrary local testimony and they elected to depart. After reviewing the contents (fictional), returned to them book *The Shadow over Innsmouth,* by Howard P. Lovecraft, published by the Visionary Press, Everett, Pennsylvania, 1936. Keep photo of note for file. Spurgeon address: 3607 Marmion Blvd., Toledo 3, Ohio. (Attachment)

66 College St.
Providence, Rhode Island
February 9, 1937

Dear Zad—

Young Crawford has printed the enclosed, which I hope will reach you safely. Fear all is up with me.

To your good health—HP.

BOY IN SUMMER

Foster, Rhode Island, August 1896

The soft morning song of the birds in the grove just north of his bedroom window gradually woke the boy from his dreams. And vivid dreams they were, centering on his exploits in the narrow passages of the John Harrington cave a few days before. That day, he had pilfered matches from the match-safe in Uncle Jim's and Aunt Jane's parlor and, after eating a hearty breakfast of hotcakes, disappeared out the screen door, ignoring old Paris Shippee's admonitions that he listen for the dinner bell. Heading across the open meadows to the land of his grandpa's friend Judge Johnson, the young boy had known in his heart that the explorations planned for that day wouldn't allow him to listen for the dinner bell. And in the dream all the marvelous discoveries he made in the narrow passages of the Harrington cave, lit by the matches pilfered from his aunt and uncle, were magnified a hundred times until a rusty old key—which had perhaps once opened a can of sardines—opened the door to vast interior caverns of hidden mysteries. Even the boy had been somewhat alarmed to find dusk already well settled when he emerged from his explorations, and as he ran home across the open fields he could hear the voices of old Paris Shippee and of his uncle calling for him.

"Whar yew ben, boy?" said old Paris as the boy ran into view. "Thank God you're safe," contributed Uncle Jim, summoned by Paris's cries that the prodigal had returned. But it wasn't until he came into the kitchen and found his mother in tears that the boy had nearly broken down himself. "In my day," said Uncle Jim, "I'd a-bin razor-strapped good for sech an exploit," but kindly Aunt Jane just gave the boy a hug and said she'd known all the time that he'd be all right. "Now, Howard, I was afeared we'd have to eat without you, but now you're here we shall all sit down gratefully to a fine supper." And so they did. Afterward, the boy slept well, despite all the excitement and emotion of that day of exploration. Uncle Jim would talk about his young nephew's explorations for years afterward. "He'd a-dun thet wild old fust John Herendon well—out amongst the bears and Injuns," he'd say of his young nephew.

And what a wonderful two weeks it had been with Uncle Jim and Aunt Jane! The Phillips household in Providence had been in mourning for Grandma Robie since her death in January, and the invitation from Uncle Jim and Aunt Jane to Howard and his mother had been a godsend. Uncle Jim had even sent the pony cart into the city to fetch them from the handsome edifice his younger brother Whip Phillips had built on the corner of Elmgrove and Angell. Despite the open fields that still bordered the Seekonk River to the east of his home, the young boy would have more space to roam on his uncle's farm. Besides, the city was becoming a dangerous place, and one couldn't be sure any longer that a person met along the street would be a kindly neighbor. So the boy and his mother had plunged into two weeks of rural retreat. Not that the small hamlet of Moosup Valley couldn't be lively: only a few days after his arrival, the boy had been treated to a Grange supper and introduced to more relatives—Howards and Whipples and Tylers and Fosters and Places and Kennedys—than he could ever remember. Despite being relatively poor, the country folk seemed to enjoy life just as well as people in the city—and the boy had certainly relished all the attention paid Whip Phillips's grandson and the luscious country ham and fresh boiled corn served at the Grange supper, topped off with strawberry shortcake with fresh whipped cream.

Most of the vacation was his very own—exploring the countryside and playing with his newfound friends, the Dexter sons and daughters, themselves refugees from the Providence metropolis. The beauty he found in the city, along the unspoiled banks of the Seekonk River, was quieter and deeper here—the little brooks and tributaries of the Moosup River, the swampy places and frequent rock outcroppings, were all tinged with quiet mystery. Perhaps the mystery was deepened by an aura of ancestral presence that even a six-year-old could feel. For here were the boy's roots—where five generations back, his Place grandmother's ancestor Enoch had settled, some forty or fifty years after wild old John Harrington first settled here. And as for the Phillipses, this was their ancestral territory, too—an ancestor known as "Great Jeremiah" having once owned much property to the north.

Along the Moosup Valley road one might still find the memorials of the past generations—the private burial grounds of the Places, once so thick in this area, according to Uncle Jim, that the entire stretch of Moosup Valley Road and the hamlet itself had once been known as "Placetown." The young boy found these secluded and sometimes neglected burial grounds places of fascination, and his mother pointed out to him with especial pride the handsome banked lot in which her grandfather and great-grandfather Place, both named Stephen, rested. Both Uncle Jim and Grandpa Whip Phillips could remember the younger Stephen well—and the kindly Batteys, who now lived in the Stephen Place household where the boy's mother had been born, allowed the visitors to tour the home, which they had kept up well. Both of Uncle Jim's boys—Walt and Jerry Phillips—and their families managed to pay calls while the boy and his mother were visiting; but the boy found most poignant the graves of the little boys and girls of Uncle Jim and Aunt Jane who had not survived to have their own families, in the little plot up the steep slope opposite the farmhouse. When Uncle Jim told the boy that he and his wife would also be buried there, the boy, only recently introduced to mortality by the death of his grandmother, began to cry. Aunt Jane scolded her husband, and the tears were soon dried. Most of the loved ones of former generations had died before photographers had swarmed over the land, but Aunt Jane's parents, old Job Wilcox Place and his wife Asenath Pierce Place, had lived well into their eighties, and their stern photographs looked down on the old familiar rag carpets from the parlor walls. Uncle Jim told the boy that this had been the home of Job's brother Abraham; he and his wife Nabby were without children and had left this home to their niece Jane and her husband.

Indeed, few Places were now left in the vicinity of Moosup Valley. Aunt Jane's younger brother Henry and his family had moved to the Providence metropolis a few years ago. Their cousin Job D. Place and his family farmed way up north of Foster Center. The only Places left along Moosup Valley road were old Christopher Place and his wife Nancy Blanchard Place. Christopher and Nancy now lived in the household of their only daughter Jennie and her husband Jim Bennis. Despite his seventy-six years, old Christopher still helped Jim and Jennie Bennis and their children with the farm work. And the boy came to visit him— this old man who had spent all his years working the rocky soil of his native town and hardly been to Providence more than a dozen times.

"So, yew be Whip Phillips's gran'sun," the old man had greeted the boy with his rough, raspy voice. (Uncle Jim had told the boy that old Chris Place was not a well man.) "Yer mom thar I dew re-call well; she war a lively gal back when she cum ter visit here over summers in the '70s and '80s. Married up ter Bostun, I heered—always sed she shudda chusen a Moosup Valley feller." At this even the quiet Nancy Place ventured to reproach her husband. "I knowed Whip's and Jim's pa and ma real well—them boys wuz left orfins when Robie died of the fever in the summer of '48 and Jerry was kilt in his mill thet same winter. Mary Stanton cum in and tuk ker of them boys and thar sister—did yew know yer gran'pap an' Uncle Jim hed two sisters? Sadly gone these many years—Susie, who war a stunning gal and thar favrite of all, of a fever jest three years arter her ma, in '51, afore she cud even marry, and Abbie, in the prime of her life, in '73. Abbie married a Dixon feller over Connectycut way, and ef yew stay long enuff by Uncle Jim ye'll meet yer Dixon cuzins, fer sure."

It seemed old Christopher wanted to tell things to the boy. "Yew know, I kin re-member futher back then even Jerry and Robie Phillips wot bot ther mill from Billy Blanchard. I dew re-member Jerry's pa Aseph Phillips, wot took over the farm of his pa Jim over whar tha Luther Road hez ben cut, and married Ben Whipple's dawter Esther. I 'member him personal, fer when he wuz an olt man in the summer of '27 and I wuz a boy uv seven—jest a year old than yew be—he lernt me to cut swamp hay. Thet summer and the next three years I wukked as a hand—which is ter say, did chures—on old Aseph's farm, though by '28 and '29 he wuz too sick to wuk hisself. I 'member, he died jest a few days arter the Fourth of July in '29. He enjuyed his lest Fourth as well as a sick man cud; I member he wuz in some considrabul pain and eased it with his likker jug. I 'member well when he was laid out in his home and then buried ter the fambly yard, fer I wer thar. His widder Esther—I 'member her well, too. She muster lived ten er fifteen mur years. Even young blades like Jim en' Whip kin member her.

"I wuz mighty sorry, tew, young feller, ter hear uv the passin of yer Gramma Robie this past winter—ez fine a womun ez yew might wish. Ez fer her side uv yer fambly, I knowed 'em all well, tew. I wukked fer Robie's father young Stephen in thuh '30s and '40s, arter Aseph died. Did yew know thet young Stephen Place an' Jerry Phillips married sisters—Sally an' Robie Rathbun? Uncle Jim's Aunt Nabby war thar sister and Mary Stanton wot keered fer Jerry's and Robie's orfins war thar niece, the dawter of thar sister Ruth. So yew see ez haow we're all fambly out here by Moosup Valley. Here in Placetun', as they uster call it, the woods wuz thick with Places—we had mur Stephens than yew could shake er stick at, en' I knowed must uv 'em. Old Stephen died afore I wuz born, but they dew tell me I wuz tuk ter the fun'ral uv his widder Martha in '22. Preacher Stephen wuz a mur remut relashun— but I heared him preach onct—same summer I lernt swamp haying from yer two times great granpa Aseph. I think it may ev bin the lest time he ever preached, fer he wer woful decrepit and died soon arter. Even today thar's a shoemaker Stephen in thar township."

"Naow, Chris," offered old Nancy, "I think yew have bored thet poor boy enuff with tales of thar past. Let's say we let him play with yer grandchilrun."

"That's wot chilrun's ought ter dew—play," said the old man. "Naow, young feller, yew be getting along and see yew don't go pulling thah har o' my grandawters. And dew bee-have when yew go ter meeting with Elder Kennedy this Sunday. He dew be my kinsman and wun uv thar few uv my generashun left hereabouts."

And the boy flew out the door to leave the old sick man to visit with the adults. He did indeed comport himself well in Elder Kennedy's meeting, and he even liked it better than the services at the Baptist Church in Providence. There was much to tell his Grandpa about his wonderful two weeks with Uncle Jim and Aunt Jane—and Grandpa even presented him with a book once owned by Stephen Place the younger. The boy advanced in strength and in wisdom, but he never forgot his summer in Moosup Valley. Later he wrote of it, and kept its memory alive. But much more of that magical summer in the life of the boy remains to be told.

THE HAUNTING OF HUBER'S

(From the Casebooks of Wilmott Watkyns, Psychic Investigator)

I

One of the very first professional cases I ever handled involved an institution I loved when I was growing up in the northern reaches of the city of Cincinnati. I was surprised to receive a call from Sol Huber, owner of the famed Huber's Teepee, a local institution founded by his father Israel Huber in the 1930s.

"Wilmott, I've heard you're getting a good start in your professional career," the ever-courteous Sol began. "I never thought I'd have any business along your lines, since the food and hospitality business is a pretty worldly affair. But it turns out I could use your help. I wonder if you would stop by mid-afternoon sometime this week. We're officially closed for food service between 2 and 5, but I think I can wrestle something out of the kitchen for you."

"Just so long as you can get me some of the hot slaw with bacon, I'll be all right," I told him. "And it so happens I've got a slot open Tuesday at three P.M."

"The hot slaw, I can handle that anytime between opening and closing of doors," said Sol. "Something more elaborate I might have to work on between the kitchen shifts."

"Well, I'm on a diet, anyway," I said.

"You attractive young ladies are always on a diet," said Sol.

"Now, you're just trying to get a discount," I replied.

"Oh, no, strictly professional basis. Going rates," said Sol.

"Well, I ask for a retainer of $500, and then it's a $50 per hour charge plus out-of-pocket expenses," I replied.

"It will be well worth it," said Sol. "I'll see you Tuesday at three."

II

I had occasion to think of Huber's Teepee and Sol several times before three P.M. Tuesday rolled around. When I was growing up with my brother Bobby, it was my parents' favorite choice for Sunday dinner. Our father was an attorney for a large firm downtown and took the streetcar to work Monday through Friday. He usually ate his lunch at a cafeteria or lunch counter downtown unless he was meeting with clients. But the evening meal was a "family affair" six nights a week. I still remember what an excellent cook mother was. But preparing meals from scratch and cleaning up afterwards was a lot more work back in the 1950s than it is now, with the advent of microwaves and prepared foods. So Sunday dinner at Huber's was a real treat that mother and in fact the whole family looked forward to each week.

Izzy Huber had started the Teepee back in the 1930s. The original building was done in the so-called "vernacular" style and resembled an Indian teepee extended with wings for serving areas. The kitchen was in the center, and what I remember best about the original building, still in place in the 1950s but much expanded with new wings, were the fishtanks lining the walls, with all their glorious shell formations and colorful fish.

The Teepee was always a fairly classy place despite its humble beginnings. The menu leaned toward steaks and seafood (even lobster tails!), but there were also homestyle offerings like chicken croquettes, served in a rich cream sauce. (Needless to say, I adored the croquettes, although they didn't help me fight the battle of my teenaged waistline.) There was also the chopped liver appetizer with matzoh to tempt me as well. Or matzoh-ball soup with chicken broth. Beef brisket and potato pancakes were some of the other traditional, homestyle items on the Teepee menu. There were always lots of good desserts, too. Needless to say, we usually went home well-filled. I can recall Father with his Sunday paper and Mother just dozing on Sunday afternoons after midday dinner at Huber's. Father got to be on a first-name basis with Izzy Huber. Sol was about a decade my senior, so he was in his college years at UC during the heyday of our family dinners. Needless to say, he was destined to follow his father into the family business.

Huber's expanded numerous times over the years. The original teepee structure finally bit the dust in a remodeling in the sixties. By then, I was off to college myself. But Father and Mother still numbered among the Huber's faithful when Sol called me during the summer of 1974, two years after my graduation with a magna cum laude degree in psychology. I guess Father had kept Sol posted on my rather unusual line of business. Not that I didn't take a mix of "ordinary" private investigator work in the early years of my career.

So when I arrived at Huber's promptly at three P.M. the following Tuesday, it was like old times, although both the restaurant and its parking lot looked larger than the last time I was there, perhaps a few years before.

Sol appeared almost immediately when I announced myself at the hostess's desk. At that hour, only the bar was officially open.

"Wilmott dear, you're a sight for sore eyes," said Sol, giving me a light hug.

"Good to see you, too," I responded. "Looks like the restaurant business agrees with you."

"I guess it must run in the blood," said Sol. "My dad Izzy is in his mid-sixties now, but he still comes in most evenings for the dinner crowd. He's got some customers who've been with him since the beginning in 1934, and he likes to see that they're treated well."

"I think we Watkynses have been pretty steady customers ourselves since the early 1950s," I said.

"And that's just why you're getting the red carpet treatment now," said Sol. "Allow me to show you to your booth."

We swept past a stairway leading to a lower-level banquet facility into the darkened main dining room. Sol seated me right at the first booth. "I've made sure we kept the slaw hot," said Sol, "but I thought you might like to begin with some chopped liver and matzoh. I seem to remember your liking that."

"You've got a good memory," I said. "Chopped liver with matzoh and hot slaw sound just like the thing to get an eager psychic investigator fired up for her next case."

"Save a little room for chiffon pie with coffee afterward," said Sol. "So, do you want to eat in peace or can I sit down with you and explain why I invited you over?"

"By all means, have a seat," I said. "It will be interesting to see if you consume any of your own wares."

A waitress on special assignment from her normal duties in the bar at this hour was standing by, and Sol motioned her over. "Would you care for anything to drink?" he asked me. "On the house," he added.

"Well, since I'm not yet officially on duty, I'll have a whiskey sour," I said. "Mother always has a whiskey sour when she dines at Huber's."

"And a fine lady she is," said Sol, in his most complimentary manner. "Jerrie, you can bring us two sours on the rocks," he said, "and then start us with the chopped liver and matzoh, followed by hot slaw."

Jerrie went about her efficient way, and soon we had our drinks in front of us. The chopped liver with matzoh wasn't long in coming, and I helped myself first.

"How do you make this stuff so good?" I asked.

"Professional secret," said Sol.

"Not that I'm about to open Watkyns Wayside Inn right down the street," I offered.

"You never know," said Sol.

We chatted back and forth a little longer. I ate my fill of chopped liver with matzoh, and when I declined any matzoh ball soup, the hot slaw followed. Served in a wooden bowl, the hot slaw had a traditional vinegar base. The delicious chunks of fried bacon added something special. It was a winner for its very simplicity. Yet, when competitors tried to imitate its success, there was always something missing.

"It's really just cabbage, vinegar, and spices—plus of course the bacon," said Sol, "but I guard the exact recipe with my life. I suppose you could come close to the mix of spices by experimentation, although there are a couple items you might not guess. But getting the bacon just the way we serve it is pretty tricky. Only my most trusted kitchen employees work with the hot slaw. Of course, many of the people back there have been with us for decades. They tend to stay."

"Must be the nice employers," I said.

"Now, you're just trying to influence me," Sol responded.

"So, after this treat, let's talk business," said I. "I wouldn't mind some coffee, and when we're finished we can decide whether there's room for that chiffon pie."

The efficient Jerrie served the coffee within moments of my asking, and at last Sol was ready to launch into business.

"You know we are sitting at this very moment in Booth #1," said Sol.

"Ah, you're just trying again to impress me," I responded. "I told you from the start, no discounts."

"Check it out for yourself," said Sol. "Each both has a small numbered plate at mid-table position, right under the table lamp, and see for yourself, this is Booth #1."

"Assertion verified," I responded. "I assume this has something to do with the business at hand."

"Well, it does indeed," said Sol, "since between you and me as principal and investigator, we've been experiencing a little bit of a disturbance in this booth."

"Customers fighting over the honor of occupying Booth #1?" I asked.

"Oh no, hardly that. In fact, there's been no interference with customers at all. Customers have continued to sit happily at Booth #1, just as you are doing now."

"So what's the problem with Booth #1?" I asked.

"Well, it's just that a particular customer, or I guess I should say former customer, has been lingering beyond our regular operating hours."

"I'm sure you and your father have been handling late idlers in the dining room and bar for many years," I said.

"That we have," said Sol. "This is a high-class place. We stop seating for dinner at 10 P.M. every night, but that doesn't mean you can't linger until midnight if you wish. At that point, we do start shooing everyone out. The doors are usually locked by 12:15 P.M. There's a late cleaning crew that springs into action, but if I'm on evening duty, I'm usually home easily by 1 A.M. Not bad for a restaurateur."

"So what's the beef?" I asked.

"It's our former customer, Miss Christine Allroth," said Sol. "Booth #1 was where she ate her Saturday evening dinner, 6:30 P.M.

sharp, for many years. She passed away a few weeks ago. But she's still with us, here in Booth #1, once we've closed the place down. Her wraith, rather. Just sitting there, smiling, as she always did, in her old-fashioned dress and granny shoes. It's giving the night crew the spooks. I don't know why she's coming, but I've stayed and seen her myself. Last week, I walked right up and asked her what we could do for her. But she's silent. I can put my hand right through her . . . and she doesn't say a word."

"Sol, you should be careful with a manifestation like the one you describe. So should your staff. What can you tell me about Miss Christine Allroth?"

"I can do show-and-tell," said Sol. He pulled a cardboard photo folder from the inside pocket of his suit jacket. He opened it, and there she was, a sweet old lady, a kind twinkle in her eyes, high cheekbones, spare, delicate features, wispy hair. She wore an old-fashioned dress, with a brooch at her throat.

"Miss Christine Allroth specifically devised this little photo folder to me," he said. "I attended the reading of her will downtown last week at Carter & Wade. I was specifically requested to attend by the attorney for the estate. You see, Christine Allroth lived her entire lifetime, 1890 to 1974, in the large Queen Anne frame that is situated immediately south of our restaurant on North Bend Road. I'm sure you've seen it many a time. In its heyday, it was a lovely property. Miss Allroth's grandfather, Christian Allroth, for whom I suspect she was named, was Cincinnati Dutch, German I mean. He made a fortune in manufacturing glass bottles for Cincinnati's German brewers, and he sold out at just the right time before competition scuttled the profits. With the proceeds, he built the big Queen Anne house I mentioned. In its heyday, I've been told, there were ten servants including an inside and outside staff and a separate carriage house. I guess Christian and his good frau lived the good life too seriously, because Miss Allroth told me her grandparents died before the turn of the century. Her own mother died in childbirth in 1890. So that means there was just Christine and her father Frederick."

"Tell me about Frederick Allroth," I prompted.

"Never met him personally," said Sol, "although he was still living when I was born in 1938. But my father Izzy had occasion to deal with him. Maybe you'll need to talk to Izzy about it. The long and short of it was that Frederick grew up a spoiled brat. His father sent him to the gymnasium in Germany, but Frederick didn't acquire much except dueling scars and a prejudice against the melting pot that was America. His father Christian had been active in many civic organizations and charities, and at first Frederick carried on in a weak-willed way. But Frederick never forgave Cincinnati for forsaking all things German once war was declared in 1917. Most German families accepted the reality and patriotically supported the war. They sent their boys to fight like all the rest. But not Frederick Allroth. If Cincinnati forsook the Fatherland, then he would forsake Cincinnati. He withdrew into his own narrow shell and abandoned all the civic and charitable activities with which the family was traditionally involved."

"How did all this impact his daughter?" I asked.

"She was a brilliant girl. B.A., Germanic Languages, University of Cincinnati, 1912. M.A., same subject, 1914. She taught German at Hughes High School in Clifton from 1914 until 1917. It was my understanding that she worked on a Ph.D. degree at the University of Cincinnati. But when the declaration of war came in 1917, Hughes and everywhere else in town dumped German. Hughes offered her replacement duties, but Frederick Allroth insisted that Christine resign immediately. From 1917 until 1946 Christine was under her father's thumb in the family homestead on North Bend Road. She kept virtually none of her school friends. If you didn't have a German name, you didn't enter Frederick Allroth's house in those years."

"If it's the house I'm thinking of," I said, "it's a dump. I wonder it wasn't leveled years ago. I'm sure Huber's hasn't been happy to have it as a neighbor."

"That's a long story," said Sol. "It is a dump now, but that wasn't the fault of the lady who had to live there. But I am getting ahead of myself. After the death of Christian, there were some contractions, but it was still a substantial and well-maintained household when Frederick staged his great withdrawal in 1917. All the non-Germanic staff then departed. Frederick eliminated the gardener and his assistant in favor of a contract landscaping firm, and tore down the carriage house, replacing it with a nondescript garage. He kept about half the inside staff his father once maintained, although cutbacks continued throughout his life. You see, Frederick was never good for any business. Perhaps he thought himself too good for that. He was living off the capital accumulated by his father, and it was a diminishing amount."

"By the time Huber's opened in 1934, the Allroth manse was beginning to show its age. Izzy acquired all the present property by 1938, and as you know we've expanded to fill it. Already by the 1940s we could have used more parking space, and seeing the declining condition of the Allroth house and knowing something of the family background and finances, Izzy wanted to acquire it. He told me the story many times of knocking at the Allroth door round about 1940 and being shown into Mr. Allroth's parlor. Herr Allroth entered wearing a monocle and military-style coat. My father tried to explain his purpose in coming, but Allroth cut him short. 'We don't want no dirty Hebes on this property,' said Allroth. 'Get out.' And he showed my father the door. My father never forgot that, and he never crossed the property line again. Izzy you know is the salt of the earth and a big believer in the American ideal. Hard work, big rewards. Get along with everyone. Izzy and his parents left Poland early in the century to get away from people who thought like Frederick Allroth. He didn't—in fact he doesn't—like to think that there are people with those same attitudes right here in America. But so it was."

"I'm surprised that Christine Allroth ever became your customer, coming from such a background," I offered.

"Christine was nothing like her father," replied Sol. "In fact, the very opposite. Broad-minded, tolerant, in every respect a lady. But you're right about one thing. The Hubers didn't get to know her until after Frederick Allroth died. He and his property went downhill during the 1930s. I think the family lost money in stocks. By the mid-1930s, Christine was doing all the inside work, including the cooking. The automobile must have been sold sometime during that decade as well. A landscaper still cut the grass, but didn't do much beyond that. Frederick himself was heavily involved in the German-American Bund. He was dead-set against war with Germany, but Hitler resolved matters by declaring war against the United States after Pearl Harbor. Once the war broke out, the F.B.I. kept a close watch on Allroth and his associates. By the last phases of the war, Allroth, like many of his associates, was pushing an alliance with the Nazis against the Bolsheviks. But Hitler went down, and Frederick Allroth didn't survive him for long. He died the next year, 1946. I think he was a year or two short of eighty. The Allroths had withdrawn from the Lutheran church to which they had once belonged when services in German were dropped in 1917. I've been told that only Christine and the undertaker accompanied Frederick Allroth to his burial in the family plot in Spring Grove Cemetery.

"We found out that Frederick Allroth left his daughter with a cruel dilemma. She was to enjoy the right to the estate so long as she lived in and maintained the family home. So soon as she abandoned it, the remainder of the estate was to go to some obscure cultural foundation in Germany. Christine was fifty-six years of age when her father died in 1946. She hadn't held a job since 1917, when she resigned from Hughes High School. She had never taken commercial courses, and Germanic Languages never come back into the Cincinnati high school system.

"One day the autumn after her father died, she came to the restaurant in the afternoon and asked to see my father. She explained who she was and apologized for the conduct of her father. She asked if she would be welcome to patronize the restaurant, and my father assured her she would be. He again stated his desire to purchase the Allroth property, and Christine explained her cruel dilemma. I think $100,000 was about the sum my father could have expended for the entire Allroth property after the war. That would have kept Christine comfortably for the rest of her life, but the cruel dilemma was that the Allroth estate was structured so that the proceeds of any sale would go to the cultural foundation in Germany, not to Christine. She would be left penniless. So she had to refuse my father's offer, even though she would have much preferred to move from the rambling Queen Anne to a comfortable apartment in one of the nearby side streets with their quaint gas lighting. So, although Christine could not accept my father's offer to purchase Allroth house, she did take up his offer to become a patron of Huber's Teepee. She was a faithful one at that and dined at Huber's nearly every Saturday night, with rare exception from 1946 until her death a few weeks ago. Since our remodeling in 1965, Booth #1 was her reserved spot. My father and I and our staff knew this gracious lady well."

"It sounds like Saturday dinner at Huber's was a happy part of her life, hardly the excuse for a haunting," I commented.

"Exactly so," said Sol. "Not that Christine Allroth did not broaden her life in numerous ways after the death of her father. She almost immediately resumed active membership in Immanuel Lutheran Church, from which her father had resigned in 1917, to protest the dropping of German-language services. Her best friend in her high school and college years had been Bertha Whitacre, and Christine resumed her acquaintance with Bertha after a breach of nearly thirty years. Bertha Whitacre had gone on to a business degree from University of Cincinnati and had a responsible clerical position with Union Central Life Insurance Company. Bertha and Christine discussed whether Christine could take an entry-level clerical position at Union Central and share quarters. But Christine decided in the end to live within the terms of her father's will. Bertha also tried to stir Christine's interest in resuming her Ph.D. thesis work at University of Cincinnati, where Germanic Languages had long since been restored. But Christine decided that the idea was beyond her financial and her physical capabilities. So she continued to live out her life in the Allroth home on North Bend Avenue.

"She took a practical tack in many ways. You had to admire her. She had none of her father's chauvinism. She quickly sold most of the family furnishings, beyond the few simple items she needed for her own housekeeping. The porcelain and silver, anything of value, was sold to increase the capital available. By the 1960s she was living in just a bedroom and kitchen on the main floor of the vast, sprawling house. The city inspectors were aware of her cruel predicament and took a lenient view toward the decaying condition of Allroth house. Christine struggled on bravely, and a last exterior painting, with necessary carpentry repair work, was undertaken about 1962. By 1965, Christine took another major decision. For $5,000—a major expenditure from her declining capital—she purchased a mobile home that was installed so that it linked with the service door of the family manse. She moved all her simple remaining furnishings into the mobile home and thereupon cut off all utilities in the main house. An extension cord ran from the trailer to the front parlor of the main house, providing power for a single light on a timer. If the obscure German cultural foundation had had an active presence, I suppose they might have raised a stir and claimed that she had abandoned Allroth house. But the estate attorney showed no sign of raising any objection.

"And so Christine Allroth continued to come to Huber's for her Saturday night dinner year after year," remembered Sol. "She was very simple in her tastes. She would order a glass of white wine and then enjoy our chopped liver appetizer and hot slaw. Almost invariably, she would order the chicken croquettes, our lowest-priced entrée. Customarily, she would finish just one of the two croquettes, and take the other home to consume later. She would forego dessert, unless we insisted upon something 'on the house' for her birthday or another special occasion. She was grateful that there was a Kroger's supermarket just north of us, where she would do small amounts of shopping—as much as she could carry in a tote bag—several times each week. Virtually everyone knew to go to the back service entrance at her home, where the trailer was parked, but there was a considerable to-do four or five years ago when some young pranksters were hurt on Halloween when some rotten boards on the front porch of the main house collapsed. Some voices in the community said that Allroth house should be condemned. A compromise was reached whereby the stairs leading to the unsafe porch were removed. Nevertheless, the controversy consumed more of Christine's modest remaining assets.

"We tried very hard to make Christine's eightieth birthday celebration in July 1970 a special event," said Sol. "She was still recovering from the stress of the porch collapse and all the attendant controversy. My father Izzy called the pastor of Immanuel Lutheran and Bertha Whitacre, and the three of them conspired to host a surprise eightieth birthday party for Christine. Huber's paid all the expenses, and Christine was delighted to occupy the head of the table with her pastor, her friend Bertha, and six members of the Ladies' Club of Immanuel Lutheran. Christine was not generally a demonstrative woman, but she gave my father a hug in thanks for her surprise birthday celebration.

"The death of Bertha Whitacre in 1972 was a severe blow to Christine, although she continued bravely with as much of her own daily routine as her stamina would allow. For years, she had maintained a small garden at the back of Allroth house, and 1972 was the last year she was able to do so. Fortunately, one of her friends in the Ladies' Club provided her with transportation to and from Immanuel Lutheran on Sundays. But Christine began to miss occasional Saturday evening dinners at Huber's, which she would explain on account of illness. She was seen less and less on the street and in Kroger's with her tote bag. My father and I finally concluded that her funds—apart from the real estate she could not touch—had now fallen to a critically low level. Christine was a generous tipper, and if her dinner bill came to $3.50 she would tip the staff an additional $1.50 and leave $5.00 in payment. We knew that Christine would never accept charity.

"So, after 1972, my father vowed he would feed Christine Allroth for that weekly $5.00. We had for some years had a valet parking service, and my father began to insist that we drive Christine home from her Saturday evening dinner. Somehow, her single left-over chicken croquette increased to an even dozen, accompanied by potatoes and vegetables, when the leftovers were packed in the kitchen. These extensions of courtesy Christine accepted with grace. She would even tell my father that her leftovers were exceptionally good and that she had enjoyed them 'all week.' Within the last year, Christine grew weaker. There were times when she experienced confusion or slurring of speech, and we thought she might be experiencing mini-strokes. Finally, this past spring she suffered what must have been a more serious stroke and was hospitalized for several days. The social workers wanted to place Christine in a care center, but she insisted upon returning home. For his part, my father thereupon instituted 'delivery service' for Christine's weekly meal. She still insisted upon paying $5.00, 'including tip.' But by summer she seemed to rally and began to appear once more at Huber's for her Saturday evening dinner. A final stroke, however, took her peacefully in her sleep three weeks ago. By way of contrast to her father's, her funeral was well-attended. My father officially deputed me to attend on behalf of the Huber family. It was a command not to be ignored. I was of course happy to pay tribute to a dear lady."

"So Christine Allroth loved this place so well she doesn't want to be away from it in death?" I suggested.

"That seems to me a reasonable suggestion," said Sol. "With her death, any incentive to preserve the decayed remains of Allroth house has been removed, and I understand that the City of Cincinnati has begun long-delayed condemnation proceedings. Hauling away the vast amount of lumber Christian Allroth's workmen used to build that house will be an expensive proceeding, and I wonder if the sale of the land will clear all that much more than the cost of the demolition. My father wants to determine whether the residual beneficiary of the Allroth estate, that German cultural foundation, has any crypto-Nazi ties before making any bid on the property—much as he would like to have it for additional parking space. I don't believe that Christine had any sentimental attachment to the house whatsoever. She had long since abandoned it, not only, I am convinced, because she was unable financially to maintain it, but also because she found it oppressive. Christine wanted to be included in the American dream, not excluded. It saddens me to think what her life might have been had she been able to complete her thesis at the University of Cincinnati.

"Not having control of any real estate, Christine had little to bequeath in her own will. As you know, I was called to the reading of her will by the attorney for the Allroth estate. She had apparently destroyed all family mementos before her death. She left a pittance of furnishings, well-used but neat clothing, and a bank account containing approximately $3,500. No wonder she was worried about expenses! After payment of final expenses, she left everything to charity, with the exception of a single bequest: the photograph I showed you, which she left to me. Of course, I accepted the bequest with humility. I offered to help with any expenses, but the attorney assured me that $3,500 would provide all the necessary. He has promised to get back to us about the residual beneficiary of Frederick Allroth's real estate trust when he learns something more. Carter & Wade seldom deviates from '100% business' in the conduct of their affairs, but Samson Carruthers, who handled the Allroth estate, seemed touched by Christine's situation. He told me that he knew well everything my father and I had done for Christine and that he would do his best to steer the real estate our way if possible. 'There was only a pittance of furnishings and personal possessions—hardly worth handling,' he commented. 'The furniture and clothing went to charity. There was still a bequest of an antique brooch to Christine's friend Bertha Whitacre, but since Bertha predeceased Christine, the brooch fell into the estate and it realized $150—enough to pay the gentleman we hired to dispose of Christine's other personal property. This gentleman told me there was a Huber's chicken cro-quette dinner with all the accompaniments in Christine's refrigerator—still in fine condition to consume, which he did.' In a way, I felt that was a backhanded compliment to Huber's long friendship with Chris-tine Allroth. So I am left to wonder, what have we left undone? Why is she coming back?"

"I want to give it some thought," I told Sol. "Before long, you're going to have to be getting ready for the Saturday-night crowd that un-til recently included Christine Allroth in Booth #1. Now, don't do any-thing to disturb her wraith. Let it be. Let me know at once if it makes any sign. Tell your staff to stay calm. I do not think Christine will do anything to cause anyone any concern."

"Can I interest you in that chiffon pie before you depart?" asked Sol.

"I'll take you up on that if I succeed in laying this ghost for you," I replied. "But you can mail me my retainer at my business address," I continued, handing Sol my business card. "And I do thank you for to-day's refreshments. They brought back good memories of good times. I can see why my Mom and Dad keep coming back."

"We have many old customers," said Sol. "Christine Allroth was one of the dearest. We never held her father's harsh words against her. If there is something we can do to lay her ghost, to make her rest in peace, we want to do it."

"I'll take it all into consideration," I replied. "You'll hear from me soon. Let me know if anything unexpected occurs. And remember, don't disturb the ghost."

"Instructions noted," said Sol, as he ushered me to the door. There was still plenty of light, so I took the occasion to walk across the vast parking lot of Huber's to view Allroth house. There stood the vast hulk of wood baking under a hot late afternoon sun. The last paint job of 1962—green with red trim—was still in some evidence, although very dull and flaked in many places. The ground-floor windows had all been boarded up as protection against vandals—a recent development. I walked around to the service entrance and found only cinderblocks remaining behind the lattice work where Christine's trailer had once been parked. The grass was cut short and too browned out to need any further cutting for the near future. I could see the small flower bed that Christine had tended at the rear of the house. I looked at the windows of the upper floors of Allroth house but could see nothing but darkness. What did I hope to see? The face of Christine? Or of Frederick? Or of Christian Allroth? I didn't know. I only knew that I had much to ponder as I walked back to my car in Huber's parking lot and drove to my own apartment. If only Christine had been able to have her own apartment and to be free of the vast, dark encumbrance of Allroth house, I thought. She might have been able to depart this life more happily. She had left in remembrance of herself just two simple items—a brooch now in the hands of jewelers and a photograph left to Sol Huber. After that last meal of chicken croquettes had been consumed by the clean-up man, the photograph Sol had seemed to be all that remained in this world of Christine Allroth—except for the wraith that was frequenting the booth she had so often occupied on Saturday nights at Huber's.

II

During the ensuing week, I chatted with both Samson Carruthers and my friend Chuck Norringer of the Cincinnati Historical Society. Mr. Carruthers assured me that Allroth house itself was (with the exception of one cheap lamp in the front parlor) totally empty when Christine Allroth died. He remembered that an antiques dealer had purchased the remaining contents of the main house when Christine moved her own effects to the trailer in 1965. Nary a scrap of personal information concerning the Allroths went with the furniture remaining in the main house. Christine had quite evidently gone through everything with a fine tooth comb before committing the contents of the main house to the antiques dealer. The brooch and the photograph were the only significant personal effects found in Christine's trailer. If there was ever a cache of material concerning the Allroth family in Christine's possession, it seems that she disposed of it before her death.

My friend Chuck Norringer was able to develop only a very slender dossier on the Allroth family for me. He did find a sketch of Christian Allroth (1841–1898) in a large subscription book of *Prominent Citizens of German Origin of Cincinnati, Ohio* published in 1895. (That's actually an English translation for the original work was in German.) There was little disagreement with the account Sol Huber had provided me of the family. I did learn that Christian's wife was Edwiga (Mackensen) Allroth (1843–1895). The book also gave the date of birth of their son Frederick Allroth as November 8, 1867. Chuck was able to provide only a very slender file of newspaper cuttings concerning the elusive Frederick Allroth. A *Post* article dated May 18, 1917, listed Allroth among citizens signing a petition against the dropping of German language courses in the public school system. An *Enquirer* feature of July 8, 1935, concerned the activities of the German-American Bund in the Cincinnati area and mentioned Frederick Allroth as a member. Chuck told me he had heard that the local F.B.I. office had a file on Frederick Allroth. But this was long before the days of the Freedom of Information Act, and even with the passage of years and adoption of the Act I haven't been motivated to seek further information on that sorry character Frederick Allroth. A little bit of work did produce Frederick's death certificate. He had died July 31, 1946, aged seventy-eight years. So he'd had about a year to stew in his juices after Nazi Germany went down. About Christine Allroth we could find nary a record. U.C. could verify only her 1912 B.A. and her 1914 M.A.

By Thursday I was ready to call Sol Huber. He told me that the manifestations were basically unchanged. Shortly after closing, her wraith would slowly materialize in Booth #1. The wraith seemed content simply to sit. The cleaning staff was starting to get used to the manifestation. They noticed a slight chill when in the immediate proximity of the manifestation, but no sense of malevolence. I asked Sol if I and a professional colleague could stay after hours the following Saturday to observe the phenomenon. He gave us a 10 P.M. dinner reservation and said the security guard would let us out when we were finished. We asked for a table with a clear view of Booth #1.

My colleague and I had a good dinner that Saturday evening at Huber's. Despite old time's sake, I deviated from the chicken croquettes. By 11:30 P.M., my colleague and I were the only ones left in the main dining room. Both Sol and his father Izzy were on duty that evening and came by our table to wish us luck in our investigation.

"I never believed in ghosts until Christine came back to haunt us," said Izzy. "I did my best to do all I could for her."

"I don't think there's any hostility underlying this," I offered. "We'll take a look tonight and then give you some further counsel."

With that Sol and Izzy bade us good luck.

By midnight the cleaning crew began their work. About 12:15 A.M. a mist seemed to form in Booth #1, and within a few minutes it manifested itself into the wraith of an elderly lady. She seemed to be smiling and she ignored us and the clean-up crew, whose members went about their work while keeping their distance from Booth #1. The manifestation went on for about an hour and a half. We activated some electronic sensing equipment, and I tried a flash photograph. The wraith exhibited no disturbance. Then about 1:45 A.M. the wraith began to dissolve into mist. Within five minutes the manifestation was over. My colleague and I gave Booth #1 a thorough going-over after the wraith disappeared. We found nothing of a suspicious nature. The security guard let us out around 2 A.M. We stopped a moment to observe the baleful hulk of Allroth house in the moonlight.

The next afternoon, I called Sol Huber. "I think you should put up with this for awhile," I advised Sol. "Let's see what happens when Allroth house comes down. I hear through the grapevine that that's going to happen soon. It's possible that the disappearance of Christine's 'prison' will free her wraith from this haunting. I would say she's having dinner with you but taking care not to disturb your paying guests. My guess is that she spent about an hour and a half with you on Saturday nights when she was living."

"Well, you're right," said Sol. "She would come promptly for her 6:30 P.M. reservation, and we could count on her booth's being free for an 8 P.M. reservation."

"Hang tight," I said. Sol agreed to comply.

I did get the results from our previous session at Huber's. Photo: negative. Electronic activity: indistinguishable from background (appliance operation, etc.).

III

The next week, I checked with Samson Carruthers concerning the handling of the estate. As I had heard through my sources, pressure was building to demolish Allroth house. Mr. Carruthers had found that Frederick Allroth's legatee, The Field and Forest Society, was a Nazi-era organization and no longer existed. He had petitioned the probate court to allow demolition of Allroth house and sale of the property. The net proceeds would be placed in trust until a suitable disposition could be determined. He anticipated that a local charity might eventually be named to received the proceeds originally intended for The Field and Forest Society. He volunteered that he had discussed the entire matter with the Hubers, and that they had decided not to make a bid on the property. He had had several contacts, however, from an apartment developer who wanted to build a 40-unit residence on the property. Mr. Carruthers was also able to provide me with the name of the jeweler who purchased Christine's brooch from the estate. Fortunately, it had not been sold. I managed to acquire it for myself for $200, a modest markup.

IV

The probate court acted more quickly than either I or Samson Carruthers had anticipated. Permission was granted for demolition of Allroth house and sale of the property. The sale came first and the Allroth estate realized $150,000 from the apartment developer. The demolition quote came to $95,000, so some $55,000 was left for a residual heir to be named. The neighbors and the city all wanted the decaying hulk of Allroth house gone. Bulldozers and crane arrived on the scene on the first day of August and almost immediately began their dusty work.

I made it a point to stop by that day. The crew supervisor assured me that Allroth house was totally empty. "Lots of rotten wood," he said, assuring me that his wrecking crew had to exercise due care.

By the end of the first day, all that remained of Allroth house was a heap of wrecked lumber. Dump trucks removed that the following day, and by August 3 the bulldozers had removed every sign that Allroth house had once stood on the property.

I called Sol Huber and asked if he could have me and my colleague for another late dinner that evening. He assured me he could, so my colleague and I arrived promptly at 10 P.M. We ate very lightly, for I wanted to see if the demolition of Allroth house would have any effect on the appearance of Christine's wraith. I had taken the liberty of wearing Christine's brooch.

Huber's closed the doors at midnight, and by 12:15 A.M. Christine's wraith had not appeared. I began to believe that the demolition of Allroth house had finally freed Christine's spirit. We were about to depart at 12:45 A.M. when mist began to form in Booth #1. It seemed less substantial than formerly, but it was definitely still there. Within minutes, the mist resolved itself into Christine's wraith. She smiled as usual. The clean-up staff had already finished their work, so only my colleague and I and the security guard remained.

At about 1:15 A.M. I resolved to walk up to Booth #1. "Christine, your prison is destroyed," I said in clear tones. "I saved your brooch. May I keep it in remembrance?"

Up to now, the wraith had made no response. But she nodded her head "yes" in answer to my inquiry.

"Do we need to do anything else to free you from this posting?" I asked.

But almost immediately the wraith began to dissolve into mist. Despite being late, Christine was honoring her regularly scheduled departure at 1:15 A.M. Within minutes, the mist was gone.

V

I called Sol Huber the next afternoon and advised him of our results. He expressed a hope that our work was done. But I asked him to have the security guard continue to monitor the main dining room carefully between midnight closing and 2 A.M. and to report the results back to me. After a week of observation, I heard back from Sol Huber.

"Jim McGinnity reports that Christine is still visiting us, but for a shorter period," Sol reported. "She's as regular as a wraith as she was as a living customer. She's materializing about 12:45 A.M. and dematerializing about 1:15 A.M. Like clockwork. Same smile. Jim hasn't ventured to have any interaction."

I told Sol about the discussion I had with the wraith concerning her brooch. "I think we need to interact about the only other physical possession she considered important enough to bequeath," I told Sol. "Can you stay with us tomorrow evening until Christine appears? And bring her photograph?"

Sol said he'd be happy to do this. We asked Sol if we could forego dinner and arrive about midnight. He expressed some disappointment, but agreed with our plans.

VI

Jim McGinnity admitted my colleague and me when we arrived at Huber's at midnight the following evening. Sol soon joined us.

"Not often I host a spook convention," he bantered.

"I hope you won't have to anymore, after tonight," I offered.

"Will you have a drink before we start?" Sol asked. "I'll tend bar personally," he offered.

We stuck to ginger ale, but kept Sol company in the bar until about 12:30 A.M. Then we all took our places at the table directly across from Booth #1. Jim McGinnity lurked in the background, in case of need.

"I'm going to show her the brooch again, and then I want you to show her the photograph," I instructed Sol, in a whisper. "Just let me do the talking."

He nodded agreement.

Christine appeared at 12:45 A.M., like clockwork. She was smiling, as usual.

We didn't wait long to approach her booth. I took Sol's hand and we walked over to Christine's booth.

"I will always cherish this brooch in memory of you," I said in a firm, clear voice.

Christine looked directly at us—I could feel Sol flinch—and nodded her head in agreement.

I nudged Sol. He took the photograph from his jacket and opened it.

"And what shall we do with your photograph?" I asked. "Your friend Sol and I want to do the right thing."

Christine touched her hand to her heart, then pointed to the photograph in Saul's hand, then pointed to the wall of the booth.

Sol couldn't help blurting out: "You want me to install your photo on the wall of Booth #1! In honor of our best customer!"

Once again Christine nodded her head yes.

It was only a few minutes before 1 A.M. But mission accomplished. Christine's wraith dissolved into mist.

VII

Sol was bursting with plans, and we didn't get out of the restaurant until 2 A.M. Lamination, frame, inscription, he wanted to settle everything in his mind, and get our agreement, before we departed. I was bone-tired, but wanted to be as patient with Sol as I had been with Christine. After all, I remembered, he was my client.

During the week, we agreed with Sol that the installation of Christine's memorial plaque on the wall of Booth #1 should occur between lunch closing at 2 P.M. and dinner opening at 5 P.M. on the following Saturday. Sol reported that Christine was keeping shortened hours between 12:45 A.M. and 1 A.M. every evening.

I had been in touch with Christine's pastor during the course of our investigation. I asked if he and two or three of Christine's friends from the church Ladies' Club would like to attend the unveiling of the plaque at Huber's Teepee. He was surprised at the suggested hour of 12:30 A.M. on Saturday night, but called me back the next day to say that he and his wife and two other church ladies would meet us at Huber's at the requested time.

I informed Sol, and he said that Izzy and Sally Henderson, Christine's regular waitress, would be there as well.

With military precision, Sol called me at 4 P.M. on the following Saturday to let me know that the installation was complete. A small moveable screen was being used to hide the plaque until the official unveiling. In deference to Christine's memory, no one would be seated at Booth #1 that evening. He indicated that he, Izzy, Sally Henderson, and Jim McGinnity would look forward to seeing me and my guests that evening. I asked if Sally could serve a glass of white wine when the wraith appeared. Sol said he was sure she would be willing to do so.

VIII

All the guests arrived promptly by 12:30 A.M. Sol and Izzy escorted us to the table opposite Booth #1 and introduced us to Sally Henderson.

Like clockwork, mist began to form in Booth #1 at 12:45. Within a moment or two, that mist resolved itself into the wraith of Christine Allroth.

Sally Henderson didn't waste a moment. She walked right up to Booth #1 and served a glass of white wine to Christine's wraith.

"You look lovely this evening, darling," she said. "We've missed you."

Then Sol and Izzy approached the table.

"Christine, everyone deserves to be remembered. You were such a faithful customer and friend of Huber's that we've decided to remember you right here in Booth #1." Izzy reached over and removed the screen.

Christine focused right away on her portrait. Huber's staff had done a beautiful job. A small lamp illuminated Christine's portrait, which had been framed in gilt. A nameplate read: CHRISTINE ALLROTH: 1890–1974: FAITHFUL FRIEND.

"I hope you like it," Izzy offered.

The wraith touched her hand to her heart.

"May we join you this one time?" Izzy asked.

And Christine nodded her head yes.

So Izzy and Sol slid into the booth opposite Christine.

She focused on them and seemed happy for the company.

Izzy motioned Sally Henderson to sit beside Christine, and she did.

I approached the table and showed Christine her brooch. The pastor and church ladies joined me.

Christine looked us all over and then touched her heart again.

Then an amazing thing happened. With her ghostly hand she raised her wine glass to her lips, and drained it.

I expected a clean-up, but nothing of the sort was needed.

There was no resolution into mist. Christine's wraith disappeared into nothingness immediately upon draining her wine glass.

Jim McGinnity must have acted instinctively to raise the lights.

Christine's wine glass stood empty on the table.

The pastor and his accompanying ladies seemed especially affected by what had happened. I returned with them to our table, and Sally Henderson served us all soft drinks. Izzy and Sol remained seated in Booth #1 for a few more minutes. Then they joined us at our table and thanked us all for coming.

I was tempted to predict that we had succeeded in laying the ghost of Christine Allroth. But despite my few years, I decided that it would be best to hold my tongue. By 1:15 A.M. we adjourned.

IX

By the spring of 1975 the new apartment building just south of Huber's on North Bend Road was ready for occupancy. It is still a handsome building today. Only a few oldtimers remember Allroth House.

But even today Christine's memorial portrait and plaque still adorns Booth #1 at Huber's. Izzy has passed to his reward, but Sol still presides and has a new generation in training. I think the Hubers would sooner stop serving hot slaw and chopped liver than remove Christine's memorial. It isn't easy to get a reservation for Booth #1, but Sol tells me a reservation is always available for me whenever I want it. Being businessmen, the Hubers decided to forego telling the story of Christine's haunting.

Needless to say, her wraith never appeared again after that final evening at Huber's.

The reality of this world is that most of its occupants are soon forgotten. I don't think that's a tragedy for the majority of us who are blessed to lead rich and full lives. But Christine Allroth was so forgotten in her own long life that I think her spirit could not rest until some posthumous memorial was created. I trust that we did all the right things.

Mr. & Mrs. Christian Allroth and Mr. & Mrs. Frederick Allroth all had individual markers in the Allroth lot in Spring Grove cemetery. So Samson Carruthers expended $2,500 of the residual estate to create a comparable marker for Christine Allroth. Legal expenses went through another $5,000 or so of the residual estate, so that eventually about $47,500 went to a Cincinnati nature conservancy. I understand that most of the money was used to create an Allroth Memorial Aviary in their main building. I have yet to see it.

I often wear Christine's brooch and remember her when I do. She was, after all, one of my very first cases.

LOVECRAFT'S PILLOW

Stephen King's introduction to the English translation of Michel Houellebecq's monograph *H. P. Lovecraft: Against the World, Against Life* (San Francisco: Believer Books, 2005) has stirred a lot of controversy in the Lovecraftian world, a world made suddenly much larger with the publication of Lovecraft's *Tales* in the prestigious Library of America series earlier the same year. I'm not going to get into the controversies, because my focus is on King's account of the idea for a story to be titled "Lovecraft's Pillow." King writes of wandering around downtown Providence one Saturday afternoon during the 1979 World Fantasy Convention. He writes of encountering a downtown pawn shop, with all the usual gewgaws in the window:

> While I was looking in at all this rickrack, Mr. Idea Man spoke up from his Barcalounger at the back of my head, as he sometimes does, and for reasons no writer seems to fully understand, Mr. Idea Man said, "What if there was a pillow in that window? Just an ordinary old pillow in a slightly dirty cotton slip? And suppose somebody curious about why such an item would be on display—a writer like you, maybe—went in and asked about it, and the guy who ran the pawnshop said it was H. P. Lovecraft's pillow, the one he slept on every night, the one he dreamed his fantastic dreams on, maybe even the one he died on.

Later on in his introduction, King writes:

> "Lovecraft's Pillow" wasn't written that weekend in Providence, and has never been written since. If you would like to try your hand at it, Reader, I bequeath it to you . . . not to mention the bad dreams that are sure to follow any serious effort to do such a thing justice. As for myself, I no longer want to go inside Lovecraft's pillow, to visit whatever dreams may remain caught there, and I have an idea that's a point of view with which Michel Houellebecq could sympathize.

This narrator's account of "Lovecraft's Pillow" probably isn't quite what Stephen King was expecting when he wrote this introduction. But nevertheless, since all the principals are now removed from the stage, it seems an appropriate time to tell it.

My late friend Tom McInnerney (1937–2004) was the man the media called in Providence whenever a story arose concerning the iconic figure of Howard Phillips Lovecraft. Tom interned at the *Providence Journal* as early as the mid-fifties, and he covered many beats for the newspaper after he went on staff full-time after his graduation from Providence College in 1959 until his retirement in 2002. Regrettably, Tom didn't have a very long retirement, but he was still doing special features for the newspaper right up until his sudden death two years ago. The Lovecraft beat was simply one of the many he covered for the *Journal*. As a young intern, he had covered the story when the Mumford House at 66 College Street was moved up the hill to 65 Prospect Street where Lovecraft fans come in droves to see it even today. In the mid-sixties, the *Journal* sent him out to Sauk City, Wisconsin, to interview Lovecraft's publisher August Derleth on the re-emergence of HPL. When markers for Lovecraft and his mother were placed in the Phillips lot in Swan Point Cemetery in 1977, Tom was on the beat. His groundbreaking article "Lovecraft's Family Speaks," with interviews with Ethel Morrish and other relatives, is remembered by many.

In 1990, Tom was there to report on the Lovecraft Centennial Conference and the dedication of the Lovecraft memorial on the John Hay Library lawn. He "scooped" interviews with Frank and Lyda Long and Maurice Lévy during the Conference and got the "inside" story on the municipal participation in the memorial dedication from none other than Vinnie Cianci himself. Over the years, he interviewed many Providence booksellers on HPL's appeal, ranging from H. Douglass Dana (who bought the remainder of HPL's library after the death of his aunt Anne Gamwell in 1941) to the owner of the College Hill Bookstore on Thayer Street. He interviewed HPL's friends Cliff and Muriel Eddy numerous times over the years and drew forth some unique insights. (He got the story on HPL's mugging on the way home from the Eddys' in East Providence and the fact that he sometimes carried a pistol to protect himself on his nocturnal wanderings after this incident.) He interviewed Brown professor Bob Kenny and was the first to publish Kenny's recollection of HPL as a ticket-seller at a downtown Providence theater. In 1997 he covered that year's Ne- cronomiCon for the *Journal* and went with some intrepid fans to ex- plore Phillips family sites in rural Foster.

Tom had much broader interests than Lovecraft and received many awards for his municipal reporting over the years. In his own way, he loved Providence and its people, and I like to think he left the town a better place. He had a special affection for the "ordinary" people of Providence, and of course that meshed well with his interest in Love- craft, since despite his eccentricity, HPL was very much an "ordinary" citizen of Providence (certainly, no celebrity) when he lived there. Randy Everts got there first, but Tom also interviewed the De Magistris family who operated the quarry that Lovecraft held a mortgage on. I think he also knew Lovecraft's barber and doctor, and I know that he did some work on that waterfront diner, Jake's, whose hearty food Lovecraft adored. Aside from the Lovecraftian Guide to Providence, another of his projects was a book titled *We Remember Lovecraft*, contain- ing the recollections of Providence folk who remembered him. I wish I knew what became of that manuscript. Maybe the Lovecraft boom will see its emergence. Tom would have been elated by the appearance of Lovecraft's *Tales* in the Library of America—it's really a pity he didn't live another year to witness that publishing event. I'm sure he would have had the whole story—how Lovecraft was outselling Gertrude Stein, how Providence was reacting to its native son's appearance in the prestigious series, etc., etc.—but, alas, he didn't live to see it. But Tom's death and Stephen King's recently published introduction do allow me to tell one story that Tom told me in confidence.

Of course, Tom was there for the World Fantasy Convention held in Providence in 1975. He reported the whole story for the *Journal*. He had been in touch with the organizers of the convention in advance, and there was some discussion of a "Providence Remembers HPL" panel chaired by Tom. The panel was announced in at least one preliminary program, but then Bob Kenny and Muriel Eddy had to cancel. So Tom decided to cancel the panel, with regret. But he did bring along one friend from his "Providence Remembers HPL" stable. A fifty-five-year-old veteran driver for the Rhode Island Transit Authority, Andy Kot made a rather unlikely guest at a convention of Lovecraft fans, most of whom were half his age or less. But in fact that was exactly what Andy Kot was—a Lovecraft fan from HPL's own hometown of Providence. In fact, Andy only attended the convention on Saturday evening, with Tom as his guide. Andy had worked a full Saturday split shift, but Tom talked him into coming over to the convention hotel when he got off from work. He made a rather unusual figure in his RTA driver's uniform and his cloth satchel workbag. (HPL used to carry a similar cloth satchel for personal possessions.) He and Tom spent some time in the dealers' room, where they browsed with great interest and Andy made a few judicious purchases. They spent some time watching a Lovecraft movie (maybe *The Dunwich Horror*) and then ended up attending some of the convention parties.

Andy was rather shy, and Tom stuck close to him to make sure he was comfortable. About midnight, they wandered into a suite party where Forry Ackerman was one of the guests. Forry had corresponded with HPL as a young fan; in fact, he even managed to have a bit of a "quarrel" with HPL regarding the appropriateness of publishing Clark Ashton Smith's stories in science fiction magazines. Anyhow, Forry was regretting that as a former correspondent of HPL, he was as close to a personal association as any of the fans in the room that evening were going to get. Tom looked at his friend Andy Kot, and was surprised when Andy spoke up, "I knew HPL." Forry—a few years Andy's senior—looked as if he was about to launch into a skeptical dismissal, when Tom nodded at Andy and said, "Andy, you can't leave all the fans here with just that bare assertion. Why don't you take a seat and tell us a bit about your personal association with HPL?" With that Forry, who had been reigning supreme in the suite, gestured Andy into the armchair previously occupied by himself, and with some encouragement from Tom, Andy told his story, more or less as follows:

> My name is Andy Kot and I was born in Providence in 1920. I attended Classical High School and was a graduate of the Class of

1938. I worked as a teller at Industrial Trust Bank from 1938 until I was drafted in 1942. I was in the D-Day invasion of Normandy and received a Purple Heart. When I was released from the service in 1946, my uncle Gus got me a job as a driver with Rhode Island Transit Authority. I received my twenty-five-year pin in 1971. I was a fan of *Weird Tales,* and H. P. Lovecraft was my favorite author. This was as early as 1932 or 1933, the depths of the Depression. I knew Lovecraft lived in Providence, but I didn't have his address and I never expected to meet him. My mother Marina did housekeeping, and Alice Sheppard at 66 College Street was one of her clients. On Miss Sheppard's recommendation, she started to work for Mrs. Ann Gamwell in the upstairs flat in the same building in 1934 or 1935. The name Ann Gamwell didn't mean anything to me at that time.

By 1936, I had a notebook of Lovecraft stories in tear-sheets from *Weird Tales* and other magazines. I was thrilled when Providence was featured again in "The Haunter of the Dark" in the December 1936 issue of *Weird Tales,* which appeared on the newsstands in November of that year. I had a few "fan" contacts, and that year I also bought *The Shunned House* from Robert H. Barlow and *The Shadow over Innsmouth* from William L. Crawford. I worked after school and Saturdays at Elmwood Market, so I had enough pocket money to afford such occasional luxuries. My father had been a successful house carpenter but he died in 1923. I still live in the little house on Elmwood Avenue that he left free and clear to my mother, who died just a few years ago.

It was Christmas 1936 and my mother made our humble home as festive as she could for my two older sisters and me. We went with Uncle Gus and his family to Midnight Mass, and upon return home my mother gave us our presents. She said to me: "Andrzej, I know you don't think your ignorant mother knows anything about *Weird Tales* and those writers you like, but see what your mother has for you." With this, she handed me a small envelope. "Mr. Andrew Kot" was written on the face in a neat hand. The reverse side was printed "Mrs. Annie E. P. Gamwell, 66 College Street, Providence 3, Rhode Island." I could vaguely recall that my mother worked for a Mrs. Gamwell at that address. I tore the envelope open with carelessness that I later regretted. The note inside was dated "Providence/Tuesday/December 22, 1936." It read: "Dear Mr. Kot:/I will be at home Sunday, December 27, 1936, at 2 P.M., and pleased to make your acquaintance at that time. Sincerely yours, H. P. Lovecraft."

Mama explained that she had recently learned that Mrs. Gamwell's scholarly nephew, whose rooms she also attended to every Tuesday morning, was none other than my favorite author H. P. Lovecraft. On her most recent visit to 66 College Street, she had discussed me with Mrs. Gamwell and Mr. Lovecraft, and received the invitation. Needless to say, I was filled with anticipation. I don't think I slept much that night, despite the fact that I had to report to Elmwood Market the following Saturday morning, December 26, at 8 A.M. (I worked Saturdays 8 A.M. to 8 P.M. and after school from 4 P.M. to 8 P.M.) By Saturday night, I was tired enough to sleep, but still filled with anticipation. On Sunday, December 27, I went with Mama and my sisters and Uncle Gus and his family to 6:30 mass at St. Albert's, but I don't think I heard a word. Mama prepared a Sunday breakfast for us afterward, but I only had thoughts for my invitation to 66 College Street. I determined that I would ask the distinguished Mr. Lovecraft to sign my two books and the cover sheet of my notebook of tear-sheets, which was titled "The Works of H. P. Lovecraft."

I stayed dressed in my best suit and counted the minutes until it was time to catch the streetcar at 1:15 P.M. I was in downtown Providence by 1:45, and Mama had provided exact instructions on how to get to 66 College Street. It was located in a rustic court just behind the main library at Brown University. It was just a few minutes before 2 P.M. when I rang the door bell marked "A. Gamwell." I was surprised when a speaker next to the doorbell announced in a female voice, "Is that you, Mr. Kot?" When I confirmed that it was I, the voice announced, "Just come right up the stairs when I buzz you in," at which a buzzer sounded, and a door opened to reveal a stairway. I climbed up rapidly and was greeted by an elderly lady at the top. "We're happy to have such a handsomely dressed guest," announced Mrs. Gamwell, who introduced herself. "But I know it isn't I you wish to meet," she said. "I'll show you into my nephew Howard's study." With that, she knocked at a doorway immediately to our left, and announced, "Howard, your guest Mr. Kot is here."

Immediately, there was the sound of feet, and H. P. Lovecraft himself appeared at the door of his study. He appeared rather gaunt, dressed in robe, pajamas, and slippers. "Mr. Kot, I'm glad to meet you," he said, extending his hand. "Please come into my study and have a seat," he said, with a gesture of his hand. "I hope you will forgive my appearance—especially after you yourself have dressed so handsomely for this occasion—but I am recovering from a case of grippe which I've had difficulty shaking." I entered his book-lined study. It was filled with old furniture and had many decorations on the walls and on top of the bookcases. Years later, when I saw the photographs of the study that Robert H. Barlow took after Lovecraft's death—they were reproduced in *Marginalia*—I was moved, because it looked exactly like the study as I saw it two days after Christmas in 1936.

"I understand that you are quite a reader of my humble work," he offered, and I confirmed that I'd been reading his work in *Weird Tales* for nearly five years and had in fact found quite a few earlier issues with his work in local bookshops. I showed him the binder of his stories which my Uncle Gus had helped me to construct and also my copies of *The Shunned House* and *The Shadow over Innsmouth*. "You have quite a comprehensive collection of my work," said Lovecraft, looking through my notebook. "Even the early things from the first year of *Weird Tales*, and, my goodness, 'The Colour out of Space' from *Amazing Stories*, and even 'Cool Air' from *Magic and Mystery*. How I wish I might have a published book of my stories as handsome as your binder!"

"I wish so, too, Mr. Lovecraft," I offered, "although *Shunned House* and *Innsmouth* are both nice to have. I like Mr. Utpatel's drawings for *Innsmouth*."

"Those little devils Barlow and Crawford have been busier than I imagined," said Lovecraft. "*Shunned House* is really a handsome printing job—a friend of mine named Paul Cook, a printer by trade, originally did it in 1928, but the Depression struck before he could get it bound and he has sent the unbound edition to my young acolyte Bobby Barlow. Utpatel's weird drawings are one of the few positive things about *Innsmouth*—not that I am not happy to have it in print, but young Billy Crawford has let slip far too many mistakes. In fact, if you do not object, I would like to keep your copy of *Innsmouth* for just a few days so that I can correct at least the worst of the mistakes with razor and pen."

"Certainly," I said, with a bit of hesitancy, then asking, "Mr. Lovecraft, I would be honored to have you sign my books and notebook."

"An honor to do so, especially for a Providence reader," he said. "You know," he continued, "there are really very few readers for weird fiction in my native city. It is always a pleasure to meet one." He was sitting next to me in another chair, but with this, he rose, went to his desk, and inscribed *The Shunned House* and my notebook to me. He left *The Shadow over Innsmouth* on his desk, slipping a note into its pages. "Here you are," he said, returning to his chair. "I hope you will be pleased with the inscriptions—as pleased as I am to encounter a reader in my native city. My late elder aunt Mrs. Clark shared my taste in weird fiction—as did my grandfather, Whipple Phillips—but alas they are gone. My younger aunt Mrs. Gamwell shares my taste in colonial architecture but has no special fondness for weird fiction."

With that Lovecraft engaged me in conversation, mostly about myself and my aspirations. I think he was somewhat disappointed to learn that I was not an aspiring writer, but he consoled himself with the thought that all writers need good readers. I enthused over "The Haunter of the Dark"—his latest story in *Weird Tales*—and asked him if he intended to write any more stories set in Providence. He said he had in mind a multi-generational tale of vampirism set in nearby Benefit Street, but that it might be years before he could summon the time and energy to write it. He pointed out to me through his west window the spire of St. John's Catholic Church on Federal Hill, which he told me inspired the Starry Wisdom Church in his story. We must have engaged in conversation for forty-five minutes or an hour. He succeeded in setting me at ease despite our differences in age and in sophistication.

At about 3 P.M., Mrs. Gamwell knocked at the door. "Howard, I have some cake and tea ready in the parlor."

"I hope you will join us," he said, pointing toward the door. We crossed the hallway and entered the parlor, where a lit Christmas tree adorned one corner. "This is the first tree we have had since we all lived in my grandfather's house on Angell Street in the 1890s," said Lovecraft. "A recent literary check—payment for 'The Shadow out of Time' in *Astounding Stories*—enabled us to make this addition."

Walking over to the tree, he bent down and recovered a small, wrapped package. "We did not forget our holiday guest, either," he said, handing the package to me. I opened it with care and found inside an inscribed brochure titled *The Cats of Ulthar*. "Young Bobby Barlow—with whom you have corresponded—printed this for me as a surprise last Christmas," he said. "I thought you might enjoy having one of my remaining copies. It is an example of the appearance of my work in amateur publications—the only home my work has found aside from professional pulp magazines."

We were soon seated at a small table, where we all shared tea and cake. I can remember that Mrs. Gamwell poured boiling water into the teapot and then filled a tea ball with loose tea to prepare our beverage. The small cakes were similar to what I would call kolaczki. Mrs. Gamwell also engaged me in conversation about myself. She complimented me as a handsome young man and expressed the hope that my mother would keep her informed of my progress.

"My nephew Howard is the last of my immediate family," she said. "I myself had a boy who lived to be about as old as you are now, but I lost him to tuberculosis. His name was Phillips Gamwell. I had a daughter as well, but she died only a few days after birth." I consoled her for her losses, but she said, "I am very lovingly cared for by my dear nephew. It is always a pleasure to greet young men and women who are interested in his literary work. My late sisters Lillie and Susie—the latter was Howard's mother—had much more refined taste in literary matters than I myself. But Howard and I do share a love of Providence and of olden times. Our flat in this fine colonial home is really a marvel—I never expected to live in such a wonderful place. We even have a number of things here that had been in storage since my father's home was broken up following his death in 1904. Your mother helps us keep everything beautiful. We really have so many blessings."

By 3:30 P.M., we were ready to say farewell. I recovered my satchel with my inscribed treasures and my present. "Mrs. Gamwell will let your mother know when I have corrected *Innsmouth* and it is ready for you," said Mr. Lovecraft. "Have no fear, humble book that it may be, I know you value it, and I will attend to it very soon. You will forgive me, I hope, if I do not escort your to the doorstep in my present attire," he said, showing me to the stairway. "If I were feeling better and properly dressed," he said, "I would should you around the immediate neighborhood." I assured him I was delighted with my visit and thanked him again for his present, and for inscribing *The Shunned House* and my notebook. The door at the foot of the stairs clicked behind me, and soon I was on my way down the steep College Street hill. I looked up behind me and saw Mr. Lovecraft standing in his study window. He waved at me, and I waved back. It was the last I was ever to see of H. P. Lovecraft.

Tom remembered that Andy was peppered with questions from the young fans in the hotel room. Andy coped as well as he could. One fan asked, "Did you ever get your copy of *Innsmouth* back?" which prompted Andy to complete his story:

> Yes, I did, although under sad circumstances. On Tuesday, December 29, my mother told me that Mr. Lovecraft's condition had worsened, and that he would be delayed in correcting and inscribing my copy of *Innsmouth*. I wrote him a thank-you note and asked him to take his time with *Innsmouth*. My mother could return it to me whenever it was ready. I showed my Uncle Gus the inscription in the notebook he had helped me to construct—"For Andrew Kot / A good reader & collector / from my own native Providence / who assembled this collection / of my humble work— / a finer collection than / any publisher has deemed / worthy of issuance / With kindest regards / H. P. Lovecraft / Dec. 27, 1936." Uncle Gus was no fan of weird fiction, but he was proud of the notebook and proud to see it inscribed to me by my favorite author. "Maybe someday he will be world-famous and this book will be valuable," my uncle speculated. Little did he know.
>
> School resumed Monday, January 5, 1937, and soon I was fully occupied with classwork and my work at Elmwood Market. But I kept Mr. Lovecraft in mind and asked my mother about his condition every Tuesday evening. Alas, the news became grimmer and grimmer as the weeks passed. By late February, my mother confided in me that Mr. Lovecraft was dying of cancer. We agreed that we would not trouble him or Mrs. Gamwell about my book. On Tuesday, March 9, my mother reported to me that Mr. Lovecraft was in terrible pain and that arrangements were being made to take him to the hospital. She said that he was terminally ill. We didn't take the daily newspaper, so my mother learned on Tuesday, March 16, that Mr. Lovecraft had died in the hospital on the previous day. Mrs. Gamwell told her there would be a brief funeral service at Knowles & Sons on Thursday, March 18—family and close friends only.
>
> And so it went into the spring. My mother said that Mrs. Gamwell seemed at first to be wholly prostrated by the loss of her nephew, but gradually her resources of inner strength pulled her through her grief. On Tuesday, May 4, my mother brought the unexpected news that Mrs. Gamwell would like to see me on the following Sunday, May 9. She said that I could come about 2 P.M., as on my prior visit to 66 College Street.
>
> So, once again, I took the streetcar in my best clothes to visit 66 College Street. Buzzed through the door, I met Mrs. Gamwell at the

top of the stairway. "Andrew, it is so kind of you to come to visit me," she said, leading me to her own sitting room and inviting me to have a seat. "I know that it was my nephew who was your friend. He was so delighted to find another reader in Providence. He talked and talked to me about that notebook of his stories you made. He wished that he had copies to send to all his friends around the country."

I assured Mrs. Gamwell that I was happy to see her and condoled her on her loss.

"I never expected that I would outlive my nephew," she said. "He was not only a dear friend and close relative but also a source of much good counsel and advice. Now I have not only my own affairs to take care of, but there are already questions to answer regarding Howard's literary work. I just this week received a letter from the editor of *Weird Tales* asking if there were any unpublished works by Howard that he could use. Young Bobby Barlow has taken everything relating to Howard's literary work in charge—by Howard's specific request—so I am relying on his good advice. I wish Albert Baker, who is the family attorney, had had the chance to meet Bobby while he was in Providence. I would value his estimate of the young man."

I told Mrs. Gamwell that I had corresponded with Mr. Barlow and purchased a copy of *The Shunned House* from him.

"I am not sure whether that story has been in *Weird Tales*," Mrs. Gamwell wondered.

"Not to my knowledge," I said.

"But I ought not to trouble you with all my worries," said Mrs. Gamwell. "Tell me how you are doing in high school. Your mother tells me she is very proud of your achievements."

So we engaged in conversation about myself, and Mrs. Gamwell served tea and cake, just as she had after Christmas, when HPL was still with us. She suggested that we visit HPL's study before I left. It seemed much the same as it had when I visited just after Christmas, although one bookshelf had been partially emptied of books. "HPL left the first selection of his books to young Bobby," said Mrs. Gamwell, "and he selected a modest number of weird titles which he crated and I am storing in the attic for him. Other books he mailed according to HPL's specific bequests—for example, his copy of Cotton Mather's *Magnalia Christi Americana,* which he left to his dear friend Mr. James Morton of the Paterson, New Jersey, Municipal Museum. But Bobby felt I should make disposition of the majority of Howard's library. I haven't reached any decisions yet. But I do have one thing for you—in fact, the principal reason for your visit," she said.

With that, she took a small book from the top of the table-desk in the center of HPL's study and handed to me. "There—there—is your copy of *Innsmouth*—signed and corrected for you. Howard kept in mind that he had it on loan from you, and how much you valued it. Despite his illness, he asked me to remind him from time to time of his promise to attend to it. Despite his pain, I know that he worked on it on several occasions in January and February. By March, he could do nothing, and March 10 we sent him to the hospital. I quite forgot about your little book until quite recently, when I found it on HPL's desk. Please—take a look," she said, handing the book to me.

I opened the cover and found on the flyleaf this inscription: "For Andrew Kot— / My only published book / Sincere regards, / H. P. Lovecraft / February 28, 1937." The hand was shaky, but still unmistakable.

"I think that Howard must have signed it the last time he worked on it in February," said Mrs. Gamwell. "I don't know that he signed a thing or did any more work after that Sunday," she said. "He was in too much pain."

I thanked her profusely and asked if she might wish to keep the book as a keepsake. "No, I still have a shelf copy here in Howard's study," she said. "After he worked so hard to correct this copy despite his illness, I know he would want you to have it."

When I later examined the book in detail, I found that Lovecraft had indeed corrected all the errors with penknife and ink. I put the book in my satchel and thanked Mrs. Gamwell again.

"Your mother has been a great help to me during these difficult days," she said. "She will keep me posted on your progress, and perhaps we will have the good fortune to meet again. I know you will never forget my nephew and his generosity to a young fan from his own native city." I assured her that I would not and departed into the warm spring weather.

Bear in mind that no one had yet read Lovecraft's great novel *The Case of Charles Dexter Ward,* but I had already acquired a small Providence guidebook to educate myself better about my own native city that HPL loved so well. Instead of heading directly home, I walked to Prospect Terrace, which HPL had loved so well. I walked down Jenckes Street to Benefit Street, and back along Benefit Street to College Street. I noted number 135, which HPL had told me was the site of his story "The Shunned House." It must have been close to 5 P.M. before I reached home. Mother was anxious to learn of my visit to Mrs. Gamwell. At her urging, I wrote a thank-you note that she bore to Mrs. Gamwell the following Tuesday.

My mother continued to work for Mrs. Gamwell through the middle of 1940, when Mrs. Gamwell had to enter a sanatorium in Newport. She, too, was suffering from cancer. I had not seen her personally since our meeting on May 9, 1937, but I had received a graduation card, with $5 check, from her in June 1938, when I was graduated from Classical High School. I had aspirations to attend college, but economic necessity forced me to start work right away as a teller at Industrial Trust Bank, where I worked until I was drafted in 1942. My mother and I learned that Mrs. Gamwell had passed away at the end of January 1941. We did not learn anything about the disposition of her estate.

I did splurge $3.50 to place an advance order for *The Outsider and Others,* the first collection of HPL's work from Arkham House. It was published toward the end of 1939. I remember my excitement when it arrived in the mail. Here at last was a finer collection of HPL's work than the notebook I had so carefully assembled. I couldn't keep track of Arkham House and its publications while I was in the service. When I returned to Providence in March 1946, my Uncle Gus got me my present job with Rhode Island Transit Authority. I have driven the Elmwood Route for nearly thirty years and am now a senior driver.

My friend Don Grant got me back into the loop on Lovecraft and obtained for me copies of *Beyond the Wall of Sleep, Marginalia,* and the World *Best Supernatural Stories.* I also got to be good friends with H. Douglass Dana, who I learned had purchased the remainder of HPL's library after Mrs. Gamwell's death in 1941. Over the years, I think I must have purchased nearly a score of books from HPL's library from Mr. Dana. I think I am proudest of owning his copy of Stormonth's *Dictionary,* which has the ownership signature of his father, W. S. Lovecraft. One could still buy books from Lovecraft's library at reasonable cost into the 1950s. Mr. Dana also sold me new titles from Arkham House as they were published. Since the fire that closed Dana's several years ago, I've been a bit out of touch, but I'm proud to say I purchased copies of L. Sprague de Camp's and Frank Belknap Long's new books on HPL in the dealers' room earlier this evening. I'm looking forward to reading them.

Tom could see that the strain of so much attention was beginning to wear on his friend Andy Kot, and began to look for an opportunity for a graceful exit. Then one fan popped up: "So do you have any HPL relics other than your signed books?" After a bit of hesitation, Andy responded:

I'll tell you probably the strangest story I have to tell. Mr. Grant told me that a used furniture dealer, Abraham Sakovitz, had bought most of the furniture from Mrs. Gamwell's flat, after a few things were given to family and friends. I found Mr. Sakovitz still in business in a somewhat decrepit business district off North Main Street. He didn't immediately recognize the name of Mrs. Gamwell and knew nothing of H. P. Lovecraft, but when I described the location of 66 College Street just behind the John Hay Library, he recalled the Gamwell-Lovecraft flat in detail. He said that all the bookcases from HPL's study and most of the other furniture had sold quite readily. He had left only the daybed from the alcove off the study and some miscellaneous china. He showed me the humble folding daybed, with a dusty brown cover with a pillow tucked under it. Then some china, among which I recognized the teapot and cups that Mrs. Gamwell had used on the two occasions when I visited 66 College Street. So I asked Mr. Sakovitz how much he wanted for the tea set and the daybed. He commented that the tea set was not complete but was still nice Victorian ware. There was the pot, four cups, and six saucers. He said he wanted $2.50 for these. If I took the tea set, the old daybed was mine to have for free. So we reached our bargain.

I didn't yet have an automobile (I was not to acquire one until 1955), but Mr. Sakovitz suggested a cab company that would take me and my acquisitions home at modest cost. I adopted his suggestion and soon found myself home only $4.00 the poorer. I gave my mother the tea set, and she was delighted to have something from 66 College Street, which she remembered so fondly. I had a comfortable bedroom of my own, and a study-library in the dormer room in the attic, where I installed my new daybed. Under the dusty brown cover were sheets—somewhat yellowed but still in decent shape—and the pillow in its case. My mother cleaned everything up beautifully for me. The pillowcase proved to be special—with "W.V.P. & R.A.P." embroidered at one corner. Those initials, by the way, stand for HPL's maternal grandparents, Whipple V. Phillips and his wife Robie A. Place. So, you see, in addition, to owning a few books signed by

H. P. Lovecraft, I have also had the honor, from time to time, of sleeping in his own bed, on his own pillow.

Tom said the hands went up by the fives and tens with more questions for Andy Kot, but that with this they gently but firmly made their farewell. Forry Ackerman was a gentleman. "I stand corrected," he said, before Tom and Andy left. "Nearly forty years after Lovecraft died, we've had the honor of meeting a resident of his own city who not only met him, but from time to time sleeps on his bed. Thank you, Andy Kot!" Andy took a gracious bow, and departed with Tom.

By then it was 1 A.M., and Tom insisted that Andy take a cab home. Tom didn't believe that Stephen King was in that room at the Biltmore Hotel where Andy told his story, but King was at the convention and probably heard about the story from Forry or others. And that's as much of the story of Andy Kot and Lovecraft's pillow as the world has known until now. Andy's mother Marina Kot had died in 1972. Andy himself retired from the Rhode Island Transit Authority in 1980, at age sixty, after thirty-four years of service. He continued to live in his mother's house on Elmwood Avenue, which he kept in beautiful condition. Andy himself died on August 24, 1992, aged seventy-one, of a massive heart attack suffered while working in the backyard garden at his home. Tom McInnerny stayed in touch with Andy over all these years and intended to tell the "rest of the story" about Andy and Lovecraft's pillow. He didn't get the story told by 2002, when he retired from the *Journal,* but he shared his notes with me. With the publication of Stephen King's introduction to *Against the World, Against Life* (2005), the time seems ripe for offering Tom's notes on the strange story of Andrew Kot and Lovecraft's pillow to the world at large.

*

Charles (Karol) Kot and Marina Wesolowski wed, July 31, 1917, Providence, RI, St. Albert's Church. 1920 U.S. Census, Charles, carpenter, born ca. 1892, Poland, naturalized, 1911; Marina, housewife, born ca. 1895, Poland, naturalized 1912. Children (all baptized St. Albert's Church, Providence, RI): Helena, born June 6, 1918 (bapt. June 11, 1918); Ruth, born September 21, 1919 (bapt. Sept. 25, 1919); Andrew

(Andrzej), born December 15, 1920 (bapt. Dec. 22, 1920). Charles Kot, died, Providence, RI, July 29, 1923, aged thirty-one, killed in construction accident. Marina Kot died, September 6, 1972, aged seventy-seven. Helena m. 1935 Walter Pilowski, resided Warwick, RI, family of six, died 1995. Ruth m. 1941 Fred Mazurkiewicz, resided Providence, RI, family of four, still living 2000. Andrew, graduated Classical High School, cum laude, June 1938. Teller, Industrial Trust National Bank, June 1938–February 1942. Drafted February 1942. D-Day Invasion, June 1944. Purple Heart, December 1944 (Battle of Bulge). Honorably Discharged, February 1946. Hired, Rhode Island Transit Authority, March 3, 1946. Retired December 31, 1980. Died, Providence, RI, August 24, 1992. Burial Kot Lot, Elmwood Cemetery, Providence, RI.

ca. 1960. I meet Andy Kot for the first time. He works split shift for RITA driving Elmwood Avenue bus, 6–10AM, then 4–8PM & is wearing his RITA uniform. Upon occasion he will spend part of his midday break using the HPL Collection at the John Hay Library. When I meet him he is reading in Sarah Susan Phillips's commonplace book, an unusual choice. He says he's done some exploration in Foster RI and is taking notes on HPL's Place relations. He has met Cliff & Muriel Eddy but doesn't know them well. Is good friends with H. D. Dana and has purchased lots of HPL books from him. Met HPL once toward the very end of his life. His mother did light housework for Annie Gamwell. We talk about the wrecking of HPL's childhood home at 454 Angell Street. Says he talked his way inside before demolition began and managed to "rescue" a sample of the original wallpaper from the parlor. He also made a chart of the floor plan—probably much altered from Whipple Phillips's days. He wishes he had had the resources to "save" 454 Angell Street and 66 College Street *in situ*. At least the latter wasn't wrecked. He tells me he sleeps on HPL's daybed and drinks tea from Annie Gamwell's tea set—all purchased from a junk dealer after he returned from wartime service. I am wondering whether this guy is on the level. I've met a number of Lovecraft "fans" over the years, and some of them have been pretty strange. But then, so was HPL—from the perspective of ordinary Providence people who met him.

ca. 1962. I run into Andy Kot for the second time, this time at Dana's bookshop. He is talking with Mrs. Dana about John Vetter's purchase of the bulk of the remaining books from HPL's library. He wishes he had bought more of them—he must have a couple dozen, most purchased for $2, 3, 4 or 5. He is proudest of owning HPL's copy of Stormonth's *Dictionary*—a copy that had belonged to HPL's father, W. S. Lovecraft, and bears his ownership signature. Mrs. Dana thinks she probably has another fifty or so books from HPL's library left and some miscellaneous papers—but they are going to be expensive. Kot gives me his telephone number and invites me to visit his home on Elmwood Avenue—"I have a few things you might like to see."

September 2, 1962. Finally connected with Andy Kot and visited his home on Elmwood Avenue on a Saturday afternoon. (With his seniority, he can often get Saturdays off. Has worked for RITA since 1946.) Greeted by Mrs. Kot, small woman with a perpetual smile, about seventy years old. She serves us tea and cake using "the Annie Gamwell tea set." Mrs. Kot tells how she used to work for Mrs. Gamwell, 1934–40. She was recommended by the downstairs neighbor, Alice Sheppard. Only found out that Mrs. Gamwell's nephew "Howard" (whose rooms she also cleaned) was the writer H. P. Lovecraft in 1936. Her high school son was a big fan of HPL's work in *Weird Tales,* and she mentioned this fact to Mrs. Gamwell. HPL had her son to visit just after Christmas in 1936. Signed his HPL books and tear-sheets and gave him a cat story book (i.e., *The Cats of Ulthar*) privately printed in Florida. HPL died in the spring of 1937, and her own work for Mrs. Gamwell ceased when the latter had to enter a nursing home in the summer of 1940.

Andy has pursued his interest in HPL over the years. Mrs. Kot & Andy show me the immaculately kept house & grounds. There is a beautiful Marian shrine in the garden. Andy takes me up a back staircase to his study-library in a dormer room in the attic. In one alcove is the HPL daybed, where he tells me he often sleeps. In another alcove is a bookcase, and Andy shows me a number of items on a table in the center of the room. Here is that poorly made book *Innsmouth,* carefully corrected with penknife and ink, and with a shaky but obviously authentic Lovecraft signature dated February 28, 1937. He only got this book back after HPL died. Here are *Shunned House, Cats of Ulthar,* and a collection of tear-sheets in a notebook, all signed to Andy Kot by HPL on December 27, 1936. He has a number of other, early items: *Notes & Commonplace Book* (Futile Press), *The Outsider & Others* (with original AH shipping case postmarked November 24, 1939), *Dream-Quest of Kadath* (Shroud Publishers). He missed some items during his wartime service, but Don Grant helped him catch up.

During his high school days, he was in touch with fans like Robert H. Barlow, William L. Crawford, Nils H. Frome, F. Lee Baldwin. He missed out on Francis Laney and the *Acolyte* because of his wartime service, nor does he have Bill Evans's *Fungi from Yuggoth.* He has met George T. Wetzel, who is the bibliographer of HPL's amateur press appearances. (He shows me his set of Wetzel's *Lovecraft Collectors Library* published by a New York fan publisher.) He tried researching some of the Providence amateur journalists, but hasn't gotten very far. Once was introduced to Harold B. Munroe, a childhood friend of Lovecraft, who now works in the juvenile division for Providence County. His brother Chester P. Munroe—perhaps an even better friend of HPL— died during the war. He shows me the HPL daybed & lets me examine the embroidered pillowcase with the W.V.P. and R.A.P. initials. Offers to let me lie on the daybed, but I decline. "I am no literary man," he says, "but I have the strangest dreams when I sleep on that bed with that pillow. It's almost as if I am in HP's stories or even some of them that he never lived to write."

He never kept *WT* because his mother objected to the Brundage covers, but he preserved all the Lovecraft stories in tear-sheets. He confides that some of his dreams are of an erotic nature; there is a re-curring dream of a city of monoliths in the Pacific, where bare-breasted maidens are sacrificed to alien gods. Wonders if some of these same elements are sublimated in the Lovecraft fiction. Andy knows well the Foster farm house with the magical murmur of the brook and the eld-ers in their graves on the hilltop and the ancient decaying house in Benefit Street where HPL's "family epic" was to take place—a differ-ent one from the "Shunned House" at 135 Benefit. He missed out on the Lovecraft "boom" in the mid-forties but expects that another one is coming. Has heard from Don Grant that August Derleth finally plans to reprint the Lovecraft fiction in three AH volumes. The collector Jack Grill from Brooklyn visited him a few years ago, but he declined to sell anything. Grill has had some success in finding amateur publications containing HPL's work. He met Wetzel when the latter paid a research visit to Providence. Wetzel did his research at the Franklin Institute in Philadelphia, which has a collection of amateur journals (the Edwin Hadley Smith Collection) including HPL's own. Kot is clearly authentic but just as clearly a little weird. I resolve to keep in contact, but to keep a certain distance as well.

Summer 1968. Talk with Kot over the telephone. He's pleased as punch with the AH hardcover and the Lancer paperback reprints of HPL's work. He had the wallpaper sample from 454 Angell Street reproduced and has papered his study-library on Elmwood Avenue with the reproduction paper. Also trying to acquire some Victorian furniture to "re-create the ambience of 454." Has been spending a lot of time at the Elmwood Branch of the Providence Public Library—with its James N. Arnold collection of genealogical data. He wants to learn more about HPL's family, since "they recur in his dreams." Did I know that Whipple's sister Susan Esther, who died unmarried in the 1851, was the most beautiful of all the Phillips women? And that her younger sister Abbie Emeline had a son whom she named after her brother Whipple? He also has a pane from an upper bedroom window at 454 Angell—thinks it might have been HPL's own bedroom. He's thinking of installing it in his study-library. To help him see the "other worlds" he experiences when dreaming on the HPL daybed. He would like to launch into a dissertation on the Place family relatives—has been spending much time with the Sarah Susan Phillips commonplace book at the John Hay Library. There are some Place family burial lots in Foster RI that he would like to visit soon.

July 15, 1970. Visit to Kot home on Elmwood Avenue. Greeted by Mrs. Kot as ever smiling, but she is thinner & I fear she may be failing. Andy ushers me up to his study-library. It is completely papered in the 454 Angell Street reproduction wallpaper. He has acquired several ponderous Victorian relics to match—it must have been quite a struggle to get them up the narrow back stairway. One of the dormer windows has been completely replaced—he has installed surrounding panels of colored glasswork, with the 454 Angell Street pane in the center. Somehow, the pane has a blue-gray coloration—perhaps glazing that he has added. "You wouldn't believe the things I see through that pane in dream," he tells me. "I've seen the sequel to Randolph Carter's adventures and Nyarlathotep's return engagement in Providence. I can't begin to tell you what I've seen in the Vale of Pnath or on the low, domed hills in the dark countryside. If only I had the power to write, I feel that I could recreate Lovecraft's worlds on paper." I ask, gently, if perhaps he needs more rest. "No, between doing my job and caring for mother, everything fits exactly. There is just the perfect slot for dream." He's been to College Hill bookstore and has a good sample of the recent Lovecraft paperback editions. "I'm told they're even going to do the poems in paperback, which amazes me," he comments. "Someday, every word that Lovecraft ever wrote will be in print," he prophesies.

September 7, 1972. Call from Andy Kot to advise that his mother has died. He found her dead yesterday evening when he returned from work. Visitation will be the evening of September 9. I promise to call.

September 9, 1972. Attended the wake for Marina Kot. Andy introduced me to his sisters Helena and Ruth and their families. He knew mother was failing, but wanted to do nothing to upset her. He dreamed of mother last night while sleeping on the HPL daybed, and she told him he was now freer than ever to explore.

February 17, 1973. Andy Kot just called. He didn't realize it was 3 A.M. He had awakened with a start in his study-library from a particularly vivid dream. He was being borne by night-gaunts to a secret destination in Leng, but then they released him and he was falling . . . falling . . . I suggested that perhaps it was time to get some professional help. He is apologetic about disturbing my sleep, but he feels that professional intervention would destroy his dream life. "With mother gone, I don't have much else to keep me alive. I could almost drive the bus in my sleep." I urge him to get some rest, even if he won't see the doctor. He agrees that he has a professional responsibility to drive safely. He loves the people he drives on his route.

October 29, 1975. Andy says he will come to World Fantasy Con Saturday evening, Halloween. He will meet me in the lobby of the Biltmore Hotel about 8:15 P.M. after his shift ends. He's been working Saturdays as a favor to a younger driver who needs the day off.

October 31, 1975. Kot at WFC. Buys the de Camp and Long books on HPL in the dealers' room. Watches The Dunwich Horror with me for awhile—pretty poor stuff. We agree to visit some of the room parties. Tells the story of his meeting with HPL in the Ackerman Suite. Then goes on to tell about the HPL daybed and Annie Gamwell tea set. There is a small local fan contingent present—mostly University of Rhode Island but a few locals. I hope no one is going to bother Andy.

February 6, 1976. Call from Andy Kot. He has had Ben Silver, from the local Providence HPL fan contingent, over. Silver is about the worst of the new Kalemites—fawning, full of never-completed projects. Silver is a college dropout and works for a shady antiques dealer part-time. Andy is totally unable to set anything down on paper, which puts him a notch above Ben, who wastes the paper he writes on. He can only "publish" in the lowest order of "fanzines"—and yet he sends me every monster-devours-sorcerer story that he writes in the hope I'm going to proclaim a new Lovecraft in the *Journal*. I advise Andy to watch out with Ben Silver.

June 11, 1976. Frantic call from Andy Kot. The worst has happened. Ben Silver has made off with the Annie Gamwell tea set and—worse yet—not the HPL daybed itself but the HPL pillow. Calls not returned. I advise Andy to file a stolen property report and change the locks.

July 27, 1976. The Annie Gamwell tea set has shown up at the antiques dealer where Ben Silver works, labeled "Gamwell-Lovecraft tea set" and offered for $1,000.00. This fellow's been in trouble with the law before. I advise Sergeant Cromwell of the Detective Bureau and alert him to Andy Kot's stolen property report.

July 29, 1976. Call from Andy Kot. He's got the Gamwell tea set back. The dealer let Sergeant Cromwell have it without a protest. Silver denies taking it. But the word is he has been fired by the antiques dealer.

January 5, 1978. "In the Vale of Pnath" by Ben Silver went to press in *Nightrealm* in December. This is so otherworldly, so unlike anything Silver has ever written before, that all the Providence Kalemites are astounded. George Michalik of Cthulhu Press is talking about offering Silver a book contract. I talked with Andy Kot. Kot says of Silver: "He's stolen my dreams. He's got the HPL pillow." I try to explain to him that a pillow is going to be a lot more difficult to recover than a tea set. He protests that his stolen property report intricately describes the case with the W.V.P.–R.A.P. embroidery. I promise to discuss the matter with Sergeant Cromwell.

May 1978. "The House in the Willows" by Ben Silver makes the latest *Otherworlds* anthology published by Doubleday. "Pnath" was a powerful, dreamlike narrative of fifteen pages, but this is a ninety-page novella, God help us, in the classic HPL style. Michalik says Silver is taunting him that he should have signed him when he could. "I'm going to be the next Stephen King—just you watch!" Silver tells Michalik.

October 1978—Michalik says that Doubleday has paid Silver a $5,000 advance for *Night of the Gods*.

December 8, 1978. I talk with Andy Kot over the telephone. "I don't dream anymore, I just drive my bus," he tells me. He says he has read "The House in the Willows"—"that's straight out of my dreams, the dreams he stole from me. It's the Benefit Street story HPL never lived to write." When I tell him about *Night of the Gods*, he tells me straight out—"That's the Tahitian dream—the city of the monoliths. I can't bear to think about Silver's writing that as if it were his own." Andy and I discuss the practicality that we can't very well accuse Silver of stealing dreams. I tell him with regret that Cromwell had declined to follow up on the W.V.P.–R.A.P. embroidered pillowcase—"insufficient value," said Cromwell. "Even that tea set was borderline. But I'm going to be the laughing stock of the PPD if I get a warrant to search for a pillowcase."

March 31, 1979. Michalik tells me that Silver is in trouble with Doubleday. He has failed to deliver the manuscript for *Night of the Gods*. Local rumor is that the $5,000 advance has plunged Silver into a dope-sex wonderland from which the promised novel will emerge only with difficulty. Silver is bragging he will still pull it off before Doubleday demands return of its money.

June 8, 1979. Maybe the miracle Ben Silver predicted is going to come off. A dope and prostitution bust hit his pad last week. Thinking of my need, Cromwell took along the description of the embroidered pillowcase and—what do you know—this relic has been recovered and returned to its lawful owner, Andy Kot. As for a pillow, Cromwell tells me that Silver was apprehended in flagrantibus with his latest paramour, and that there were pillows (of all sorts and descriptions) strewn over the room. "I got your embroidered antique, now give me a break," says Cromwell. Silver is faced with a dope and public nuisance bust but apparently has enough of his cash advance left to finance a lawyer.

June 13, 1979. Call from Andy Kot. "No dreams. It's the pillow—not the case. So long as Silver has the pillow, he's going to keep stealing my—no, HPL's—dreams." I tell Andy I think we have no alternative except to let the matter run its course. Cromwell's not going to do a pillow bust, but Silver doesn't have the strength to keep up his charade.

December 1979. Silver hands us a defeat. *The Night of the Gods* is out from Doubleday. In this version of HPL, the human race are sex slaves for the Old Ones. If Lovecraft dreamed this, thank goodness he didn't write it. Michalik says Doubleday had second and third thoughts about the manuscript, but decided to go ahead with it. Needless to say, it's become an instant bestseller, into six printings within weeks of publication. Silver is even making the rounds of the talk shows, and Doubleday has him booked into a bookstore tour in February–March. Michalik says Doubleday is hesitating on a new advance; Silver says it's got to be twenty times what they paid for *Night of the Gods*.

January 1980. Call from Andy Kot. Says Silver called him to taunt him about the new book. "I've got that pillow locked away where you and the Providence cops will never find it," Andy says Silver told him.

"Whenever I need a new half-a-mil, I just lock myself away with cuddly-duddly for two weeks and I'm golden. So ——— you, Kot!"

April 1980. Call from George Michalik. Verdict on the Silver tour—successful despite the best efforts of its "star." Silver appealed to his fans—and some of the females virtually threw themselves at him. He was coarse and rude to the bookstore and hotel staffs and especially to the travel agency staff who accompanied him on the tour. Supposedly, he did $500 damage to his hotel room in Philadelphia. "What do you expect from a rock star?" I ask Michalik.

July 1980. *Publishers Weekly* reports the deal for the next Silver novel—Doubleday will pay $125,000 upon signing and $125,000 upon delivery of the manuscript, all as advance on royalties.

January 1, 1981. Andy Kot calls to wish me a happy new year. He hung up his RITA uniform for the last time last night. They threw a party for him at the Elmwood car barn that included several of his longtime customers. "Come spring, it's going to be just me and my garden," says Andy.

March 22, 1981. News from Sergeant Cromwell. Silver's been evicted from his penthouse suite at the Biltmore Hotel. He agreed to self-commitment to Blackstone Hospital. Cromwell says that the Biltmore had to hire a contractor to clean out the incredible mess in Silver's suite.

March 27, 1981. "He's Raving He Can't Write It!"—the Silver story hits the trade journals. Doubleday may be out its $125,000 advance to Silver. Cromwell tells me that George Enos of A&B Cleaning Service got the job of cleaning out Silver's Biltmore suite. The Biltmore is claiming Silver did over $5,000 worth of damage.

April 1, 1981. I talked to George Enos of A&B Cleaning. There was an incredible mess in the Silver suite at the Biltmore—half-eaten containers of food, human waste, scraps of paper, you name it. There is indeed a battered old pillow with a large safety pin and a cardboard tag scrawled "HPL's Pillow." He can't release any property for thirty days, pending a claim by Silver or his attorney.

April 12, 1981. I talk with Ben Silver's attorney Joel Brinkman. "Ben's about at the end of the road," says Brinkman. "He's got just $10,000 left of that $125,000 advance, and no book to deliver to Doubleday. $5,000 of that money has got to go to the Biltmore for damages, and I'm going to need the other $5,000. How Ben's going to pay Doubleday or Blackstone I have no idea at this point. So if there is anything of value in that mess George Enos cleaned out, I've got to realize it for Ben. I've put in a claim."

May 5, 1981. The story is that the Silver trove from the Biltmore includes scraps of "manuscript" that Silver's "fans" may be willing to pay for. Lovecraft's pillow, or the property so tagged, is likely to be the subject of contention as well. Doubleday is reportedly sending someone in to examine the manuscript material.

May 31, 1981. An amazing story—Doubleday has agreed to pay an additional $125,000, per its contractual agreement, to take possession of the Silver manuscript material recovered from the Biltmore. That leaves Silver $135,000 to the good, of which $15,000 is going to Brinkman, $5,000 to Enos, $5,000 to the Biltmore, and $110,000 to Blackstone for ongoing treatment of Ben Silver. Brinkman gives me the good news. "Ben says to give the [expletive omitted] pillow to Kot. He says he stole it and now he's sorry."

June 1, 1981. A subdued ceremony in the offices of Brinkman, Post & Gumbel. Andy Kot identifies the Lovecraft pillow as his property, and it is returned to him after he signs a document releasing Silver from all further liability. I tell Andy I'll await the verdict.

June 2, 1981. Phone call from Andy Kot. "It's authentic. Now I've got more than my garden to look after in retirement." Andy and I agree he should keep the Lovecraft pillow a private matter. Thank goodness for HPL and his reputation that the entire matter never hit the paper.

August 1981. *Azathoth and Other Horrors* by Ben Silver is published by Doubleday. It's pretty slim pickings, but it's been promoted as the "last" of Silver and Doubleday feels it will do reasonably well, although nothing like *Night of the Gods*. Silver needs every penny he can get to pay his bills at Blackstone, and word is there is a new Doubleday contract in the offing, for a collection to include "In the Vale of Pnath," "The House in the Willows," and Silver's truly terrible earlier work including "The Eldritch Summoning of Ali-Bin-Hotep."

May 1982. Publication of *Last Enchantments* by Ben Silver by Doubleday. Everything that's left to publish, including the worst of the worst. The book contains a postscript by Silver in which he writes: "I tried to steal the worst of Lovecraft's dreams. Now I know better. They were never meant for this world. Farewell, reader." George Michalik, who is usually in the know, tells me that Silver has been released from Blackstone and placed in a supervised living program somewhere in the Midwest, far away from Lovecraftian dreams. Brinkman is still handling Silver's financial affairs. There are still residual rights remaining to be sold.

August 1990. Lovecraft Centennial Conference in Providence this month and I'm trying to convince Andy Kot to put in an appearance. What if we could get Belknap Long, Harry Brobst, and Andy Kot together on a "We Knew Lovecraft" panel discussion? But it's not going to happen. Brobst backs out because of the potential emotional strain. Ditto for Kot. We all know that Belknap made it thanks to the strenuous efforts of some of his friends. What little he had to say in his soft voice probably wasn't worth the hell his friends went through, but then again the sight of Maurice Lévy conferring with him on the conference stage may have been worth it all. I guess we'll never know. I myself think Kot would have been good, but his cautiousness in recent years has been extreme. "I'm still dreaming," he told me, "but Howard doesn't mind so long as I keep it to myself. I found a nice lady out in Foster who's willing to rent me a sleeping room, and sometimes I spend my weekends there. Of course, I take the pillow along. I wouldn't want to be without my dreams. I've been using Joshi's *Lovecraft's Library* to buy some of those books I missed at Dana's—not the actual ones that belonged to HPL, but the same titles. Some of them help me with my dreaming. You'd be amazed at some of the things he knew." I'm sure I would. But now it's his centenary and he belongs, if you will, to the ages.

August 25, 1992. I got a call today Harry Erdmann, next-door neighbor to Andy Kot. Andy collapsed and died in his garden yesterday afternoon. Massive heart attack. He had left Mr. Erdmann a note to call me if anything happened. Perhaps he had a premonition. Erdmann had a key to Andy's house, and we agreed to meet there at 4 P.M. Erdmann said we should go to a fireproof safe Andy had in his study-library. He also had the combination. We opened it up found the following document:

> I, Andrew Kot, being of sound mind, make this my last will and testament.
>
> I name my friend Thomas McInnerny and my neighbor Harry Erdmann as co-executors of my estate.
>
> I want to be buried according to the rites of the Catholic Church in my father's lot in Elmwood Cemetery.
>
> I bequeath my daybed, my tea set, and my W.V.P.–R.A.P. embroidered pillowcase to Thomas McInnerny.
>
> I bequeath the sum of $5,000 to Harry Erdmann.
>
> I bequeath the sum of $5,000 to St. Albert's Catholic Church, Elmwood Avenue, Providence, Rhode Island.
>
> I bequeath all my books to the H. P. Lovecraft Collection in the John Hay Library at Brown University.
>
> I order and direct that my executors Harry Erdmann and Thomas McInnerny destroy my H. P. Lovecraft pillow.
>
> After payment of my funeral expenses, I bequeath all the rest of my estate, real and personal, in equal shares to my sisters, Helena Pilowski of Warwick, Rhode Island, and Ruth Mazurkiewicz of Providence, Rhode Island.
>
> Signed: Andrew Kot Dated: December 28, 1991
>
> Witnesses: Harry & Louise Erdmann

Reader, after due submission to the Probate Court of the City of Providence, we did as the testator directed. On an October morning, after all due approvals had been secured, Harry Erdmann and I burned the Lovecraft pillow in the furnace of Erdmann's home. You are *not* going to find it in a pawnshop, no matter how long and hard you search. Andy had over 100 titles that Lovecraft once owned, including 23 actual volumes from his library. His collection provided the impetus for the John Hay Library to start its comprehensive collection of the books once owned by Lovecraft. I understand that in this library of some 2,500 volumes there are included more than 50 actual volumes from Lovecraft's own library. Of course, they also have the magnificent December 27, 1936, presentation copies of *The Shunned House, The Cats of Ulthar,* and the Kot tear-sheet notebook as well as the February 28, 1937, presentation copy of *The Shadow over Innsmouth* along with the other Lovecraft volumes from Andy Kot's collection. Mr. Erdmann reports that a young Asian couple purchased the erstwhile Kot home and that they have reported no visitations from Leng despite the presence of the 454 Angell Street panel in the dormer bedroom. There was a film of *Night of the Gods* about 1995, but it was a flop. It's the old story—Lovecraft's work does not adapt well in the visual media. No one has heard anything about Ben Silver for years. Joel Brinkman cut the last checks in 1995, after the film of *Night of the Gods* appeared. I had the W.V.P.–R.A.P. pillowcase restored and framed. It hangs in my study today. Lovecraft's daybed brings me no strange dreams. I keep it in my study as well. Sometimes I serve visitors from the Annie Gamwell tea set. These three mementos are to be auctioned for the benefit of my estate after I die. I don't think they have any serious value for Lovecraft studies. God grant they bring their owners only good dreams.

*

Tom's three Lovecraft mementos went to auction after he died in 2004. Sotheby's handled the sale. The embroidered pillowcase sold for $10,000 and the daybed for $25,000, both to an anonymous Japanese buyer. The Annie Gamwell tea set went for a much more modest $5,000 to an anonymous Midwestern buyer. The Pao family of Elmwood Avenue in Providence have offered their attic dormer window for $10,000 on eBay. The 454 Angell Street replica wallpaper (with two unused rolls) is offered for $2,500. So far, no takers. I'm not bidding.

LENG

I was dead tired by the time I decided to pull off I-80 in the western stretches of Nebraska. I had hoped that day to complete my traversal of Nebraska on my way to a family gathering in Denver, but it was not to be. I spotted a Super 8 on the south side of the highway at the interchange and pulled off. My headlights swept up the exit ramp. I came to a stop sign at the county road, and there on the telephone pole opposite I made out a rusted sign, pointing north, with the legend: "⟵ LENG." I thought immediately of Lovecraft's hidden Tibetan domain, but I was too tired to do much wondering that a town in Nebraska should bear the same name. I turned in the opposite direction and was soon asleep in my motel room.

I remembered the sign in the morning, when I was at breakfast in the nearby restaurant. The cashier looked as if he had been around the area for some time, so when I was paying my bill, I asked him, "Is there really a town called Leng to the north of here?"

"How'd you hear of that?" he asked me back.

"Well," I said, "I saw the sign for it on the telephone pole where the exit ramp for the freeway joins the county road."

"I thought that sign had been taken down years ago," said the cashier. "Ain't really any town called Leng anymore."

"But there once was?" I persisted.

"Yeah, there was a hamlet, and in fact there still is," he replied. "Used to be a spot where nearby farmers would retire, and there were even a couple grain elevators and a Lutheran church. But ain't hardly anything there anymore. Just three or four loners that I know of, living there now. County hasn't even maintained the road all the way up there—you have to go by private road the last three or four miles."

"And how'd this little hamlet come to be named Leng?" I asked.

"The way I heard it, the founder was a man named Delbert Leng," replied the cashier. "The folks up there don't have much to do with the nearby farmers anymore. Lutheran Church has long been closed."

"Well, thank you for the information," I said.

"You ain't figuring to drive all the way up there?" he asked.

"I don't know," I said. "I have a little time in my schedule today."

"Make sure you're gassed up," he said. "No services up that way anymore. Last Texaco station must have closed up three decades ago."

I did fill my tank before departing the interstate service area. As I drove north along the county road, I tried to see the sign for Leng again, but failed to do so. But, as I had told the cashier, I did have some time in my schedule, so I decided to drive northward to see what was to be seen.

The first six or seven miles were pretty routine—well-maintained county road, adjoining well-kept farms. But, then, of a sudden, a sign appeared at the side of the road:

END OF COUNTY MAINTENANCE
TRAVEL AT YOUR OWN RISK

I slowed and found that the road visibly narrowed. From being well-maintained, the road shifted to a bumpy track that probably hadn't had much maintenance for many years. The farms seemed fewer, less prosperous, and set back deeper from the road than during the first seven-mile stretch. The bumps became so severe that I slowed to 25 miles per hour and considered whether I ought to turn around. I didn't pass a single vehicle, and there was no one behind me.

I struggled along, and then, just beyond a tree-line, I caught sight of houses. There was no marking of a town name, but surely if it was anywhere, this had to be the hamlet of Leng. I was apparently on the main thoroughfare, with scattered businesses and houses, most of which were boarded. There were only a few cross-streets, and perhaps three or four streets parallel to the main drag. I caught sight of the steeple of the erstwhile Lutheran Church a few streets over. I came to an intersection beyond which the buildings appeared to thin, and then, all of a sudden, with loud bangs, my two right tires lost pressure. Because of my low speed, I easily ground to a halt and got out to inspect the damage. They were indeed flat, and I pondered my predicament with only a single spare in the trunk. I began to regret not taking the advice of the cashier back at the restaurant. A structure with a faded Texaco sign loomed ahead on the cross-street, so I decided to see if anyone was about.

The pumps must have been closed down years ago, but I did see someone in the office. It was a young red-haired man, in jeans, with no shirt on. I stepped into the office where he sat at the desk.

"No gas here," he said to me.

"I'm not in need of gas," I said, "but I've just sustained two flat tires on the right-hand side. Can you do anything for me?"

"I'll have to take a look," he said. "If they're beyond repair, I'll have to go to the station on the interstate, and they'll likely have to order tires for you."

"Anything I can do while you take a look?" I asked.

"You'll have to arrange payment with Pastor Loomis in any case," he said, "so you'd best head back up Main Street to number 130. I'll let Pastor know what I find out."

"So Pastor Loomis pretty much runs things around here?" I asked.

"Well, I'm his employee," said the young man, "and the church does own almost all the property in town. But if you have questions, you'd better ask Pastor Loomis."

"And who shall I say sent me?" I asked.

"Eric," he said. "Not that there's anyone else who might have sent you."

"How many people call this hamlet their home?" I asked.

"You should ask Pastor Loomis your questions," said Eric, pointing up the street to number 130. So I left Eric and began the short walk to the pastor's residence.

"If he ain't in," Eric called after me, "you can just go right in and make yourself comfortable. He can't be too far."

Number 130 was a fairly well-maintained red brick home of two stories. There was a commodious front porch. I rang the bell, but no one answered. So I took Eric's advice and tried the front door. It wasn't locked, so I entered the front parlor. There was some bulky furniture that looked well-used, but not positively decrepit. I spotted a dining room toward the rear of the house, and there was a stairway ascending to the second story.

"Pastor Loomis! Pastor Loomis!" I called out, but there was no response.

Evidently, no one was home. So I took the liberty to tour the main floor of the house. The dining room was fairly spartan, and an equally spartan kitchen adjoined it. The kitchen windows looked out on a fairly extensive backyard. I didn't see any outbuildings.

I decided to forego a tour of the cellar, and just as I was walking back to the parlor I heard the front door open.

A dour-looking couple, evidently in their sixties, came through the front door. The man was of medium build, with a red face, greasy black hair, and a large nose. The woman was more spartan in appearance, with her black hair pulled into a tight bun. The man had on a well-worn business suit, but wore his shirt open at the neck. The woman wore a white blouse and a black skirt that nearly went to her ankles. I noticed she wore no ornamentation at all.

"Eric told me we had a visitor," said the man, extending his hand. "I am Henry Loomis, and this is my wife, Delbertine."

I shook both proffered hands. "I'm John Sturdivant," I said. "I'm on my way to Denver, but I saw the sign pointing to Leng back on the county road and decided to investigate."

"The end of the county road three or four miles back retards most of our potential visitors," said Loomis. "You must have been quite interested in our hamlet to continue."

"Well, it's an unusual name to encounter in western Nebraska," I said. "I had time to explore and I was curious."

"The name comes from Delbert Leng, who founded this hamlet in the 1870s," said Loomis. "He was an emigrant from the Pennsylvania Dutch country. Died in 1915. Three more generations of Delbert Lengs sprang from the loins of the original settler, and my wife Delbertine is the only daughter of Delbert IV and the last of the founder's line."

"You certainly have a long history in this village," I said to Mrs. Loomis.

She remained silent, and gestured toward her husband. "Delbertine prefers to let me do the speaking," said Pastor Loomis. "For myself, I am a relative newcomer here. Delbertine was a bright girl, and her father sent her to college back east, at Pennsylvania State. I met her there, and she convinced me to return to Leng with her after we graduated."

"And you are the pastor of the church here?" I asked.

"Well, there is hardly much of a congregation," said Loomis. "Leng had already begun to depopulate before the death of its founder in 1915. The railroads went elsewhere, and there was less and less profit in trucking grain to store here. At our height, perhaps 1890, the hamlet may have had 300 souls. By the death of the founder, in 1915, it was 150. By 1965, when I first came to Leng with Delbertine, there were only 50 people left. The post office had closed in 1950, and the Lutheran Church followed in 1961. The Texaco station closed in 1970, and the last grocery store in 1975. Today, Eric and Delbertine and I are the only permanent residents of Leng. The last retired farmer who lived here died in 1993. So you can see we are hardly a congregation."

"Yet Eric calls you Pastor Loomis," I said. "Is he your son?"

Henry and Delbertine Loomis exchanged a glance. "Eric is our adopted son," said Pastor Loomis. "Our founder Delbert Leng arrived here with many esoteric Pennsylvania Dutch traditions, which have been maintained in the family. Despite their prominence in the business affairs of the hamlet (the Lengs at one time owned both grain elevators in town), the Lengs were never the center of society here, and the other German settlers set up their own Lutheran church. Delbertine is the last of her line, and in pursuit of esoteric spirituality, we live in a state of sacred celibacy."

"So Leng is like a Shaker community?"

"In a sense," said Pastor Loomis, "although generally we do not share their orthodox Christian beliefs. But Eric is indeed our recruit from the outside world."

"And do you strive to be self-sufficient, like the Shaker communities?" I asked.

"Generally, we do not need to stain our hands with servile work. Eric does what maintenance is necessary around the hamlet. Our esoteric endeavors enable us to transact what business we must with the outside world."

"Well, I suppose the founding Delbert Leng must have made a

good fortune developing the real estate hereabout, and probably passed his wealth along to his heirs."

"In part," replied Pastor Loomis, "although Delbertine and I can create needed resources on our own, as well."

A cellphone tone interrupted our conversation. Pastor Loomis motioned for silence while he took the call.

"As you can see, we are not without modern conveniences. That was Eric, who says that your two right tires are a total loss. He has spoken with the service center on the interstate, and they have two replacements on order from Omaha for delivery tomorrow."

"I had hoped I would be able to continue on my way today," I said.

"Alas," said Pastor Loomis, "you will have to accept our hospitality for at least one evening."

"I hope I will be no inconvenience," I said.

"We keep a bedroom expressly for guests," said Pastor Loomis, "and it will be our pleasure to have you. If you will excuse Sister Delbertine, she will need to commence preparations for our midday meal soon. In the meantime, I propose to show you around the hamlet whose name you found so fascinating."

"Well, there's a twentieth-century author, H. P. Lovecraft, who described a locale named Leng, a highland in the remote regions of Tibet. I never expected to encounter the name here in Nebraska, of all places," I said.

"I've heard of Mr. Lovecraft," said Pastor Loomis. "He is not without repute in occult and esoteric circles. But we have time for a walking tour of Leng before Sister Delbertine offers the midday meal. I am sure I cannot offer sights as esoteric as Mr. Lovecraft's Tibetan region had to offer, but our Nebraskan Leng is not without its charms."

I accompanied Pastor Loomis out the front door. He led me up and down the streets of Leng. In truth, there was not much to see. The former grain elevators were ruinous. He had the keys for the former Lutheran Church and opened the doors for me. It was musty inside. There appeared to be some stained glass, but it was difficult to see because of the darkness. Pastor Loomis explained that most houses and businesses were kept boarded, for insurance purposes.

"For appearance's sake, we keep a few homes close by us on Main Street unboarded. Eric serves as town security guard and makes occasional rounds. We offered him one of the former homes as his residence, but he prefers to reside at his headquarters, the old Texaco station. You can't come into town and miss Eric. But, truthfully, we do hope eventually to attract more persons to our way of living. Perhaps one day most of the boards will come down. We have battled to keep electric service; we get our own water from wells. We lost the battle for telephone service, but cellphones have served our communications needs. The county abandoned three miles of the county road to the south of us and destroyed access from the north. We've never been an incorporated place, and I think the State of Nebraska makes no recognition of us. I'm amazed, frankly, that the telephone pole sign still survives. We get few visitors and do not advertise our existence."

The circuit of the hamlet did not require too much time. We returned to Pastor Loomis's house to find Sister Delbertine and Eric already seated at the dining room table. Eric had seen fit to don a shirt for the occasion, but otherwise he was still clad in the blue jeans he wore when I originally met him. Sandwich meats, bread, and a pitcher of milk rested on the table.

"You can see that we live quite simply here," said Pastor Loomis. "I hope you were not expecting gourmet cuisine. If you wish, Eric could drive you back to the motel and you could wait there until you car is repaired."

"No, I'm happy to accept your hospitality, since I'm going to be delayed in any case," I said.

I noticed they said no grace over their meal and ate in silence. I comported with their custom.

"We are at our studies and devotions during the afternoon," said Pastor Loomis, "while Eric must pursue his own duties around the hamlet. Let me show you to your room; of course, you are free to stroll around the hamlet again if you wish. I will call for you when supper is served around 6 P.M."

Pastor Loomis led me upstairs. The master bedroom was to the left, looking over Main Street. The guest room was on the right and looked out over the backyard. "We passed the bathroom at the head of the steps," he said. "Delbertine has laid out some extra towels for you. You will find some books of a general nature in the guest room, as well as a radio. We have no television here. If you should need to communicate with someone, I'd be happy to allow you to use my cellphone. In the event of an emergency, by all means knock on our door, but otherwise we ask for privacy during the afternoon. I shall come to call for you before suppertime."

With those words, Pastor Loomis left me. I soon heard him and Sister Delbertine ascend the stairway and close the door of their room. I did not find much of interest in the books in the guest bedroom, and I was not in the mood to listen to the radio. A window had been thrown open to combat the summertime heat, but I remembered a swing seat on the front porch and soon decided to adjourn there. I was tempted to stretch out on the seat, and before I knew it I was asleep. I did not awaken until Pastor Loomis called me for supper.

"Your adventures must have tired you out," he said.

"I found the coolness and quiet of the porch attractive on a summer afternoon," I replied.

"Well, you have slept through to supper," said Pastor Loomis. "I expect you will want to freshen up in the bathroom upstairs, and then we shall expect you in the dining room."

The dining room presented much the same aspect as it had at luncheon. Pastor Loomis was seated at the head of the table, Sister Delbertine at his righthand side, and Eric at the foot of the table. Pastor Loomis motioned me to his lefthand side. For supper, the fare was a bit more substantial. A platter of fried chicken and bowls of mashed potatoes and carrots occupied the center of the table. A pitcher of lemonade was also present.

"This is quite good cooking, a regular traditional country meal," I remarked, after partaking of what was offered.

"Sister Delbertine accepts your compliment," said Pastor Loomis, and his wife merely nodded. I wondered if I could get Delbertine to say a single word during my stay. It did not appear that it would be easy.

"By custom," said Pastor Loomis, "we eat in silence, but since you are our guest, we will adapt our custom to yours. Is there anything more I can tell you of ourselves or of our hamlet of Leng?"

"You spent the entire afternoon in your esoteric studies?" I asked.

"Well, part of that time is spent in meditation," said Pastor Loomis. "We were not perusing grimoires like Lovecraft's *Necronomicon* during all those hours. Quite a bit of modern physics, particularly what is called string theory, jives well with the traditions that Delbert Leng brought here. We believe that higher-dimensional entities currently concealed from us will play a critical role in the future of the universe."

"And you receive messages from these entities while meditating?" I asked.

"Well, that is our goal," said Pastor Loomis. "Note that we do not always achieve our goals at first attempt. But we keep on trying and refining. Every new presence—like yourself—has the potential of opening new keys."

"Well, I hope you will not be asking me to participate in some kind of spiritualist soirée this evening," I said.

"You will note that I said entity, not spirit," said Pastor Loomis. "I am afraid we of the Leng persuasion are unreconstructed materialists. No, each human being is represented by his or her genome or genetic code. I think we would rather test the saliva left on your utensils than involve you in some kind of spiritualist nonsense."

"Why so much interest in the genetic code?" I asked.

"Well, if higher-dimensional entities are to lead this universe into a new development, they must certainly control the gene space of the lower entities already in residence here," he replied.

"And so are we humans to be slaves or masters when these higher-dimensional entities are released into the dimensions we know?" I asked.

"We feel that the enlightened ones who are ready to serve the future destiny of this universe will occupy thrones. Of course, those who resist destiny must be made to serve, or perish," replied Pastor Loomis.

"Sounds rather grim," I said.

"Not for those who can anticipate what the Great Old Ones will reveal," replied Pastor Loomis.

"So you worship these Great Old Ones?" I asked.

"I told you we are speaking of material entities, not spirits. We cooperate and facilitate. We do not worship. We are beyond such myths."

"And if the Great Old Ones should fail to honor their promises to you?" I asked.

"You are descending again to myths like Christianity," said Pastor Loomis. "The Great Old Ones were, are, and shall be. They make no promises to us. We will either be within their schema or without it. I do not expect any pity for those of us who elect to be without it."

"And so you're expecting thrones here in Leng when the Great Old Ones stage their return?" I asked.

"Where we shall be enthroned, I do not know," said Pastor Loomis. "Leng is simply our staging point for the present. The future is yet to be revealed."

"Well, I hope I pass my DNA test if tonight is the night the Great Old Ones elect to return," I said.

"Eric and Sister Delbertine and I will pass over your flippancy," said Pastor Loomis. "I would advise keeping to the house once darkness descends. We have been the victim of some vandalism by neighbors who do not understand us, and Eric customarily makes his rounds armed. I would not wish you to come to any harm during your stay with us."

"So you don't envision sending me fleeing for my life like Lovecraft's visitor to Innsmouth?" I asked.

"If you play by our rules," replied Pastor Loomis, "I see no reason why you should have to leave us prematurely."

By 9 P.M. dusk was descending rapidly on that summer night in Leng. Eric had departed for his rounds. Pastor Loomis and I sat on the porch, exchanging an occasional remark. Finally, about 10 P.M., I made my excuses and ascended the stairs to the guest bedroom. There was a full moon, and I drew the shades against the moonlight. I did not find sleep very readily, since I had rested so well all afternoon. But I must have eventually fallen asleep.

A small noise awakened me. Sister Delbertine, in a robe, opened my door and stepped into my room.

Closing the door, she dropped her robe and stood there in the moonlight. For a woman of sixty-some years, she was still very attractive. She had let her bun down and her black hair fell down her back.

Her breasts were still firm and well-rounded, and she had taken good care of herself, with a flat stomach that descended in a gentle curve to the rich thatch of her pubis. She had a generous bottom and muscular, attractive legs.

And she stepped right into my bed . . .

Sister Delbertine knew all about pleasuring a man. My path to ecstasy in those early morning hours in the bed with Sister Delbertine was both extended and exquisite. She uttered no word, yet she rose toward the peak of passion herself.

But when finally I achieved my release inside her, she strode away immediately, holding one hand to her pubis.

Then I realized . . . she had wanted only my seed.

Sister Delbertine did not even stop to pick up her robe from my floor.

I don't believe I slept again that night. Toward dawn, I was awakened by the sound of hammering in the backyard. Eric, once again naked to the waist, was erecting some kind of X-frame in the backyard.

When Eric had completed his work, Sister Delbertine appeared in the backyard, once again wearing a robe.

She dropped her robe, and Eric tied her wrists to the upper reaches of each side of the X-frame. Then he laid into her with a set of knotted cords. I counted twelve vicious strokes to her upper back. And then another twelve strokes to her bottom. Sister Delbertine was left bleeding from the cruel cuts in her back and bottom. Eric untied her wrists, and it seemed to me that he whispered a few words into her ear as he did so. Then, he and she marched toward the house. Sister Delbertine bent down for a moment to pick up her robe, exposing her ample breasts to my view, but Eric urged her onward with a smart slap to her injured bottom.

I decided to wait a decent interval, dressed, and then descended the stairway. Eric and Sister Delbertine and Pastor Loomis were seated at table. Sister Delbertine wore a clerical robe of some sort that concealed her body from her neckline to her sandal-clad feet. Her dark hair was once again drawn back into a severe bun at the back of her head.

"I trust you had good rest," said Pastor Loomis.

"Not after Sister Delbertine came to take my seed," I replied.

"I told you that you would be undisturbed if you complied with our simple rules," said Pastor Loomis.

"So am I of the cooperator or of the resistor class based upon the seed that Sister Delbertine took?" I asked.

"Yet to be determined," replied Pastor Loomis. "Much depends upon your disposition as well as your genes."

"And if Sister Delbertine did as she was instructed," I asked, "why was she punished with a cruel whipping this morning?"

"Sister Delbertine had a duty to do," said Pastor Loomis. "She was bound to resist any incidental pleasure to the utmost. I regret to say, she did not."

"Sister Delbertine has a great body for a woman of her age," I replied. "You are a fool if you have given away your privilege to be one with her for some promises of the Great Old Ones."

"Do not speak sacrilege," said Pastor Loomis. "I could have Eric cut your throat in a minute for what you have dared to say about my wife."

"But you yourself sent her to my bed," I replied.

"If you knew what I was about, you could have spent your seed directly, instead of engaging in half an hour of obscene play."

"There was nothing obscene about our play," I said. "Such play is the highest destiny of man and woman on this planet, the noblest thing we can do, the very origin of all life."

"Perhaps the genesis of human life," said Pastor Loomis, "but hardly relevant to future that awaits the universe from the hidden dimensions. Sister Delbertine deviated gravely from her charge, and so she was punished. If you want to look at it from a Christian viewpoint, I as the husband punished my wife for adultery."

"But you yourself sent her to get my seed," I said.

"The sin was her pleasure and yours, not the seed-taking," said Pastor Loomis.

"If Sister Delbertine was at liberty to go, I would take her with me, out of Leng forever, to begin a new life," I said.

"Sister Delbertine may leave at any time," said Pastor Loomis. "Neither Eric nor I will impede her if she wishes to abandon her greater destiny."

"Will you come with me?" I asked Sister Delbertine.

She sat stolidly in silence.

"I assume that means no," I said, after an interval. "Then it's my time to depart from Leng."

"The tires are supposed to be in from Omaha this morning at nine," replied Pastor Loomis. "Eric will leave shortly to pick them up. I anticipate that he will have them installed on your vehicle by ten. If you will sit on the porch once you have eaten your breakfast, Eric will come to call for you when your vehicle is ready."

"And how much do I owe you for the tires and for the accommodation?" I asked.

"I have to admit that Eric set the snares that ruined your tires, at my instruction," said Pastor Loomis. "We have reason to detain those few who venture into our domain for our own investigations. So I will ask no recompense for tires or for accommodation. I might ask recompense for the use of my wife, but Sister Delbertine has already paid the price for your mutual pleasure. So you are free to go without any charge."

"I have half a mind to report you for wife-beating," I said.

"Your word against ours," said Pastor Loomis.

"Not after the sheriff sees those cuts on your wife's back and bottom," I replied.

"Sister Delbertine denies being beaten. There is no reason to inspect her," replied Pastor Loomis. "If it came to a forced inspection, she would have to confess that I discovered her *in flagrante delicto.* Any jury would empathize with me. She has been beaten many times and heals quickly. Unfortunately for one sworn to celibacy, she is a very passionate woman. Why, she has even had sex with our adopted son Eric. So you see, there is little result to be expected from any complaint to the authorities. We steer clear of them, they steer clear of us, to put it very simply."

"And Sister Delbertine is free to join me on the porch and to depart with me when my car is ready?"

"Absolutely so, if she is foolish enough to surrender her birthright in the New Order," said Pastor Loomis.

"Well, I'm headed out of here as soon as my car is ready, and I invite her to join me if she wishes."

I went to the porch. Sister Delbertine never joined me. Eric arrived with my repaired car just after ten. Pastor Loomis came to the porch to bid me farewell.

"Would you care to use my cellphone to notify anyone of your delay?" he asked.

"I'll stop down the road somewhere. You've already got my DNA, I don't need you to have my loved ones' telephone numbers," I replied.

"As you wish," said Pastor Loomis. "I wish you could look more wisely on what transpired while you were with us. But in any case I wish you a safe journey. Perhaps you will yet hear more of us and the Great Old Ones on your life's journey."

"I hope not," I replied. Eric handed me the keys and looked at me with a leer. I drove away, exercising extreme care on the three miles of unimproved road that intervened before I reached the county highway. I did not think to stop to look for the sign pointing the way to Leng. I turned onto the interstate and did not stop again for several hours, when I called my relatives in Denver to advise them of my delay.

I've never been able to discover another thing about Leng, Nebraska. Maybe I dreamed the whole thing. I thought that I identified the exit with the Super 8 Motel, but when I drove northward on the county road I passed farmsteads for twenty-five miles before I come to a town. The restaurant next to the Super 8 really didn't look all that familiar, and the staff at the restaurant didn't remember the old cashier who discussed Leng with me.

I can find no trace of Delbert Leng or of any of his descendants. If there was a Delbert Leng living in Nebraska in 1900, there is no trace of him in Ancestry. All the plat maps and real estate records just show farm country where I imagined Leng, Nebraska, to be. Nor can I find any trace of Henry Loomis or Delbertine (Leng) Loomis, as students at Penn State or otherwise. Several genealogical reference books list Adeline Leng Murphy's *Chronicles of the Leng Family in America,* privately published in Cuyahoga Falls, Ohio, in 1952, but it seems to be missing at every institution that once claimed a copy. Not one of the handful of Lengs I can find in online telephone directories will admit any relationship to the Nebraska patriarch Delbert Leng (1834–1915) or have much to say to me at all.

My subsequent explorations make me wonder if I dreamed the entire episode. Perhaps I simply haven't yet identified the exit I took, or Nebraska has subsequently closed it or redesigned it. I've wondered whether the Super 8 might have switched to a different motel chain. Perhaps Leng, Nebraska, has slipped through a crack in space-time, to emerge later in some new spacetime location. Right now, it seems as remote to me as H. P. Lovecraft's Tibetan Leng.

Yet the images of Sister Delbertine in my bed and of her being punished by Eric are burned into my consciousness to such depth that I wonder whether even death will obliterate them. I wish this story might have had a different ending. The way the story ended, I'm not sure I'd want to see Sister Delbertine again. She might have a whole new family I don't want to meet. I have the nagging dread that my own seed spilled into Sister Delbertine's body might have provided Pastor Loomis with the key he needed to ramp up the return of the Great Old Ones to this planet. I guess it's a nightmare I'm going to have to live with.

GOTHIC STUDIES

The advent of Ann Giunta to the small world of Gothic studies was surely star-studded. Her 1999 Rutgers thesis interpreting the works of Ann Radcliffe in terms of the sexual politics of late eighteenth-century England was generally acknowledged to be ground-breaking, and on the basis of it and faculty recommendations Ann secured a tenure-track appointment as assistant professor of English at the University of Wisconsin at Eau Claire. Her work *Ten Lady Gothicists* (Boxworth, 2002) provided the first scholarly look at a number of minor authoresses since the work of Montague Summers in the 1930s. Then, in 2003, Ann presented her paper "Mrs. Lawton's *Thyssilda; or, The Captive:* A Possible Influence on Lovecraft" to Professor Robert Waugh's annual New Paltz seminar devoted to the dean of twentieth-century Gothicists. Ann had discovered an unpublished 1929 letter of Lovecraft to Samuel Loveman with a passage commenting on Mrs. Lawton's nearly-forgotten novel:

> . . . Cook writes that he has obtained from an Edinburgh dealer a fabulously rare set of Mrs. Lawton's four-volume *Thyssilda; or, The Captive* in the original 1806 edition. He tells me that the heroine, taken captive by Algerine pirates, is treated to a tour of the then-Mussulman world including (believe it or not) a brief period of captivity by an heretical sect in Lebanon who still worship the Philistine god Dagon. Since it was Cook who first encouraged me to write my own "Dagon" in 1917, he has promised me an early look at his new Gothic rarity . . .

Whether Lovecraft ever got to see Mrs. Lawton's sole contribution to the Gothic realm remained unknown at that time, but Ann held the New Paltz Lovecraftians enthralled with her learned speculations on the subject. Ann had discovered that the Widener and the Bodleian owned the only recorded institutional copies of *Thyssilda* and had made thorough notes on the Widener copy before addressing the New Paltz symposium. She proposed an early reprint of Mrs. Lawton's novel with her own introduction and editorial notes.

There the matter remained for a number of years. Ann's published papers ranged over late eighteenth- and early twentieth-century English literature and were by no means confined to the Gothic novelists, although they remained her first love. She presented papers to the MLA in her subject areas every year, and in 2005 she received the coveted promotion to associate professor at Eau Claire. In a word, everything seemed to be booming for Ann Giunta. In 2006, the Gothic Studies Association appointed her chair of the committee planning for the symposium to celebrate the 250th anniversary of the birth of Ann Radcliffe in 2014. The very next year, Brown University, home of the world-renowned H. P. Lovecraft Collection, agreed to provide a prestigious home for the Radcliffe symposium, just as it had hosted the Lovecraft centennial conference in 1990.

Then, somehow, the career of Ann Giunta began to stall—and it all seemed to be related to Mrs. Lawton and her novel *Thyssilda*. In 2007, the Widener made a digital copy of *Thyssilda* to serve as the basis for Ann's edition. But, somehow, it wasn't right. At first, Ann thought there was a simple indexing problem with the digital pdf, but soon she found that entire paragraphs seemed to be transposed. When she cited specific problems to the Widener, their librarians found the same problems in their book. To Ann, the pdf text appeared more and more garbled, and she set the entire work aside for a period of six months to concentrate on other work. On a spring day of 2008, she appeared at the Widener with the pdf on her laptop, determined to make a comparison with the original. To her amazement, her pdf seemed to match the original exactly, and both of them seemed more and more garbled. Entire pages seemed now to consist of nearly random arrangements of the twenty-six letters of the alphabet. Called over to examine the original, the Widener rare books librarians remarked that *Thyssilda* had always had the reputation of being a rather bizarre book. They wondered openly if some environmental exposure during the digitization process had initiated a processing of textual bleeding from one page to its neighbors. Inquiries at the photography lab, however, produced not a single clue.

Concerned that *Thyssilda* in both the original and in the digital pdf were transforming themselves before her very eyes, Ann laboriously copied pages 51–100 of the third volume of the book in longhand into a notebook. Most of them still made some sense, although pages 77–78 appeared to be almost entirely gibberish. At the same time she made her longhand transcription, Ann copied the pdf from her laptop to a backup DVD. Then she laid her work aside for another six months, hoping that the Maxwell's demons who seemed to belaboring her Lawton project would go away. But if anything the pdf on her laptop seemed to have deteriorated further when she next examined it in the fall of 2008. What's more, the pdf she had copied to the DVD seemed to contain matching changes. Only her longhand transcription from the spring seemed to be unchanged.

The Widener librarians were noncommittal when consulted again about the precious volume in their charge. They acknowledged that some obscure process of change appeared to be affecting the volume, but declined to take any further action for the present. Word gets around in the small scholarly community. The Widener librarians disparaged *Thyssilda* as "near pornography" (so they said) and blamed the photo lab contractor for the disastrous changes affecting their copy. Boxworth canceled Ann's contract for the reprint of *Thyssilda* based upon non-delivery of the manuscript. While she had secured tenure at Eau Claire with her appointment as associate professor in 2005, Ann was not promoted to full professor at the first opportunity in 2009, and it seemed that her career might become slower-track than she had originally hoped. Certainly, no appointment at a more prestigious institution seemed to be in the offing, so Ann determined to make the best of what Wisconsin had to offer. She secured a six-month fellowship to study *Thyssilda* in the original at the Bodleian in Oxford, starting in the fall of 2009.

Ann had the good fortune to secure lodgings in the very dwelling that had once been the home of her predecessor Montague Summers when she came to Oxford. Some of the leading lights of English Gothicism, including not only academics but also independent scholars like Mark Valentine, came to make her feel welcome. She made several research trips to Mrs. Lawton's Edinburgh to see if she could discover new facts concerning the authoress of *Thyssilda*. Her friends were also kind enough to make sure that she was not lonely on the weekends and took her see most of the sights of literary Britain, including the Lake Country, Shakespeare's Stratford, Hardy's Dorset, and Baring-Gould's Devon, and much more. Before her departure the following spring, she was treated to a tour of Machen's Wales in conjunction with the annual meeting of the Friends of Arthur Machen. But day in day out each week, her work was a manual transcription of the precious original edition of *Thyssilda* owned by the Bodleian. The Bodleian, of course, had been fully informed of developments by the Widener and insisted that Ann wear white linen gloves when handling their copy. Any form of photography or digitization was strictly prohibited, pending, said the Bodleian librarians, the results of further study of developments at the Widener. So, over a long English winter, Ann laboriously copied the text of *Thyssilda* into the notebooks she had brought with her.

Ann kept her attention fixed on her work whilst at the Bodleian, but the long nights in Montague Summers's former dwelling left her ample time for speculation. She began to feel that perhaps the librarians at the Widener had some justification for deprecating Mrs. Lawton and her work. Curiously, she was unable to discover any other scrap of published writing by Mrs. Lawton apart from her novel *Thyssilda* in four volumes, uncharacteristically published by McCardle of Edinburgh rather than by a London publisher. She could discover no reprint whatsoever of the original work and only a single review, which commented:

> . . . Mrs. Lawton would fain explore the territory so thoroughly worked by Mrs. Ann Racliffe and others, but it appears she feels compelled to descend to mere sensationalism in the mode of Matthew Gregory Lewis in order to appeal to her potential readers. Where the authoress seeks to create a fearsome shiver for her readers, we fear that many of them will experience only shock and disgust at the crudities of her prose. Indeed, Mrs. Lawton would do well to return to the duties of her own domestic life if the flights of her imagination prove to be so consistently lubricious and provocative.

Of course there was little to shock Ann—well accustomed to the works of latter-day Gothicists of the gore-and-guts "shock 'em" school—in the pages of *Thyssilda*. Mrs. Lawton's account of Thyssilda's experience on Dagon's altar in the temple of the Lebanon heretics seemed extraordinary only for its seeming account of the shaving of the heroine's pubes in preparation for sacrifice:

> As soon as the guards had left, the female Acolytes of Dagon stripped poor Thyssilda of every article of her clothing, despite her ardent protests. They tied her wrists to a wooden frame above her head, and began to explore every orifice of her body. She was shorn of every single hair not upon her head with expertly wielded razors, and washed inside and out with perfumed waters. Thyssilda stood trembling with her wrists bound to the frame until there came word that the Chief Priest of Dagon was ready for her appearance on the Altar of the horrific Philistine Deity. . . .

Ann wondered if Mrs. Lawton's flights of fancy had taken her too far from domestic reality. Of Mrs. Lawton she had found only a few nuggets of information. Born Frances McKinnon, she had wed George Lawton, an Edinburgh merchant, in a dissenting chapel in that city on June 26, 1798. There was no record of any children born to the marriage. Mrs. Lawton was mentioned in her husband's will submitted for probate in 1820. Mr. Lawton was interred in the churchyard of the Second Methodist Church of Edinburgh, where his widow joined him in 1835. That was essentially the sum of all the information that Ann was able to assemble about Mrs. Lawton until unexpectedly near the end of her research fellowship a stray note regarding her from the literary manuscripts of Montague Summers (now held in Canada) came to hand:

> Lawton, Frances (née McKinnon), author of a sole novel *Thyssilda; or, The Captive*, in 4 vols. by McCardle of Edinburgh. Mrs. Augustine (iii. 59) says she was an unfortunate and that George Lawton, an Edinburgh merchant, married her out of pity. She was still a very beautiful woman, but left barren on account of her years of debauchery. It was said she led a chaste married life, but her sole novel shows that her erotic imagination was still very active. We have no account of her widowhood, but she joined her husband in the churchyard of the Second Methodist Church of Edinburgh in 1835. *Thyssilda* remains her sole published work.

Ann searched at every available English library, but could find no trace of Mrs. Augustine or of her memoir.

Ann finished the longhand transcription of *Thyssilda* into her notebooks only a week before her fellowship was up in the spring of 2010. Her paper "Frances McKinnon Lawton: Erotic Imaginer of Nineteenth-Century Edinburgh" was published to acclaim in *Nineteenth Century Studies* in the fall of 2010. On the basis of this paper, Valancourt Books signed a contract with Ann for a reprint edition of *Thyssilda*, scheduled for spring 2012. But Ann did not report for her classes at Eau Claire at the opening of winter quarter in early 2011. The editor of Valancourt has shared a disturbing sequences of e-mails received from Ann:

> 10.13.2010. Transcription of T. into electronic format nearly complete. Am using a completely different computer than the one which holds the still-changing Widener pdf. Hopefully we will have a stable text of this fabulously rare classic, from the one remaining incorrupt copy.

> 10.21.2010. THYSILLDA.DOC complete. Have printed a hard copy for myself at the office. I will edit this against my longhand notebooks before attempting to make a pdf for you.

> 11.1.2010. Have compared THYSILLDA.DOC two times against my notebooks. Each review has turned up new differences. Will conduct yet a third review this coming weekend.

> 11.8.2010. Bad news. The hardcopy print of THYSILLDA.DOC appears to be changing just as did the ill-fated Widener volume. A comparison shows that the same changes are occurring in the electronic copy on my laptop.

> 12.1.2010. Please excuse my silence. I had to lay T. aside in order to concentrate on my classes. I can't afford bad reviews of my teaching if I am to prosper here in the narrow confines of Eau Claire. My chair has even counseled me about moving away from the Gothicists. He says the V. edition of T. will be okay, but he wants me to move to broader subject areas for the future.

> 12.17.2010. Fall quarter finally over. I find T.DOC on laptop and in hardcopy print a total mess. There are whole pages of gibberish just as I experienced with the Widener pdf. I wonder if some books are truly

cursed from their birth—perhaps some authority has decreed that an impious work like T. shall not be further replicated. Widener copy wrecked, Bodleian under close guard, my longhand notebooks with only me to vouch for their authority. I begin to wonder if I should make an appointment with the university health service. When I think of the determined Ann Giunta of 1999, Ph.D. fresh in hand, and the wreck I am now, I wonder what the future may hold for me.

12.31.2010. Anent your story regarding your visit to examine the Summers mss., I can say that last Saturday old Monty appeared to me in dream. He was in full clerical dress and looked rather livid. He told me I must burn everything concerning Mrs. L. and T. if I want to be a godly woman—his term. Curious Monty should wait until now to appear to me, since I spent an entire six months in his gloomy former digs in Oxford. But I don't think even a ghost would want to appear in those chilly, forlorn chambers.

1.3.2011. T.DOC both on laptop and in hardcopy print a fearsome mess. Yet I don't dare entrust my notebooks to the mails—nor do I feel you would have the time to undertake their transcription. The best hope for Mrs. L. and T. may be that the Bodleian copy shall remain incorrupt until a more favorable moment. I am undecided whether I shall do the godly thing as Rev. Mr. Summers advised.

1.10.2011. Yes, I think we are best advised to cancel T. in the V. reprint edition. I haven't been to classes yet in 2011 and I'm unsure whether I shall appear. I don't want the black mark of a mental health consultation in my university health record, but I don't know what other course of action I may have.

1.14.2011. I just spoke with the Dept. Chair who says he'll give me leave if I keep an appointment with the university health service tomorrow. I don't know if I shall or not. The Chair applauds me for canceling the V. edition of T. and says I should sever all Gothic connections. "A woman of your talents . . ." and so forth. And yet the Gothic was the whole origin of my academic rise—shall I have to surrender even my chairmanship of the Ann Radcliffe 250th anniversary committee?

[Ed. Note] Ann Giunta never appeared at the Eau Claire university health service on January 15, 2011. Her parents filed a missing persons report for her on January 22, 2011. The notebooks containing her longhand transcription of *Thyssilda; or, The Captive* are also unaccounted for. Lovecraft scholars report that no other Lovecraft letter mentioning Mrs. Lawton or her novel has been found. It is not known whether Lovecraft himself ever read his friend W. Paul Cook's copy of Mrs. Lawton's novel. The Widener reports that its copy was purchased from a Boston dealer in 1944—whether it is identical with Cook's copy remains unknown. The Bodleian copy of *Thyssilda* was apparently acquired from a lending library liquidation before 1850. It seems probable that Montague Summers consulted the Bodleian copy of *Thyssilda*. His reference to a memoir by "Mrs. Augustine" remains untraced.

SOURCES

First periodical publication:

"Introduction"* [for "Tales of the Lovecraft Collectors"], *Moshassuck Review* 16 (dated July 1979), pp. 1–5, EOD (Esoteric Order of Dagon amateur press association) Mailing 27, Lammas 1979.

"Collector the First: Major Geoffrey Hopkinton-Smith (1857–1943),"* *Moshassuck Review* 16, pp. 5–8, EOD Mailing 27, Lammas 1979; *Moshassuck Review* 17 (dated February 1980), pp. 1–10, EOD Mailing 29, Candlemas 1980; *Moshassuck Review* 18 (dated February 1980), pp. 1–7, EOD Mailing 31, Lammas 1980.

"Collector the Second: Dean Alan Edgerton Noble (1876–1959),"* *Moshassuck Review* 19 (dated February 1981), pp. 1–6, EOD Mailing 33, Candlemas 1981; *Moshassuck Review* 20 (dated May 1981), pp. 1–6, EOD Mailing 35, Lammas 1981; *Moshassuck Review* 21 (dated September 7, 1981), pp. 1–8, EOD Mailing 36, Hallowmas 1981.

"Collector the Third: Charles Wilson Hodap (1842–1944),"* *Moshassuck Review* 22 (dated December 30, 1981), pp. 1–15, EOD Mailing 37, Candlemas 1982.

"Collectors the Fourth and Fifth: David Parkes Boynton (1897–1956) and Another Gentleman of the Hope Club,"* *Moshassuck Review* (dated September 10, 1988), pp. 1–14, EOD Mailing 64, Hallowmas 1988.

"Collectors the Sixth and Seventh: Miss Susan M. Rounds (1780–1878) and James N. Arnold (1844–1927)"† (as "A Pair of Old Shears"), *Moshassuck Review*, pp. 20–37, EOD Mailing 76, Hallowmas 1991. Reprinted in Peter A. Worthy's electronic magazine *Black Book* 3 (2003), pp. 44–61.

"Life and Death,"† *De Tenebris* 2 (dated December 5, 1976), pp. 2–4, Howard Phillips Lovecraft Amateur Press Association [aka Ne-

---

*First collected in *Tales of the Lovecraft Collectors*, Moshassuck Press (25 copies), 1989; reprinted, Necronomicon Press, 1995.
†First collected in *Lovecraft's Pillow and Other Strange Stories*, Moshassuck Press, 2011.

cronomicon APA], February 1977. Reprinted in *A Hoax and a* Retraction, Moshassuck Press (19 copies), April 1989.

"The Squirrel Pond,"† *Moshassuck Review*, pp. 1–5, EOD Mailing 49, Candlemas 1985.

"Innsmouth 1984," *De Tenebris 10* (dated Spring 1985, "typed March 10, 1985"), pp. 1–6, Howard Phillips Lovecraft Amateur Press Association [aka Necronomicon APA], Mailing 25, March 1985.

Boy In Summer,† Moshassuck Press, August 20, 1996, 100 copies, grey paper wraps + interior pages [1]–[4]. Published for the one hundredth anniversary of Lovecraft's birthday visit to Foster RI, August 1896. Also distributed in EOD Mailing 96, Hallowmas 1996.

Lovecraft's Pillow,† pp. 1–18, EOD Mailing 136, Hallowmas 2006.

"The Haunting of Huber's," "Leng," and "Gothic Studies" were first published in *Lovecraft's Pillow and Other Strange Stories*, Moshassuck Press, 2011.